The
Princess
in
Opal
Mask

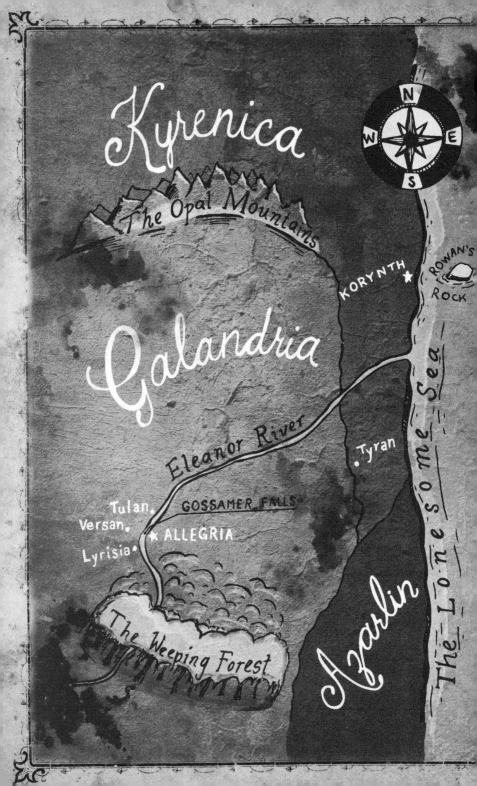

The Princess in the Opal Mask

in the

JENNY LUNDQUIST

RP | TEENS
PHILADELPHIA · LONDON

Books published by Running Press are available at special discounts for
bulk purchases in the United States by corporations, institutions, and
other organizations. For more information, please contact the Special
Markets Department at the Perseus Books Group, 2300 Chestnut
Street, Suite 200, Philadelphia, PA 19103, or call (800) 810-4145, ext.
5000, or e-mail special.markets@perseusbooks.com.

ISBN 978-0-7624-5109-8
Library of Congress Control Number: 2013946853
E-book ISBN 978-0-7624-5116-6

9   8   7   6   5   4   3   2
Digit on the right indicates the number of this printing

Cover and interior design by T.L. Bonaddio
Edited by Marlo Scrimizzi
Typography: Berling, Lavanderia, and Trade Gothic

Published by Running Press Teens
An Imprint of Running Press Book Publishers
A Member of the Perseus Books Group
2300 Chestnut Street
Philadelphia, PA 19103–4371

Visit us on the web!
www.runningpress.com/kids

This dedication is split equally between my sons:
Noah Robert and Thomas Austin.

I love both of you all the way to forever and back again.

PROLOGUE

"Standing at the edge of the mountain, grasping the most colorful stone she had ever seen, she did not yet understand how it was going to change the course of history. . . ."

ELEANOR OF ANDEWYN HOUSE:
GALANDRIA'S GREATEST QUEEN

Not everyone who attends the coronation wishes the young queen well.

As the townspeople gather in the great hall of the young queen's palace, many object among themselves. Construction has just begun. The great hall is the only completed room and already her palace is by far the grandest structure in Allegria. The townspeople see the glass windows—the first in the city—and glimpse the blustery, inky night beyond. They wish their own homes were so sheltered.

The wind howls and flickering candles paint shadows on the walls. At the end of the hall is an altar, which displays the young queen's crown, as well as the large stone that started it all. The First Opal. The jewel glints in the candlelight, showing veins of gold cracked through deep blue, as if lightning is trapped inside. A man whispers that if he had discovered the opals in Galandria's soil, instead of young Eleanor Andewyn, it would be *his* coronation they'd all be attending.

An elderly woman stands among the crowd. Hatred burns in her heart. Time will pass, but her son will never be returned to her. The young queen's army has seen to that. She weaves among the people, spreading her discontent like poisonous seed.

The whispers go still as the young queen and her newly appointed council of advisors—her "Guardians"—appear at the back of the hall. The young queen's expression is pained.

She is having trouble accounting for her floor-length gown, which trails behind her.

The townspeople cheer and clap as she ascends the aisle. But in the privacy of their own hearts, many hope she will trip and break her neck.

They are bitterly disappointed when she does not.

The young queen kneels before the altar. Ambition burns in her heart. The crown has been purchased, not just with precious stones, but with blood. The people doubt her now, but time will pass. She will build a dynasty. One day her son will also rule Galandria.

A Guardian places the crown on the young queen's head. She jolts slightly under its weight, yet her smile does not waver. This is her first test as a queen. She will not fail.

She stands and lifts the First Opal, raising it over her head. She turns to face her people. She is triumphant. She is their warrior queen.

She is also off balance.

The young queen stumbles backward and trips over her gown, dropping the opal, and she lands on her side. Loud gasps erupt, followed by a shocked hush descending over the crowd.

But Eleanor stands up, eager to reassure them. It will take more than a fall to stop their new queen.

However, the people's attention is not on her. Instead it is on the First Opal. There on the ground sits not one large stone, but two. The First Opal has broken in half.

The old woman sees her chance. Fate has smiled upon her. She points a bony finger at young Eleanor and proclaims, "An omen! Just as this stone has split, one day this kingdom shall also split in two!"

The old woman's triumphant stare locks with the young queen's dismayed one. Neither can look away from the other.

The old woman is not a witch; she cannot curse a kingdom. She is simply an angry mother who has lost her son. And the young queen is not a prophet; she cannot foretell the future. She is simply a new mother who wants to protect her kingdom and her son.

But both the old woman and the young queen understand that the right words, spoken at the right time, can become more powerful than a thousand swords. The right words scatter like seeds. They are watered by rumor and grown by time.

Until one day, they become legend.

Three Hundred Years Later . . .

PART ONE

*"Given her humble origins,
few could have imagined the heights
she would one day ascend."*

ELEANOR OF ANDEWYN HOUSE:
GALANDRIA'S GREATEST QUEEN

CHAPTER 1

ELARA

omewhere in the kingdom of Galandria, someone knows my real name.

When I was a small child I was dumped on the Royal Orphanage's doorstep, like a sack of rotten potatoes. In return, the orphanage dumped me with the Ogden family and told them to choose a name for me. Mistress Ogden called me Elara, after a girl from her childhood village. ("Dirtiest, most disgusting brat I've ever known," she's fond of saying.)

One day I intend to find the name I've lost. And when I do, I'll declare the name Mistress Ogden gave me worthless, just as she has always declared *me* worthless.

Somewhere in this wretched kingdom, someone must remember me.

I tell myself this as I stare at the honey almond cake I've baked for Mister Blackwell's visit tonight. I had hoped to surprise Mistress Ogden with the cake and finally show her that I am not the inconvenience she says I am. I don't need her to love me. I gave up on *that* a long time ago. But I do need a place to live.

I woke up early and gathered extra wood for the brick oven. But instead of the masterpiece I envisioned, the cake is lumpy and scorched. Nevertheless, my stomach rumbles. I despise dinners with Mister Blackwell, but at least I will eat well tonight for a change.

"Elara!" bellows Mistress Ogden. *"Is something burning in there?"*

"No!" Cursing, I brush a lock of sweat-soaked hair behind my ear and sprinkle flour on top of the cake, hoping to disguise the blackened crust. Why didn't I think to make frosting as well?

Mistress Ogden storms into the kitchen. Her silvery-blond hair is tied back with lavender ribbons, in the fashion most respectable Galandrian women prefer. "It is stifling in here. What have you done?" Her eyes, the color of blue disdain, land on the misshapen lump. "What is that?"

"It's a cake." I wipe my flour-coated hands on my skirt, a hand-me-down from Serena, Mistress Ogden's daughter. "I thought with Mister Blackwell coming tonight that—"

"That what? You'd bake a monstrosity and serve it to our guest?" She props open the back door with a rock. Outside, rain batters the Ogdens' unkempt yard, turning it into a muddy marsh, and cool air wafts into the overheated kitchen. She picks up the cake and pitches it out the door.

"You didn't have to throw it away," I say, and my stomach rumbles again.

She snorts. "That thing was nearly as hideous as you are. . . ."

She launches into one of her tirades, so I carefully arrange my features into a look of penitence. Then, as always, I tune out every word she says. It's a game I've played since I was young. What I do is imagine a poor, starved kitten. I imagine feeding it Mistress's words, the same words she has repeated over and over throughout the years like an oath. *Worthless. Unwanted. Unlovable.* I imagine the words are being devoured and stripped of their power, that they are carried away to someplace else entirely.

A place where they can no longer hurt me.

"Besides," she finishes when she has finally exhausted herself, "have you forgotten how important tonight is?"

As if I could. My life at the Ogdens' has always depended on Mister Blackwell, the director of the Royal Orphanage, and the four hundred worthings he brings the Ogdens every three months. Their payment for allowing me to live with them.

I turn away and begin stuffing rags into the window sill, intent on keeping my mouth shut. Through the smudged and cracked window, the Ogdens' untended almond orchard stretches into the fog-laden landscape. The wood around the windows is old and rotting, giving the rain a clear path into the kitchen, where patches of mold fester on the walls.

"Grab the bag of flour and make an apple tart," Mistress commands. "That should be easy enough for you to do without screwing it up. Are you listening to me, Elara?"

"I can't make the apple tart," I say and turn around. "We're almost out of flour."

"How is that possible? I gave you plenty of worthings for flour yesterday." She grabs the nearly empty flour sack and gives it a shake, sending white puff clouds into the air. Then she plucks a wooden spoon from the counter and raises it over her head, as though she intends to strike me.

Without thinking, I reach up and grab the spoon. Mistress and I lock eyes, each of us holding either end while we silently mark this moment. The moment where we both understand I am no longer afraid of her.

I remove my hand. "Wooden spoons leave marks, remember?"

She slowly lowers the spoon. With Mister Blackwell visiting she must appear to love me, and a black eye or a bruised cheek won't fit with the image she wants to project. And tonight she intends to wrangle not just the worthings from Mister Blackwell, but also get tickets to the birthday masquerade for Princess Wilhamina Andewyn, Galandria's "Masked Princess."

"Mister Ogden took most of the money," I continue. "He had a debt to pay at the Draughts of Life. . . ." I break off, because there is nothing more to be said. If Mister Ogden didn't visit the village tavern, partaking in cards and drinking ale so frequently (and Mistress didn't love expensive things), the Ogdens wouldn't need to depend so heavily on the stipend they receive from the orphanage. Ogden Manor might not have fallen into disrepair, and they wouldn't have had to let go of their servants one by one, until there was only me. The only servant they are actually paid to keep.

"Forget about the apple tart then," she says. "Go to the Draughts and fetch Harold. You are to return with him immediately and start on the stew."

"Yes, Mistress. Your every wish is my most desperate command." I bow sarcastically in her direction. Then I leave the kitchen, before I decide to grab a wooden spoon of my own.

❧

While I'm pulling on my cloak, Serena hollers for me to come to her bedroom.

When I arrive, she is scrutinizing herself in front of a mirror. She has Mistress Ogden's silvery-blond hair. She's plump and apple-cheeked from a lifetime of being given the best the Ogdens could afford. Today she is wearing the green silk dress Mistress bought the day after Mister Blackwell last visited.

She holds up first a powder blue frock and then a lavender one, the colors of the Andewyn family crest. "Which do you think the Masked Princess will prefer?"

"She has a name," I snap. "And I don't think she'll care two figs what you're wearing. You don't even know if Mister Blackwell can get Mistress tickets yet."

Serena frowns at her reflection. "Mother will find a way.

She always does." She holds up the lavender gown again and turns her head side to side. "Yes, I think lavender will do quite nicely. I'll need you to wash it and return it to my room when you're finished."

"It'll have to wait. Your mother has sent me to the Draughts again."

"Later then," she says, pursing her lips. "And say hello to Cordon for me."

I stare blankly back at her. Cordon is the son of Sylvia, the woman who owns the Draughts of Life. He is also my best friend. He has been since I can remember, though lately we don't talk as much as we used to. And ever since we were children, Cordon and Serena have never gotten along well.

"I will if I have time," I snap. "Between you and your mother I have quite enough to do already."

Serena's expression softens. "Things would go so much easier if you didn't antagonize her all the time," she says, and I know she must have heard us in the kitchen.

"Really, you think so?" I say. "You think if I was all sweetness and smiles she'd ask someone else to do the cooking and the cleaning?"

Serena stiffens and her expression of concern vanishes. "You are her servant. What she asks is nothing more than what is proper."

"Servant," I scoff. "Most families aren't paid sixteen

hundred worthings a year to house a servant."

"You're lucky to be here at all," she replies coolly, and holds out the lavender dress. "After all, if my family hadn't taken you in what would have become of you?"

I pluck the dress from her outstretched hand. The word *family* twists in my stomach like a cruel vice.

❧

When I finally step outside, I pull my cloak tight against the rain and wind. My boots squelch through mud as I make my way from Ogden Manor down the narrow path through the woods leading into town. Overhead, a canopy of almond tree branches blooms with tiny white and pink blossoms. Despite the rain, winter is finally giving way to spring.

I kick a muddy stone as I walk. There was a time when I believed Mistress Ogden was my mother and I thought she was the most beautiful woman in the world. I would have said anything, done anything, to have her smile at me. But over time I realized her smiles—like her love—would never be given to me, and that instead of trying to earn her favor, I needed to learn how to survive her wrath.

And now, all these years later, I have other concerns. One day those bags of worthings from the orphanage will stop coming. And when they do, what is to keep her from tossing me out of Ogden Manor? I don't know exactly when my birthday is, but I think I turn seventeen sometime this year. I doubt the orphanage will continue paying the Ogdens after I've come of age.

One winter when I was very young, the appointed night for Mister Blackwell's visit came and went and he never appeared. Mistress said she refused to provide a place for me if the orphanage wasn't going to pay for it, so she threw me out of the manor. I spent the night shivering in the Ogdens' barn, hoping I wouldn't freeze to death.

Mister Blackwell arrived early the next morning. A tree had fallen across the road, delaying his carriage. Like the great performer she is, Mistress immediately transformed into a loving and concerned mother. Mindful of how cold it had been in the barn, I played along. After Mister Blackwell left, we never spoke of that night. But the message was loud and clear:

No worthings, no home.

Sometimes when Mistress Ogden has sent me into town to buy food or supplies, I've wondered what would happen if I just kept walking? If I walked through the entire village of Tulan and continued beyond it, walking away from one life to find another.

Necessity stops me every time, though. Without a way to provide for myself, where would I go?

The snap of a twig and the sound of something, or someone, shuffling through a bush makes me stop and turn around. I shield my eyes against the rain but see nothing except for a couple of squirrels chasing each other up a tree.

I resume walking and my hand closes over the dagger I keep hidden in the pocket of my cloak. Another twig snaps. I turn around again, hoping to find more squirrels. But this time I see a flash of deep green fabric disappear among the fog and almond trees.

I leave my hand on my dagger and sprint the rest of the way to the tavern.

CHAPTER 2

ELARA

*T*he Draughts of Life sits at the edge of Tulan's meager town square. Dusty and old, it reeks of ale and desperation, frequented by men who've watched the price of grain rise higher and higher while their wages sink lower and lower. It's not a place that easily welcomes outsiders. But an unaccompanied young woman is another matter entirely, so I reach for my dagger again as I step inside.

But the first face I see isn't that of a man in search of comfort. It's the face of a child, one I know well.

"Timothy, what are you doing here?"

Timothy, a small boy of about eight, stares back at me with frightened eyes. He jumps slightly at the sound of a man loudly cursing. "Cordon said he'd try to find some leftovers for us."

Last month Timothy's father, a soldier, was recalled to Allegria, Galandria's capital, amid fears that war with Kyrenica was imminent. Most days his family doesn't have near enough to eat.

"All right. Stick near the wall and stay quiet." I raise my voice in case anyone's listening. "And if someone gives you any trouble, I want you to yell for me or Cordon."

Sylvia waves me over. She is taking orders from a table of men who look as though they've had more than their fair share of ale. One of them smacks her on the rump. Sylvia's eyes narrow and her lips thin, but she says nothing. Like everyone else in Tulan, she barely makes ends meet and can't afford to lose customers, no matter how ill-mannered they are.

"Back again, sweetheart?" says a scruffy, unshaven man with oily blond hair, a Draughts regular. "What's a pretty thing like you doing in a place like this?" His arm slithers around my waist. "Care for a friend tonight?"

I pull out my dagger and point it at him. "I've got enough friends, thanks."

That shuts him up and he turns away cursing. Sylvia bites back a smile and points to a table where Mister Ogden sits. "He happened upon a winning streak for once. Good luck bringing him home."

Mister Ogden is short and squat with a nose the size of a pimply squash, which is flushed beet red. Even from here I can see the shiny gold worthings stacked near his elbows as he examines his cards.

"Are you all right?" Sylvia continues. "You look a bit pale."

I hesitate before answering, mindful others are within earshot. I'm almost certain someone was following me, but I don't want anyone in this tavern thinking I'm a scared little girl.

I turn and stare at the tavern entrance, as though I'm expecting a ghastly villain to appear. Instead, the door opens and Mister Travers, Tulan's schoolteacher, steps inside.

I exhale.

"I'm fine," I tell Sylvia. "I'm just hungry. We've run out of most of the supplies we stored for the winter, so we've been saving our food for Mister Blackwell's visit tonight." What I don't say is that Mistress's idea of "saving food" means forcing me to go hungry while she, Serena, and Mister Ogden eat smaller meals.

Sylvia nods and tells me that Cordon is in the kitchen if I want to see him, then leaves to deliver more ale. I decide I'll wait to approach Mister Ogden until he's lost most of his worthings, which shouldn't take long, and head for the kitchen. On the way I pass two men slumped over mugs of ale, whispering.

"But do you suppose the rumors of the Masked Princess are true?" The man's eyes dart around, as though he expects the king's men to appear and pounce on him for the very thought.

"Which ones?" asks his companion. He hiccups and adds, "Took the wife to see the Masked Princess wave from her balcony last year. You ask me, she looked like nothing more than a rich brat."

Inside the kitchen, Cordon is filling a basket with stale bread and mushy apples. He smiles when he sees me. His eyes are as gray as the sky outside, and his unruly blond hair hangs in his face.

"Figured I'd see you in here sooner or later," he says as he finishes up with the basket and moves on to stir a pot of bubbling stew. "I already tried to tell Mister Ogden to go home, but he wouldn't hear of it."

"Thank you," I say, stepping closer. The warmth of the hearth is a relief after walking in the rain, and the smell of the stew makes me lightheaded.

"Serena asked me to talk to him. Convince him to cut back on the ale."

"How nice of her," I say curtly, although I can't remember when Serena and Cordon could have had that conversation. Serena is never required to bring her father home, as Mistress Ogden feels that the Draughts is too rough a place for her.

Cordon shoots me a wary look and changes the subject, "How did the cake turn out?"

"Crispy," I answer. "Mistress tossed it out."

"I told you I should have helped. I'm a much better cook than you are." He gives me a sly grin and I smile in return, cheered for the first time all day.

"All right," I say, laughing. "Next time you're in charge of convincing Mistress not to toss me out."

Cordon stops smiling. He looks down and begins stirring the stew with fast, efficient strokes. An awkward silence falls between us and I wish I'd kept my mouth shut. Ever since he came of age things have been strained between us, and I wonder if he remembers our childhood promise.

"Maybe you should talk to Serena," he says finally.

"Serena?" I repeat, surprised. "Why would I want to do that?"

"Maybe you can work out a different arrangement with the Ogdens," he says. "Serena would help you; I'm sure of it."

"I doubt Her Royal Highness could be bothered to lift one lazy finger on my behalf."

"She's not lazy," Cordon says, frowning. "She's just used to being waited on. And she's good with her mother. You should talk to her."

"Right. And since when do you make it your business to know what Serena's good at?"

"Don't be unkind. She's changed. Serena's not the girl she once was. She's grown softer, kinder."

I stifle a snort. The thought of Serena being a kind-hearted girl is laughable. Serena is the kind of girl who once threatened to tell Mistress I hit her if I didn't stand under a beehive. She wanted to see how long it would take for one to sting me. (Two hours, as it turned out.)

Of course, that was before I toughened up. Before I started studying Mistress and the way she persuaded others to do her bidding. Once I learned the delicate art of manipulation, I found I could convince Serena to do what-ever I wanted.

Do you know, Serena, I heard a woman talking in town, and she said that standing in a swamp will give you fairer skin? It must be true because she was beautiful. . . .

"Serena cares for you in her own, complicated way," Cordon continues.

"There's nothing complicated about being a spoiled brat," I say.

His features darken and he picks up the basket. "I need to give this to Timothy," he says stiffly. "Can you look after the stew?"

He brushes past me, and I'm left wondering why my words angered him.

Just then the door opens behind me, and a shadow casts across the wall. Hot breath brushes my neck and gooseflesh pimples my arms. It must be the oily-haired man, coming to see if I've reconsidered his offer of "friendship." As I reach for my dagger, a hand grabs my shoulder. I give a shout and whirl around and my dagger nearly slices Mister Travers's arm.

"I'm so sorry, Mister Travers," I say, sighing with relief as I slide the dagger back into my pocket.

Mister Travers moved to Tulan a month ago and is the best teacher I've ever had. I've always enjoyed school because it is the one place I can escape Mistress. Yet she always seemed to find reasons for me to stay home to cook and clean, saying it was useless to waste an education on me. In the past my schoolteachers, charmed by Mistress, always overlooked my absences. But Mister Travers makes it a point to visit Ogden Manor every time I miss, which irritates her to no end. Thanks to him, now I hardly ever miss school.

"I'm sorry, Elara," he says. "I didn't mean to scare you."

"You didn't scare me," I lie, although it looks like Mister Travers is the one who is scared. Sweat pours from his brow and his eyes seem strangely unfocused. I step closer to him and get a strong whiff of ale. "Is there a problem?" I ask.

"Your whole existence has been a problem," he whispers. His voice sounds haunted. But before I can take in his words, I notice the inside of his cloak.

It's lined in a deep, emerald green.

I step backward and the heat from the stew warms my back. "Were you following me, Mister Travers?"

He removes a handkerchief from his cloak and mops his brow. Although he doesn't reply, I realize I have my answer.

"Why were you following me?" I reach my hand back into my cloak and grasp my dagger. It occurs to me that although Mister Travers seems kind, I don't know him well at all.

"I am sorry I scared you . . . I had wanted to . . . that is, I thought I should—" He breaks off, and closes his eyes. When he opens them he says, "They've found me."

"What?" I step forward. "*Who*'s found you?"

"The Guardians. Ever since I came to Tulan I have wanted to speak with you. But I had to wait, I had to know for sure, and now it seems I have waited too long to tell you. . . ." He breaks off and his eyes stray to the door.

"The Guardians?" Sighing, I release my dagger and place a hand on Mister Travers's shoulder, as though he is a confused child. "I think you've had too much to drink. No one is coming after you. Let me make you a cup of—"

"No! You must tell no one you saw me today," he whispers intently. "I have something important to give you." Quickly, he reaches into his cloak and removes a book. An expensive one, judging by the brown leather-bound cover. He hands it to me and I read the title: *Eleanor of Andewyn House: Galandria's Greatest Queen.*

Eleanor Andewyn was Galandria's founding queen. She grew up in a family of miners and it was she who first discovered opals in Galandria's soil. She used her newfound wealth to unify all the villages and form our kingdom. Her family, the Andewyns, built the Opal Palace in Allegria and has ruled Galandria for centuries.

But why this should matter to me, I don't understand.

"Take it," Mister Travers says in response to my confusion. "I shall be going away, and the time has come for you to keep it."

"But why?"

"Because it was your mother's," he answers. "And she intended for you to have it."

CHAPTER 3

WILHA

*F*rom my chambers in the Opal Palace, I hear the people chanting my name. It is not my birth name they chant, but the other name. The one that has always overshadowed everything else. Their cries pelt in through the open window, insistent and demanding, like a nettlesome song that you cannot get out of your head.

Masked Princess!

Masked Princess!

Masked Princess!

A gust of wind blows into the room, and I bring a hand to my face. Instead of skin, my fingers brush the smooth, painted metal of my mask. It is cold and wet with stray raindrops.

Behind me, Arianne, my father's secretary, runs through my itinerary for the rest of the day, while my maid, Vena, begins tugging at my corset. I gasp as it pulls and puckers tight.

"How's that?" Vena grunts. She doesn't wait for an answer and begins fastening up the buttons on my gown. Her movements are hurried, as I know she hates touching me.

"It is a bit stiff," I murmur. "Could you—"

"Princess, try to concentrate, please?" Arianne says with annoyance. "Matters important to Galandria require your attention. After your appearance on the balcony, you have your training session with Patric. After that the king has asked you to visit the children at the Royal Orphanage. . . ."

Vena finishes buttoning my gown. I turn around to face Arianne, who peers at the parchment she holds and continues. "In addition, the daughter of the king's physician is having a wedding in three days. His Majesty feels it would be best if you attended."

"Please tell the king that if he wishes me to be there, I shall. But if he leaves it to my discretion, I should like to remain here."

Vena gives Arianne a look that says *I told you so*.

Arianne continues as though I have not spoken, "Master Welkin delivered your new mask today. He says it is his greatest work yet." She grimaces her disapproval, to remind me that I should have met with the mask maker myself, and holds up a large lavender velvet box.

I open the box and sigh. The metal mask is painted in gold leaf and encrusted with red, orange, and yellow fire opals from Galandria's wealthy opal mines. Small diamonds line the holes cut for my eyes. As I lift the mask from the box, the opals catch the candlelight and sparkle like a sunset. The mask is beautiful, yet I cannot see it as anything more than a sentence I must carry out.

I only wish someone would tell me what crime I have committed.

Although this mask is much brighter than the one I am currently wearing, they are identically shaped. Every mask I own covers my entire face, with the exception of my chin, my lips, and the top of my nose. When I was younger, I would stare at the shape of my masks and try to comfort myself with the thought that at least they left me enough space to breathe.

"Master Welkin is designing several more masks," Arianne says. "They should be ready in a week so you will have your pick for the birthday ball."

I utter my thanks and gratitude, for I know it's expected of me, then turn and enter my closet. I take a few uncomfortable steps and turn back to tell Vena my corset really is too tight, but stop when I hear Arianne whispering.

"Spoiled is what she is. Doesn't appreciate anything the king does. He gives her the world and asks that she only make a few appearances."

"Spoiled freak, you mean," Vena whispers back. "If my family didn't need the worthings, you wouldn't catch me anywhere near her. The palace pays good money after what happened to Rinna. I'll bet you under that mask she's just as ugly as they say she is."

A true princess would not allow her servants to speak about her so. But at hearing the name of my former nanny, I draw back so they cannot see me. The fear that Vena may be speaking nothing less than the truth steals my voice.

Quietly, I turn back and move deeper into the closet. Rows of golden gowns and jeweled silken dresses seem to go on for ages. Glass cases holding every mask I have received since birth line the wall in front of me.

The cases are made of thick glass that is said to be unbreakable, and can only be opened by a jeweled key, a key which always hangs around my neck. Dozens of other decorative keys hang from the chain as well, forming a thick jeweled necklace. The keys clink and jingle as I remove the necklace and open a case. I place my new mask inside the case and close it again.

I stop to look at myself in the mirror next to the cases. The mask I am wearing is painted black, and black opals that shine with veins of sapphire trail like tears down either side.

I glance backward to make sure Arianne and Vena have not stepped into the closet. When I see they haven't, I untie the mask and stare at my reflection. My eyes are green, and my nose is small. My hair is brown, the same color, I am told, as my mother's. There is nothing remarkable about me. Yet surely, there is nothing horrendous either?

"Princess!" Arianne snaps. "It is nearly noon!"

I sigh and tie the mask back on. Every Friday at noon, I appear on the palace balcony before the crowd. The stares are agony. People look at me, not as someone they may wish to know, but as a macabre curiosity, a freak that both intrigues and repulses them. Men hold their children tighter, fearing that the rumors may be true, and I have the power to harm their family. Beautiful women glare at me, feeling upstaged by the grandeur of my jewels and dress. The peasants worship or revile me, calling out their well wishes or ill will in equal measures.

None of them want to look past the Masked Princess's costume and see the girl underneath.

❧

*T*he chanting grows louder, until it seems the palace walls shake in anticipation. I hurry down the corridor with Arianne and Vena following closely behind. A group of nobles who have come to call on my father sweep out of our way. One woman discreetly brings her hand to her eyes as we pass, in case I suddenly decide to rip off my mask and curse everyone with my abominable face.

Patric stands in front of all the other guards at the entrance to the balcony. His black hair, broad shoulders, and strong arms and legs give him the distinct build of a soldier.

"Good afternoon, Princess." His voice is formal and he bows appropriately.

I nod. "Good afternoon, Patric." I am careful to match his tone.

"Will you be joining us on the balcony today?" Vena, standing beside me, tucks a lock of brown hair behind her ear.

"Not today," he answers, though he looks at me as he speaks.

"Pity," Vena says in a lilting voice. "A stray arrow might be worth the risk if it were *you* coming to a lady's rescue."

"Stray arrows are nothing to joke about," Patric says curtly. "Especially while the princess stands beside you."

"Of course. Please forgive me." Vena curtsies in my direction, yet I read the irritation in her eyes.

"Forgive me for detaining you, Madame Arianne," Patric says with a brief glance in her direction. "I have come with a message for the princess. We will have to cancel our training session today." He pauses, and I read the slightest disappointment in his eyes. "After your appearance on the balcony, the king requests your presence in his study. We are instead to have our lesson early next week."

I nod briefly, as though he is just another guard.

Patric bows and leaves, and while Arianne gives instructions to the other guards, Vena leans in close, her eyes lingering on Patric's retreating figure. "During your training sessions, does he mention anyone? He is of age. Is he betrothed?"

"I wouldn't know. I do not make inquiries of his personal life," I say, dismayed to realize this is the truth. I turn away, unwilling to discuss Patric any longer.

Arianne orders the guards to open the doors to the balcony, and we are greeted with the smell of rain and wet cobblestones. Cheers from the crowd below mix with the roaring of the wind. Vena holds a parasol over my head and I step forward.

Even with the rain, the courtyard is packed. People are still streaming through the gilded gates, past the gardens and water fountains, and up to the stone steps, where a line of palace guards stand.

Peasants dressed in simple clothes mix with rich Allegrian noblewomen, who carry their own pastel-colored parasols. Several men and women appear to be on a pilgrimage judging by their foreign-looking robes. At the very front of the crowd are several men dressed in brown cloaks and masks made of gold thread. I know them to be "Maskrens," a cult devoted to the Masked Princess.

I look, too, at the masks some of the women in the crowd wear: simple costumed ones for the merchant class, and jeweled—but less ornate than mine—ones for the noblewomen. A scream wells in my throat, clawing for release. But I swallow it, because who will ever understand?

"Smile and wave, for Eleanor's sake," Arianne hisses in my ear. "Stop standing there looking like you are facing the chopping block."

I obey and force myself to wave. The crowd parts for two men, each of whom hold the arm of a third man. All three of them look ragged and dirty. But the third man has a bloody nose. His left eye is swollen shut; his lips are bruised. His shirt is torn, and he is fighting to free himself from the other two.

The first man says, "Masked Princess, we have a crime to report," and he gives the third man a shake. "This man stole grain from a family in our village. One of the little ones got sick from hunger and died. This man is guilty of murder!"

"We have come here to demand justice!" The second man raises his voice. "Take off your mask and curse him. Give him the punishment he deserves!"

A hush falls over the crowd. Even the wind ceases its wailing. Horror twists my insides as his words register. I grasp the balcony railing and look down at the bruised and bleeding man, who stares back at me with terrified eyes. The men who hold him are superstitious. Yet they are not asking for healing or a blessing, as some have before.

They are asking me to kill this man.

A few women gather up their children and hurry away. Several other citizens cover their eyes.

"I wasn't trying to hurt anyone," screams the bleeding man as his captors shove him to his knees. "I was hungry!"

"Everyone is hungry," shouts a peasant woman in the crowd. "Everyone except the Andewyns and the rich!"

Arianne's grip on my shoulder is vice-like. "Say something!" she hisses. "Before this turns ugly."

I look out at the crowd. The air is thick with silent expectation. I open my mouth, but no words come out.

Arianne curses under her breath and then shouts down at the men. "Take him to the courthouse if you feel he has wronged you." She begins ushering me back into the palace. "Get back inside, unless you want to be the cause of another death."

There is a sharp intake of breath from Vena and the

guards. Arianne goes pale as she realizes she has just uttered the unspeakable.

"Your Highness," she says, for once using my proper title, "I apologize. I was out of line."

I nod blindly and follow her back inside the palace. Vena hurries away, muttering something about errands.

After she is gone, I lower my voice and ask Arianne, "Did she die? After what happened, did Rinna die?"

Arianne refuses to look me in the eye. "Your father has asked to see you in his study. You don't want to keep the king waiting."

"Please," I beg. "No one will ever speak to me about her."

Arianne sighs. "It is not my place to ask questions," she says carefully. "But shortly after . . . the incident, Lord Murcendor told me Rinna had to return to her village due to family obligations."

"And did you believe him?" I whisper.

Arianne doesn't answer. But I read the truth in her eyes and know that she, just like so many others, believes I am a monster.

CHAPTER 4

WILHA

*A*ll my life I have been forbidden to show my face. Yet I don't know why. All I know is the scandal surrounding my birth. While my mother Queen Astrid lay laboring in her bed, my father ordered the Opal Palace be emptied of all its staff. A few members of the Guardian Council were summoned to the palace, and no word was heard from them, or my father, for two days. Everyone in Allegria assumed my mother had died, and possibly, the baby she carried as well.

Yet on the third day my father, King Fennrick the Handsome, appeared on the palace balcony. Tired and careworn, he declared that Queen Astrid, though severely sick, was alive and had given birth to a healthy baby girl, who they named Wilhamina. When my mother finally reappeared in public she was unrecognizable. Gone was Astrid the Regal, the strong queen who bore the monarchy with grace and compassion. Instead, I am told that she seemed a pale, haggard shadow of her former self. My father said she had been weakened by child birth and did not fully recover.

Most citizens in Allegria would have believed him, had it not been for the page who had been sent to summon the Guardians. The following night he got drunk at a tavern and swore loudly to anyone who would listen that he had heard the king shouting about the birth of his first child. That the child was not a blessing, but a curse.

When I was finally shown to the public, I was wearing a tiny, opal-encrusted mask over my face. No formal explanation for the mask was ever given. Royal officials—who themselves seemed bewildered by my father's decision to cover my face—assumed that it was a stunt, a device for King Fennrick to gain even more glory and fame for Galandria.

But many remembered the words of the page, who had disappeared shortly after his drunken confession, and other rumors began to circulate. Some believe that I was born with a facial defect and my father, brokenhearted his good looks had not been passed on, decreed I should wear a mask to hide my ugliness. Others believe that my mother looked upon me and became seriously ill, surviving just long enough to bear a son, my brother, Crown Prince Andrei, and that the mask is to ensure the protection of everyone else, lest they suffer the same cursed fate as the queen.

And one rumor that some desperately want to believe is that one look from the Masked Princess can bless or heal those in need. But I know my face can help no one.

Over the years, these rumors of the Masked Princess have spread far and wide, perhaps just as my father intended. Most sensible people in Allegria take no notice of them. Yet still, the most superstitious believe any one of them.

My father and his advisors have always assured me there is nothing wrong with me or my face. Yet it is difficult to believe them, as they never offer a real explanation for the mask. Once when I was a small child I took off my mask in front of Rinna, my favorite nanny. It was summer, and I didn't understand why I still had to wear the mask, even on the hottest of days, when all I wanted was to press my cheek to Rinna's cool palm.

I can still remember the shock and sorrow on Rinna's face, and her strangled voice crying, "But Princess, you know the rules!"

"Rinna, please," I sobbed, clinging to her. "I forgot. No one has to know. Please." Back then, I believed I would receive a good lecture and a paddling from my father, whose wrath was a fearsome thing to behold. Yet the punishment was far worse. Rinna, too noble to lie, even by omission, went to my father and reported the indiscretion.

And that was the last I ever saw or heard from her.

Lord Murcendor, one of my father's Guardians, visited me the next morning. "Rinna became seriously ill last night. Unfortunately, she can no longer be of any service to the royal family."

He paused, and added, "Is it true you took your mask off in front of her?"

"Yes," I replied in a little girl whisper. "Did that make her sick?"

"Of course not." Lord Murcendor said quickly. "But Wilha, you know what your father says. Be a good girl and keep the mask on."

After word spread in the castle about the incident, most other nannies and servants in the Opal Palace kept a careful eye on me, making sure I never again lifted my mask. And for several years afterward, I would ask what had become of Rinna, but no answer was ever given. As I grew older, and began to understand why some people would cover their eyes upon seeing me, and the whispers that always followed, I stopped asking about her. I was not sure I could handle the answer.

Oftentimes when I am alone I remove my mask and spend hours gazing at my reflection. And I cannot help but wonder . . .

Is this the face of Death?

⊶⊷

My father's private study is located just off of the Eleanor Throne Room, a large hall where he receives visitors and conducts state business. At the end of the hall on the north end is his gilded throne. On the western end, as though she is watching over the room, stands a white statue of Galandria's founder, Queen Eleanor the Great. In each of her hands she holds one of the two Split Opals she dropped during her coronation. Fifteen palace guards surround the statue and they bow as I pass through the hall.

As I enter the study my father and Lord Quinlan, the Guardian of Defense, are standing over my father's desk examining a stack of parchments.

". . . Gathered enough information and they are in pursuit of him as we speak," I hear Lord Quinlan saying. "We should have word very soon. And as for the other matter . . ."

"As for the other matter, my mind is already made up," my father answers sharply. "I will not hear—" He stops abruptly when he sees me standing in the doorway.

Lord Quinlan turns to look at me, his thick jeweled necklaces glinting in the candlelight, and he quickly gathers up the parchments. "Have a care, Fennrick," he says, as he exits the room. "Done right, war can be quite profitable." He sweeps past me with a brief bow.

My father scowls in response and signals that I should wait while he scribbles on a strip of parchment. Though still handsome, he seems to have aged overnight. I wonder if what everyone is saying is true, if war with Kyrenica is now inevitable.

My father rolls up the parchment and begins to speak. "Daughter, you are aware I have been negotiating a treaty with Sir Reinhold, Kyrenica's ambassador?" He removes a pigeon from its cage and attaches the parchment to the bird's leg. Then he releases the pigeon and it flies out the open window and into the rain.

I nod. "I am."

He rubs his temples and opens his mouth but seems to be at a loss for words. In that moment I see him, as I suspect many do, as merely a second son, never properly trained to rule. Crowned king only after his more competent older brother died of the same fever that took my grandfather the king.

"I am convinced the Kyrenicans mean to attack us. Yet Sir Reinhold plays his role well. He says King Ezebo believes Galandria is poised to invade Kyrenica. I have assured him that, so long as I am king, Galandria is committed to peacefully coexisting with Kyrenica.

"Kyrenica's strength grows each year," he continues. "So we must not be idle. We must secure peace now, when we can offer what the Kyrenicans desire. Rather than waiting until they are strong enough to take it by force."

I am unsure where my father is going with this. He does not often discuss politics—or anything else—with me. Mostly, he seems to prefer pretending I do not exist.

"And what is it they desire?" I ask.

"Mining rights over the northern range of the Opal Mountains. They have demanded that we allow them passage without interference from our army. If we do not grant them this, then they shall eventually engage their own army. In exchange, they will remove their trading restrictions on Galandria, which has been crippling our economy. And . . ."

He pauses to clear his throat. "And King Ezebo demands your betrothal to his son, the crown prince of Kyrenica."

I feel the blood drain from my face and my body goes rigid. Marry into the Kyrenican royal family? There could be nothing worse.

A century ago, Kyrenica, Galandria's premier seaport, declared independence from us. The revolt in Kyrenica was led by Aislinn Andewyn, the twin sister of my great-great grandmother Queen Rowan the Brave. Aislinn was said to be bitterly jealous that Rowan, older by a mere seven minutes, was crowned queen of Galandria instead of her.

Queen Rowan traveled to Kyrenica to resolve the dispute. She was betrayed by Aislinn, who came to be known as the Great Betrayer, and was taken prisoner inside the Kyrenican Castle. Rowan was sentenced to death. However, the night before she was to be beheaded, she miraculously escaped. Aislinn was held responsible for Queen Rowan's escape and was executed instead by King Ezebo's great grandfather, Bronson Strassburg, the nobleman who helped Aislinn incite the Kyrenicans against Queen Rowan. War began in earnest and continued for several years until Galandria was forced to admit defeat. Bronson Strassburg declared himself king of a newly independent Kyrenica and annexed several other coastal regions, leaving Galandria virtually land-locked.

And what was once a vast Galandrian kingdom, was essentially split in two. Many believe it was the fulfillment of the omen foretold in the Legend of the Split Opals, on the day of Queen Eleanor's coronation.

All my life I have been taught to believe that the Kyrenicans and their royal family, the Strassburgs, are brutal, desperate people. That they are a threat to my family, and to everyone else in Galandria.

Several seconds go by before I can respond, and when I do, my voice is high-pitched and quaking. "You would have me marry a Strassburg? A Kyrenican?"

"You would marry Crown Prince Stefan, the future king of Kyrenica."

"I have heard you say that the lowest servant in Galandria is more worthy than the greatest lord in Kyrenica. You have called them dogs. You would have me marry a dog?"

"I would have you save lives. It seems that King Ezebo does not fear the rumors of your mask, and is eager to see you married to his son. He has asked for your immediate departure. You are to leave in three months."

"Three months?" I repeat. "But I am not to marry until I am seventeen."

"You will marry at seventeen. In a year." He nods. "But we agreed that as a gesture of goodwill, I would send you sooner. And it will give you time to become acquainted with Kyrenica before the wedding."

"But . . . I thought I had another year. . . ." I feel faint and I sink into the chair in front of his desk. Why is he so eager to get rid of me?

My father shuffles the parchments on his desk, and when he looks up at me he sighs. "Be a good girl, Wilha. A good princess. Kingdoms need someone to believe in. Let them believe in you."

He stands then, as though the matter is settled. And I suppose it is.

"I will go," I say, also standing. "You know I will. But give me one thing before I go."

"A gift? Certainly. All the jewels and dresses—"

"No, not that. I want you to look at me. If the rumors are untrue, as you say they are, then please, look at me." I move to untie my mask.

"Wilha, stop!" His voice is firm. "Don't make this more difficult."

"Don't make *what* more difficult? You say that the rumors are rubbish. If that is true, then why will you not look at me?"

He does not answer. Instead, he exits the room without another word. And I am left alone with the sinking fear that has been my constant companion.

Because if my own father refuses to look at me, there must be something horribly wrong with me.

CHAPTER 5

ELARA

I cannot breathe. I cannot speak. I can only stare blindly at the book.

This was my mother's?

Before I can ask any of the thousand questions churning in my mind, the din in the tavern suddenly ceases and a loud voice calls out. "I'm looking for the man you all know as Travers."

Mister Travers pales. He seizes me by the arm and shoves me into an alcove just off the kitchen where Sylvia keeps her supplies.

"But who wants—" I begin.

"Hush!" He grabs my shoulders and stares at me with an intensity I've never before seen in his eyes. "Stay in here until I'm gone, do you understand?" he whispers fiercely, gripping my shoulders tighter until I nod. "Tell no one we have spoken."

"We saw him come in here," the voice outside the kitchen continues. "We will reward anyone who can deliver him to us."

"I saw him go into the kitchen," calls another voice.

Quickly, Mister Travers strides to the door and opens it. With a grim determination he declares: "I am the one you are looking for."

Once he disappears into the main room, I slip the book

into my cloak, cross the kitchen, and crack the door open an inch.

The room is silent. A palace guard wearing a breastplate with the Andewyn coat of arms binds Mister Travers's hands with chains. Several other guards stand nearby, eyeing the men warily, many of whom have risen from their seats and have their hands near their belt, as though they intend to grab their weapon.

"Our business is only with this man," a guard calls out. "The rest of you can resume your activities."

The guards usher Mister Travers out the door. Just before he leaves, the guard who bound Mister Travers's hands holds up a large black velvet bag. He opens it and tosses a handful of worthings to the floor. "A present from King Fennrick."

The hush that has fallen over the room breaks and the men are on the floor, scrambling over one another for the worthings. And though I haven't forgotten Mister Travers's words, the sight of the golden coins makes me plunge into the crowd, scratching, pulling, and kicking, until I've collected twelve worthings. I walk over and give eight of them to a watery-eyed Timothy.

"Take these," I say, pulling him out the door quickly. "Take them and hide them in your pocket. Don't show them to anyone, and run until you get home."

After Timothy flees, I turn in the other direction and see a guard is pushing Mister Travers into a gilded carriage.

"That's a royal carriage from Allegria," Cordon says, joining me at the door.

The curtain in the carriage parts, and a pale hand adorned with a large opal ring holds out several worthings to the guard, who accepts them and bows.

"What could King Fennrick possibly want with Mister Travers?" Cordon asks. He turns to me, looking concerned. "When he went into the kitchen, did he say anything to you?"

My hand slides down my cloak. I feel the edge of the book, hidden in my pocket. I glance back at the carriage and make a decision. "Nothing. He said nothing at all."

❧

After I finally pry Mister Ogden away from the Draughts and we begin our walk home, I wonder how Mister Travers came to be in possession of a book belonging to my mother. I consider every possibility I can think of until one of them fits.

Mister Ogden, though incapable of managing Ogden Manor, has been able to sustain a side business by systematically selling off the contents of the manor. He's made somewhat of a name for himself as an antiques dealer. Few of his customers realize it's his own possessions he sells.

If my mother left a handful of items to be passed on to me, I have no doubt the Ogdens would see it as nothing more than their right to sell them. And I'm sure Mister

Travers, being a schoolteacher fond of history, would have jumped at the chance to own such an expensive-looking book. Though how he could've found out the book was my mother's, I don't know. And if she left me a book, what else did she leave? Had there been other items that would have given me a clue to my family's origins?

But that doesn't explain why palace guards were after Mister Travers or his insistence that I not be seen with him. And the guard had said they were looking for *the man we know as Travers*. Is that not his real name?

"Harold, you're drunk!" Mistress Ogden cries as I drag him into the kitchen.

"Not a bit, dearest," Mister Ogden says and sways before sitting down heavily on the stool I pull out for him. "I've just had a wonderful run of the cards." With a flourish, he produces several worthings. "And you'll never guess what just happened at the Draughts—"

"I don't care," Mistress Ogden snaps. "You're late. Mister Blackwell will be here soon." She glares at me. "I had to start the potato stew myself."

"Mister Blackwell, bah!" Mister Ogden says, belching. "Never liked the look of that man. Calculating, like a snake—though perhaps that's why you like him so, dearest. Don't like his sneaky black eyes glaring like he thinks he's better than me."

"He *is* better than you. He's the one with the worthings."

While they bicker, I quickly hide the book in the pantry and promise myself I'll look through it later.

"Worthings? What did I just say—" Mister Ogden leans back—and promptly tumbles off the stool. His worthings scatter across the kitchen floor.

"Harold, get up this instant!" Mistress Ogden practically stamps her foot in frustration.

"The candles in the dining room are lit," Serena says, glowering as she enters the kitchen. Upon seeing Mister Ogden on the floor she rushes to his side. "Father, what's happened?"

"I'll tell you what's happened, my love!" Mister Ogden picks up a worthing and brandishes it like a sword. "I've just won at the Draughts of Life! Don't need creepy Mister Blackwell coming into my house telling me what's what. Am I not Ogden of Ogden Manor?" He spreads his hands wide, as though Ogden Manor is a grand palace, instead of the rotting dump it actually is.

Mistress and I glance at each other. She may despise me, but when she really needs something done, it's to me—and not to Serena—that she looks.

"Come Mister Ogden," I say in my most humble voice. "Dinner will be soon and I feel you should be dressed in a manner befitting your station. After all, you are the lord of Ogden Manor, are you not?"

Serena stands up. "Don't you dare talk to him like he's a fool."

"Serena!" Mistress Ogden snaps. "Accompany your father

upstairs and help him clean up."

Serena lowers her voice so only I can hear. "I don't know how you can claim to hate her so much, when you're *exactly* like her."

She stalks from the kitchen, practically dragging Mister Ogden away by the arm, and I grab on to the counter, fighting the urge to vomit. I am nothing like Mistress Ogden. I stop and take a deep breath, and imagine myself feeding Serena's words to the starved kitten.

"Set the table," Mistress Ogden commands. When I don't move she says, "Well? What are you waiting for?"

"When the orphanage brought me to you, did they give you anything from my mother?" I ask. "A keepsake, something to remember her by?" I don't mention the book, or Mister Travers, as I wouldn't put it past her to steal the book a second time.

She removes a vase from a shelf. "Your mother was probably nothing but a dirty whore who abandoned you the first chance she got. You really think she'd leave you something?"

"Please," I say, forcing the anger from my voice. "Did she leave me anything?"

"I haven't got time for your nonsense." She begins polishing the vase. "Mister Blackwell will be here in just a matter of—"

"Tell me the truth!" I move to grab her arm. My aim lands low, and my hand knocks the vase from her hands. Glass shatters on the stone floor.

Mistress Ogden stands very still. "You will pick that up immediately, or—"

"Or what?" I interrupt. "You'll beat me? Deny me more meals? Lock me in the barn again? If you're going to do something, you'd better make sure it doesn't leave any marks, otherwise Mister Blackwell may decide not to pay you tonight."

"I don't wish to play your games." She fetches a broom and holds it out to me.

I grab the broom and then hurl it across the room. It smacks the wall and clatters to the ground. I step closer to her, and for the first time ever, I see a shadow of fear flicker across her face. "And maybe I don't wish to play *your* games. Maybe it would be worth it to me to tell Mister Blackwell who you *really* are."

Mistress Ogden reaches out. Her long nails sink into my bare forearm, piercing my skin, and I gasp in pain. "Mister Blackwell will come tonight," she hisses. "And you will play your role, do you understand?" She rakes her nails down my arm, leaving small red rivers in their wake. "And if you do not, you will find yourself chained up like a common thief, as I'll have to tell the sheriff how you've been stealing from us."

"I've never stolen anything from you!"

She bends low and whispers into my ear, "It would be my word against yours. Do you think anyone would ever believe you over me?" Her nails dig deeper. "Do you understand?"

"Yes." I gasp in relief when she finally releases me.

"Now," she says, smoothing her skirts, "you will clean this mess up. You will scrape the grime off yourself. And you will make an effort to look like a respectable girl."

She turns around to leave, but turns back. "And Elara?" Her gaze flicks to my bleeding forearm. "Make sure you wear long sleeves."

CHAPTER 6

ELARA

When it comes to deception, attention to detail is everything.

The table is set with silver bowls and goblets (the ones Mistress Ogden keeps locked up so Mister Ogden can't sell them). White candles are placed before each setting and their flames flicker in the drafty dining room. It looks as though we're about to sit down to a nice family meal, instead of a performance carefully crafted by Mistress Ogden.

When Mister Blackwell arrives and Mistress Ogden shows him into the dining room, I feel a cold, cutting pain. Like a jagged piece of ice has wedged itself in my chest.

"Good evening, Elara," Mister Blackwell extends his hand, which I take.

"Good evening, sir."

He raises my hand to his lips, and it's all I can do not to snatch my arm away. Something about Mister Blackwell repulses me. He is thin. Skeletal, almost. His long black hair hangs down his back and his eyes are dark, unreadable orbs.

We take our places around the table. Mistress and I sit next to each other. She fills our goblets and nods in my direction. It's a slight, almost imperceptible incline of her head, and like an apprentice taking orders from his master, I understand. It's time to begin.

"How are things in Allegria?" I ask Mister Blackwell. I force myself to take a small, controlled bite of stew, not letting on how hungry I am.

"Well," Mister Blackwell replies. "The city is preoccupied with preparations for the princess's masquerade ball."

"Yes, I admit I have been thinking of nothing else myself," I say, affecting a breathless voice that sounds nothing like my own.

"Oh yes, the ball is coming up isn't it?" Mistress Ogden says, as though the thought has only just occurred to her. "Do you know that when she was little, Elara used to pretend she was the Masked Princess? She cut up one of her dresses— a really nice one, mind you—and tied it like a silk mask to her face."

"You did?" At this, Mister Blackwell looks at me. For once, his grim manner has vanished and he seems amused.

"Yes, sir," I lie. And for good measure I add, "I also used to stand at the top of the stairs and wave, like it was a balcony." I mimic a grand wave with a smile. Serena rolls her eyes but says nothing.

"I used to live in Allegria very briefly." Mistress gets a wistful look on her face. "I performed with the Royal Theatre Company. Once upon a time, I was quite the actress."

"That doesn't surprise me." Mister Blackwell casts an unreadable look at Mistress Ogden. And for a moment, I wonder if he knows we're all just a bunch of pathetic liars.

"I tell the girls all the time that Allegria's the most beautiful city in the world. Though it is difficult to describe to someone who has never been there." Mistress Ogden sighs. "I have so wanted to show the girls the Royal Opera House and Eleanor Square, and take them to see the Opal Palace."

"Do you intend to visit Allegria soon, then?" Mister Blackwell asks.

Mistress Ogden shakes her head. "We've had a tough few months. And a trip to Allegria costs money. Though it would be a good lesson for the girls, a bit of living history, don't you think? Something a schoolteacher just can't explain." Mistress leans back in her chair, looking utterly defeated. Her gaze finds Mister Blackwell, and I know she is gearing up for her grand finale. "I don't suppose—"

"As it happens, Elara and I saw the girls' teacher today." Mister Ogden, who, up until now has seemed content to silently drain his goblet, suddenly rouses himself.

"What?" Mistress Ogden frowns, caught off guard and clearly not happy he has changed the subject. But she doesn't let it faze her. "You mean Mister Travers?" she asks, feigning interest. "However is he?"

"Well, it was quite strange," Mister Ogden begins, and relates what happened at the Draughts of Life.

"Where do you suppose they were taking him?" Serena asks once he's finished.

"Perhaps he was a convict," Mister Blackwell speaks up. "Many criminals flee Allegria, hoping that the farther they get from the Crown, the surer they will be able to evade the justice that is due to them."

"A criminal?" Serena says. "I wouldn't have taken Mister Travers for a criminal. But then he didn't grow up in Tulan. I wonder why he chose to settle here?"

Outwardly I give no sign that the conversation troubles me. But inwardly I feel faint and my stomach churns. A possibility I hadn't considered earlier enters my mind. Why *would* an outsider choose to settle in Tulan, a small, insignificant village, unless he had a very good reason for doing so? To what lengths would a hunted man go to protect his family? If he'd had a daughter, would he hide her? Would he have gone so far to deliver her to an orphanage, only to find her later when he thought he would be safe now?

Is Mister Travers my father?

Mister Blackwell turns his dark gaze to me. "Did you see him in the tavern as well? Did he say anything to you?" His words seem casual enough, as though he's just making polite conversation. I'm considering my answer, weighing each word carefully, when I notice something that makes my blood run cold.

The large opal ring on Mister Blackwell's pale hand. Exactly like the one the man in the carriage wore.

Mister Blackwell is the man who had Mister Travers

taken to Allegria? And yet just a few hours later he sits here, acting as though he's only just arrived in Tulan, in the shabby carriage we've always greeted him in, not the royal one bearing the Andewyn coat of arms.

"Did you see him?" Mister Blackwell repeats.

My face becomes still. "I never noticed him until the guards arrived. I was talking to my friend Cordon the whole time. What will happen to him in Allegria?"

Mister Blackwell's face is a veil of shadows in the flickering candlelight. "If your schoolteacher is in some kind of trouble, he will be put in prison to await trial."

Mistress Ogden grabs my hand and squeezes it. Hard. I know I should drop it and steer the conversation back to what she really wants. But what I want is answers. Mister Travers knows something about my mother and somehow, I need to find him.

And suddenly, it occurs to me that I can.

"Well, I suppose there is no use talking about it anymore then," I say with a wave of my hand. I turn to Mistress Ogden and give her such a look of sunny adoration that she seems momentarily confused by my sudden change in attitude. "I know things are difficult, Mother"—I force myself to choke out the word—"But isn't there some way we could go to Allegria? I so want to see the Masked Princess."

The confusion on her face vanishes, and it's replaced by a look of approval. I know she hates me. But I think a small part of her grudgingly respects me for learning to be somewhat of the performer she herself is.

She shakes her head before smiling sadly. "I'm sorry, but tickets to the masquerade are just impossible to get." She turns to Mister Blackwell. "Aren't they?"

"Actually," Mister Blackwell says, "many of us in Allegria were given invitations. Perhaps the orphanage could sponsor your trip to Allegria, as well as provide you with tickets."

"Why Mister Blackwell, that would be just lovely." Faster than I've ever seen her move, she reaches across the table and snatches the four tickets and bag of worthings Mister Blackwell holds out. From the look in her eyes, I can tell she thinks she's gotten the best of him.

Yet as I listen to them speak, I'm not so sure. He knows more about Mister Travers than he is letting on. And he just happened to have exactly four tickets to a ball that's supposed to be nearly impossible to get into? I look at Mister Blackwell, at his shadowed face, unreadable black eyes, and his opal ring glinting in the candlelight. I can't help but wonder if it hadn't been his plan for us to travel to Allegria all along.

I don't care about the Masked Princess, or her masquerade ball. But if Mr. Travers is still in Allegria by the time I arrive, somehow, I'm going to find him.

CHAPTER 7

WILHA

*T*he gardens surrounding the Opal Palace are famous for their beauty. My favorite has always been an apple orchard known as the Queen's Garden. Off limits to everyone but the royal family, it is located on the south-western end of the palace grounds. Interspersed between the trees are white stone statues of every ruling queen of Galandria, from Eleanor the Great to my mother, Queen Astrid. Next to my mother's statue is an empty space, which is to be filled once a new queen is crowned.

It is a place I come to when I need to be alone, away from the whispers and the rumors. A place where, except for the guards keeping watch along the garden's wall, the only eyes that see me are made of stone.

A weak spring sun shines upon my mother's statue, and I try to find within her stone face some resemblance to myself. There is no law in Galandria, with its rich history of strong queens, decreeing the crown must pass to the firstborn son. No law saying that I, as the eldest, cannot be the crown princess of Galandria and one day have my own statue in this garden, right next to my mother's. Yet I have always known, from the time such thoughts could enter my head, that my brother Andrei would one day rule Galandria. That the next statue to grace the Queen's Garden will be of Andrei's wife.

A breeze stirs up, sending blossoms swirling from the apple trees, and for a moment it seems my mother's statue weeps pink flower petals. Her lips are pressed together. Her hair is coiled on her head, her chin is raised, and her arms are at her sides. She looks strong, as though she could stare down an entire army by the sheer force of her will.

I see nothing of myself in her.

⚜

It is several minutes later, when I am staring at the empty space where a statue of me will never be, that I hear something behind me. I turn, and see Lord Murcendor approaching. He wears a thick emerald green robe identifying him as a member of the Guardian Council.

Lord Murcendor's appearance is oft-putting to many. His sleek dark hair, pale face, and grave manner make others uneasy. But they do not know him like I do. As the Guardian of the Opal Mines, and therefore the protector of Galandria's wealth, the safety of the Andewyn family rests heavily upon his shoulders.

"You called for me, Your Highness?"

"Please do not call me that," I say. "Not today."

"Very well, Wilha." He pauses. "The last time I saw you, you were sitting here as well."

"I have a training session with Patric soon," I reply, touching the lightweight red velvet mask I am allowed to wear during our lessons. "Besides," I motion to my mother's statue, "I wanted to look at her while I still could."

"I see." Lord Murcendor settles himself on the bench next to me. "Your father told you then?"

I nod, and the tears I have been holding back the last few days start escaping. Lord Murcendor waits patiently for me, as he always does. "Father says I serve Galandria by marrying the Kyrenican crown prince," I say when I regain my composure.

"The Kyrenicans are dogs," he retorts, and I read the anger in his eyes. "Their rightful place is under Galandria's boot."

I turn to him. "Please, can you not change his mind?"

"You overestimate my influence, Wilha. It is Lord Royce who has your father's ear on this matter, and as usual he will only tell the king what he wants to hear. And what your father wants to hear, like many kings, is that he is right. During our sessions in the Guardians' Chambers, Lord Quinlan made an excellent case for declaring war and the wealth it could bring us. But your father is a fool. He is so keen to avoid a war—a war I believe we have every assurance of winning—because he and Lord Royce are too cowardly to risk going into battle. I alone argued your case and told him it was madness to hand you over to our enemy without any regard for your safety or happiness. You are the Glory of Galandria. It kills me to see so great a treasure as you pass into the hands of such despicable men."

I look away from his fiery gaze. I know he means well, but his words bring no comfort. *The Glory of Galandria* is the same thing as *The Masked Princess*. A nonperson.

I swallow. "I have been dreaming again."

For years I have been plagued with nightmares. Right after Rinna died, I used to dream that all the boys and girls in Allegria would surround me. They would slap and grab at me, and when one of them would succeed in pulling off my mask, they all promptly fell to the ground, dead.

Or I would dream that I was playing by the banks of the Eleanor River and slipped into the water. But when I tried to surface, I found I could not because my mask was too heavy. And no matter how much I thrashed about, it kept pulling me downward, until I could no longer see the sunlight.

"What do you dream of this time?" he asks.

"I dream that when the crown prince and I meet he decides the mask is not enough." I close my eyes. "I dream that he decides to lock me away in a crypt, where I am hidden from others, unable to cause harm." I breathe deeply and open my eyes. "Please, tell me what I should do."

"Do not give up so easily." His voice is sharp. "There is still time." His gaze strays to my lips and his voice lowers. "I will do everything in my power to prevent this. I will not let you go."

He continues staring, and then quickly stands up and straightens his robe. "I am afraid I must be going," he says, calmness returning to his voice. "It seems your brother has been giving his new tutor trouble. Your father has asked that I speak with him."

"Of course," I say, blinking rapidly. "Of course you must."

He leaves and I continue to sit on the bench, feeling more disoriented than before.

I give myself a small shake, trying to clear not only the fog in my head, but the unease that has suddenly sprung up in my heart.

CHAPTER 8

WILHA

*T*he day I had my first training session with Patric, my arms shook from the weight of the sword and we had to end the lesson after only several minutes of practice. After that I swore to myself I would not be the weakling I am sure everyone believes me to be. Most nights I practice with my sword, trying to memorize the footwork and techniques Patric has taught me.

In my imagination I battle an unknown, shadowy enemy. An enemy who assumes the freakish Masked Princess will be easy prey, but is shocked to discover a warrior just as capable as the fiercest palace guard.

In these moments I feel less like the Masked Princess and more like someone else. A dawning glimpse of someone I could be. Someone who is real and solid, made of flesh and sinew, blood and bone.

Of course, I win each of these imaginary battles with ease.

But in my real training sessions with Patric, he often has to repeat his instructions two, three, sometimes four times. Despite all my practicing, the techniques do not come easy.

"That was sloppy," Patric says, his mouth set in a firm line. "You are distracted today."

I do not reply. Instead, I adjust my mask and step toward him. He blocks my lunge and slaps my sword away. "Mind your position!" He takes a menacing step forward. "You're being clumsy. You're not a circus performer, though right now you look like one."

I stop, taken aback. "What is the matter with you?" I lower my sword. "Why are you being so mean?"

Patric sighs and lowers his own sword. "Princess, I wasn't being mean. I was trying to distract you and it worked. When you are facing an opponent, never pay attention to his words. Use them to your own advantage if you can, but your attention should be focused only on his weapon."

As he speaks, he raises his sword and points it at my neck. "See? What if I had been your enemy?"

"But you aren't my enemy," I say.

"You can't afford to think like that." He shakes his head. "Not now, anyway."

"What do you mean by that?" I ask, stepping back and looking from the tip of his sword and into his eyes. "Are you saying I am in danger?"

"No," he says quickly. "That's not what I said."

I stare at him, unsure if I should believe him. Patric may be my friend, but he is also one of my father's most valuable soldiers, and will follow whatever orders are given to him. Even if that means keeping things from me. "Then why have I been required to take these lessons? How many princesses are trained to defend themselves?" I gesture to the soldiers standing along the wall. "Isn't that why we have guards?"

"The lessons are for your own education, Wilha. You have nothing to worry about."

"Fine," I say, knowing it is useless to question him further. "But can we please take a break? I am feeling tired," I add, although I could easily train for another hour.

I fake a yawn for the benefit of the guards, in case any of them are watching. "Please, just give me a minute. Come sit with me." I lead him over to the bench in front of my mother's statue. I arrange my skirt over the bench and hide my hand underneath. Patric's hand finds mine and our fingers lace together.

"I passed Lord Murcendor on the way over here," he whispers. "Did he visit with you today?" When I answer yes, his hand tightens on mine. "I do not trust him. And I do not like the way he looks at you."

"He has devoted his life to protecting my family." I think of the unease I felt with him earlier, but quickly dismiss it. "And he is the only Guardian who has ever bothered to speak to me."

And he is also the only one trying to stop my betrothal, I add silently.

We sit in silence for a while until he whispers, "I heard a couple of noble boys talking in the city the other day. They are both attending your birthday ball. One of them was trying to pluck up the courage to ask you to dance."

"I envy those who don't have to go," I say. "I don't want to endure the stares."

"And I envy those who will dance with you," he says quietly, turning to look at me.

My heart thumps in my chest and I am keenly aware of the pressure of his hand in mine. And of his green eyes, and the longing I read in them.

"Vena was inquiring about you the other day," I say suddenly. "She wanted to know if you were, well . . . if there was someone else in your life." I fumble over my words, aware that my voice sounds far from casual.

"Are you asking me if there is anyone whom I care for?" he says, still staring at me.

His question hangs over us like a storm cloud and we are silent. For all my family's wealth, love is the one luxury royalty cannot afford. Something we both know well.

Our gazes hold, until he sighs and looks away. "I heard you met with the Kyrenican ambassador a few days ago," he says in a normal tone. "Do you think it is possible to avoid war?"

"I believe my father and King Ezebo will figure out an agreement that is suitable to both of them," I answer carefully.

I know it is wrong not to tell Patric of the betrothal. Yet these last few months practicing with him have seemed like an iridescent bubble: beautiful, but without tangible form.

Hard to hold on to, but easy to destroy. And to speak the words aloud, to whisper of a marriage contract, will do exactly that. And then Patric, always honorable, will see our whispered conversations as disrespectful to the crown prince of Kyrenica.

Patric squeezes my hand. "Let us get back to training, before the guards become suspicious."

Frustrated, I stand and follow him. We take our positions and he says, "All right, Princess, this time, I would like to see more aggression. You haven't learned how to properly attack, and you are too quick to assume a defensive posture."

He raises his sword. I raise mine, and he motions for me to attack.

I slash once and then twice at Patric, who easily parries my thrusts. "Wilha, wait. You aren't hacking at shrubbery. This wouldn't work in real combat. You're exposing . . ."

I continue coming at him with my sword; lunging once, twice, three times, and again. I am not fighting Patric now, or even the shadowy villain of my imagination. Instead I am slashing at the peace treaty, which marries me off to the Strassburgs as though I have no will or desires of my own.

Patric backs up as he continues to silently block my thrusts, until he trips and falls over the root of an apple tree.

Coming back to my senses and breathless from the exertion, I smile and point the tip of my sword at his chest. "I've won."

"Have you?" he asks. "Look down at your left foot."

I look. Without my noticing, Patric has drawn a dagger from his boot. If I had stepped any closer, the dagger would have pierced my ankle.

"Your strength is growing," he says. "But if I were a real enemy you would have been dead after your first lunge. You cannot just lash out without protecting yourself. And you must pay more attention to your side vision."

"I can't." I drop to my knees and lay aside my sword, suddenly tired. "The mask cuts off my side vision."

All of a sudden there are sounds of swords being drawn and a guard is yelling from the garden wall, "Protect the princess!"

Patric leaps up and seizes my arm. He jerks me to my feet and drags me behind the statue of my mother.

"Kneel down," he says. I do what he says and Patric leans over me, shielding me from view.

"What is happening? Is someone out there?"

"If so, they won't be there long enough to get close to you."

My vision is obscured by the statue, but I hear the sound of horses galloping and guards yelling. Several minutes go by. My heart hammers in my ears, and dew from the wet grass seeps through my dress.

"What is happening?" I repeat.

"I don't know, perhaps nothing. The guards have been testy lately." After a few more minutes Patric crouches down behind me. I feel his heartbeat thudding against my back as he leans close and whispers, "The guards have been forbidden to tell you or Andrei this, but things aren't going well for your father. A potential war with Kyrenica is not his only problem. The people in the villages are unhappy because food is expensive and wages are low." He pauses and adds, "Anger and hunger are a dangerous combination. Add in a little fear and it's a breeding ground for evil and unrest. And murder is the easiest way to separate the House of Andewyn from a crown they have claimed for centuries." He pauses. "This is why we have been ordered to train you and Andrei."

I look down, touched that he actually told me the truth, yet sobered by his words. We are both quiet for several more minutes until a guard calls out, "All clear!"

Patric helps me to my feet, and I brush grass from my dress. I move to step out from behind the statue, but he pulls me back.

"Wait." He stares at me, his green eyes roaming over my mask.

"Yes?" I say, very much aware that we are hidden from view.

He raises a hand, and for one horrific moment I think he intends to cover his eyes. Instead he traces a finger down the side of my mask. He leans closer until our lips are nearly touching. But then he sighs and pulls back. "Come on," he says, "we still need to practice."

I nod, thankful that the mask covers my disappointment.

He picks up my sword and holds it out to me, the look in his eyes grim. "You need to concentrate better. One day, these lessons may save your life."

CHAPTER 9

ELARA

A carriage leaving Tulan at daybreak can reach Allegria just before nightfall if the horses are strong. But between the Ogdens' overloaded coach and their half-starved horses, it takes us two and a half days, most of which I spend squashed in between two trunks of Serena's dresses—two of the many she *just had* to bring to Allegria. By the beginning of the third day I'm ready to explode.

"Serena, couldn't you have brought just a few less trunks?" I rub my sore side. "There would be more than enough room then."

"I've told you this several times," Serena says. "I don't know what the girls in Allegria will be wearing, so I can't possibly know what dresses I will need until we get there."

Mistress Ogden, who has spent most of the last two days dozing and complaining of a headache, now opens her eyes long enough to say, "Right you are, Serena." She looks at me. "If you don't like it, you can get out and walk."

"What's the matter?" Cordon says when I call out to him to stop the carriage. Mistress Ogden hired Cordon to accompany us to Allegria and serve as our coachman, thereby leaving Mister Ogden free to drink himself into a stupor.

"I'm walking the rest of the way," I say, climbing out.

"We're almost there anyway."

Next to Cordon, Mister Ogden is passed out and drooling. Cordon urges the horses onward. "Just don't fall too far behind," he says.

While I walk, I think through my plan. Somehow, I have to find a way to elude the Ogdens long enough to visit the prison and find out if Mister Travers is being held there. We're staying in Allegria for a week, so it should be an easy enough thing to do. I'll make up an excuse, or get myself sent on an errand. More difficult, is what I'll say to Mister Travers if I manage to find him. Tucked between two of Serena's trunks is a satchel I filled with the book from Mister Travers, my dagger, and the four worthings I picked up from the floor of the Draughts. I'm hoping the worthings will make a suitable bribe for the guards at the prison.

But I'm smart enough to know I have to have a backup plan. What if I actually do manage to find Mister Travers and discover he is nothing more than a crazy old man?

I stare at the Ogdens' rickety carriage. I had hoped our two days on the road would give Cordon and me an opportunity to talk, yet Serena has always seemed to be underfoot, preventing us from having any time together. It hasn't seemed like Cordon has minded as much as he would have when we were younger. Is it because he does remember his promise, and wishes he had never made it?

It was many years ago and he found me crying by the

Eleanor River. Serena had struck me and called me a worthless servant who would never amount to anything—words she heard Mistress repeat thousands of times. I cried on Cordon's shoulders and he swore Serena had no more sense than a drunk dingbat.

"But she's right," I cried. "I have no one. I can't ever expect to marry, not without a dowry. I'll spend my whole life here, if Mistress doesn't throw me out first."

"You don't have *no one*," Cordon protested. "You have me, and I won't let anything happen to you. When I turn seventeen, I'll marry you. I promise."

I glance ahead at the carriage again. Cordon turned seventeen a few months ago, and from the growing tension between us I think he remembers his promise just as keenly as I do. But still, he hasn't asked. And I'm not quite sure what I'd say even if he did ask.

I know I feel more than just affection for Cordon. But love? Sometimes I wonder if I'm even capable of loving another. I learned early on that if I was going to survive Mistress's abuse, I would have to take the little girl who cried and craved another's love and tuck her away, somewhere deep inside of me, where no one could ever find her.

All these years later, I wonder if that girl even exists anymore.

❧

As the morning passes, the forest thins out and gives way to farmland, which soon yields to gently sloping hills. I climb another hill, always keeping the Ogdens' carriage in sight, and suddenly, I'm in Allegria proper.

I've grown up hearing tales of Allegria's grandeur. But nothing prepares me for the sight that greets me as I pass through the city gates. Gray stone buildings with golden spires rise up into a blue sky; and the cobblestone streets, inlaid with shards of common lavender opals, glitter in the sunlight.

Gargoyles perch on the tops of iron lampstands and stone buildings, watching the crowd below with evil grins. The streets are packed with carriages, and the city reeks of roasting meat, horse manure, unwashed bodies, and the warm, sugary smell of fresh apple tarts. Strung across the streets are banners wishing Princess Wilhamina happy birthday. Ladies wearing costume masks and pastel-colored dresses look into shop windows. A few brown-cloaked figures wearing gold-threaded masks stand on a street corner, and I stop short when I see them. They appear to be Maskrens. I've heard of them, but I've never seen one before.

Vendors call out to passersby, begging them to buy their wares. A plump man carrying a stack of colorful fans jumps in front of me. He holds up one made of peacock feathers and white lace and shouts, "Official birthday ball fans! Cover your eyes and protect yourself from the curse of the Masked Princess! Only five worthings!"

Everyone, it seems, is trying to capitalize on the princess's birthday. One vendor parades a cart of costume masks up the street, calling out that it would honor the Masked Princess if women wore them. Another sells hair ribbons in shades of milky lavender or iridescent powder blue, calling out "Get your hair ribbons in the official colors of the House of Andewyn!"

All around me noblewomen are feverishly snatching up the trinkets. And I can't help but wonder if any of them know how many families in Tulan will go hungry tonight.

Mister Blackwell arranged for us to stay at a place called the Fountain Inn, named for its proximity to the King's Fountain, where water sprays out of the mouth of a stone statue of King Fennrick.

By the time I catch up to the carriage, Mistress Ogden has already checked in at the inn.

"Elara, get the trunks," she commands. "Our rooms are on the second floor. Mister Blackwell only reserved three, so you'll have to sleep on the floor in Serena's room."

"I'll get the trunks," Cordon says, hopping down from the carriage. "They're heavy and then Elara can—"

"Nonsense," says Mistress Ogden, "Go inside and rest up with Harold. Elara's strong as an ox, and not much prettier."

"Better strong as an ox than dumb as a donkey," I retort,

reaching into the carriage and yanking out my satchel. "Go on in," I say to Cordon, shooing his hands away, "I don't need your help."

"You never need my help," he answers. With a sigh he leaves, and a seething Mistress Ogden follows behind.

⚘

My opportunity to go to the prison comes a day later, when over a dinner of rabbit stew and cheese, Serena complains that she wants a decorative fan for the birthday ball.

"The entire city is already sold out of them," she pouts. "We should have bought one when we first arrived. I don't want to be the only girl who doesn't have one."

"Really? That's odd," I say, thinking fast. "I heard a couple of Allegrian women talking today—noblewomen, by the look of them—saying they were sending their servants across town to a shop that still had them."

I stare down at my stew. I'm planting a seed, letting them believe their next thoughts will be their own.

"Elara will go for you in the morning, darling," Mister Ogden says, drowsy from his third mug of ale. "The king is giving an address tomorrow in Eleanor Square; you won't want to miss it."

I ignore Cordon, who is looking at me suspiciously, and steal a quick glance over at Mistress Ogden. I've spent my whole life studying her. If I give any indication that I actually *want* to get sent on an errand, she'll see to it that I spend the rest of the trip staring at the walls of the inn.

"But that shop was on the other side of the city!" I protest. "It will take me all morning to—"

"You will do exactly as we say and fetch that fan," Mistress snaps. "Serena asks one small thing, as she is quite within her right to do, and you turn up your nose and sniff, just as you've done all your life—" She stops suddenly, realizing that several tables around us have fallen silent.

I give a grunt of frustration and mumble my assent to Mistress Ogden. Nothing on my face shows the triumph I feel.

Later, as I'm turning in for the night, Cordon meets me at the foot of the stairs. "What are you planning for tomorrow?" he whispers.

"What do you mean?"

"You know exactly what I mean. Now the Ogdens think it was their brilliant idea to give you free rein in the city tomorrow."

"It wasn't *my* idea that I spend all morning looking for some blasted fan to satisfy Serena's latest whim."

Cordon grins, and his gray eyes twinkle. "It was, actually. And I don't think you have any intention of helping Serena tomorrow. You've got something else planned entirely. I just want to know what it is."

"I've just got a few things I need to take care of," I say.

Cordon's grin vanishes, as though I've let him down. "When will you learn to trust those who care about you, enough to tell them the truth?"

I look away. "I do trust you, Cordon."

I leave him standing at the foot of the stairs, aware I'm telling a lie neither of us believe.

CHAPTER 10

ELARA

When I wake up the next morning, I quietly pull on my boots and grab my satchel, careful not to disturb Serena, who is still sleeping. Downstairs, I'm just about to step outside when Marinda, the innkeeper's wife, asks me to follow her into the kitchen, where a man in a black cloak waits.

"This is Gunther from the Royal Orphanage. He is here to see how you're getting on."

Gunther nods. He has a pale, pockmarked face and aloof brown eyes which travel dispassionately up and down my body. "Is your stay in Allegria going well?" he asks once his gaze finally lands on my face.

"It is, thank you."

Gunther continues to study me, his eyes moving over my features, and Marinda and I glance uneasily at each other.

"Perhaps you'd like to stay for breakfast?" Marinda asks, gesturing to a pot of porridge bubbling over the hearth.

Gunther finally tears his gaze away from me. "No, thank you," he says to Marinda. And with another nod of his head he departs, leaving us to stare after him.

Marinda frowns. "That was odd."

"Yes, it was," I agree, "but Mister Blackwell, the orphanage director, is a bit odd too."

"That's the thing of it," Marinda says. "I don't understand this business with the orphanage sending you here. I've never met Mister Blackwell. I had never heard of him before he sent us his letter and the payment for your rooms. But I've seen the outside of the orphanage, and I just don't see how they can afford to sponsor a trip for you to visit Allegria."

I hesitate, unsure how to respond. I still don't understand why Mister Blackwell pretended to know nothing about Mister Travers. But after all these years, experience has taught me he won't answer any questions he doesn't want to.

Before I can answer, I hear the stairs creaking and the Ogdens' bickering voices.

"Could you at least make an attempt to look presentable while we're here?" Mistress Ogden rants. "My father paid you a hefty dowry because he thought he was sending me into a proper noble family."

"Or maybe he was just desperate to be rid of you, dearest. Did you ever think of that?"

I hastily bid Marinda a good day and leave before the Ogdens see me and change their mind about sending me on an errand.

Outside, I make my way toward Eleanor Square. Bright morning sunlight glints off the opals inlaid in the cobblestone streets, giving the day a hazy, rainbow-colored feel. The city is even more crowded today. Several men huddle together in groups, speculating about the king's address and hoping he'll have something to say about the rising price of grain and the rumors of a brewing war with Kyrenica. I pass a group of women wearing glittery costume masks who debate over what Princess Wilhamina will be wearing during the address.

Eleanor Square is a large open area bordered by the Galandrian Courthouse on the west and the Clock Tower on the east. The Allegrian Historical Library marks the north side and on the south is the Royal Opera House. The Opal Palace, a monolith of creamy stone and twisting turrets is visible from the Square, rising up on a hill over the southern-most section of Allegria.

I buy an apple tart from a vendor near the Clock Tower and ask him to point me toward the prison.

"It's just over that way," he answers. "Make a left at the next street, and you can't miss it."

The prison is several stories high, topped by a watch tower. I approach slowly, finishing off my apple tart and watching as a man and woman knock on the entrance gate, which is opened by a palace guard. They speak with him briefly before being shown inside.

This is it. If I'm ever going to find out what Mister Travers knows about me and my family—or if he *is* my family, the time is now. I pound on the gate. When it opens, a guard with bristly black hair peers out at me.

"Yes," I begin, "can you help me—"

"State your name and the name of the prisoner you wish to see," he interrupts, leaning against the gate.

"My name is Elara, and I wish to visit Mister Travers."

He eyes me suspiciously. "There is no one here under that name."

He begins to close the gate, but I put my hand out to stop him. "He may have come in under a different name. He would have come from the village of Tulan, approximately two weeks ago." I tilt my head and let my hair fall over my shoulder. Give him my most charming smile. "Surely there must be a way to find out if you're holding someone of that description?"

It works. He returns my smile, revealing a mouthful of gray teeth. "Maybe. What's it worth to you?"

I open my satchel and remove my four worthings. Wordlessly, he snatches them out of my hand. "Stay here," he says, and shuts the gate.

While I wait, I imagine all the questions I will ask Mister Travers. Several minutes later, the gate opens and the guard emerges. "I spoke with the warden."

"And? What did he say?"

He looks pointedly at my satchel, until I open it and hand him the three worthings Mistress Ogden gave me the night before. I tell myself I'll think up a good excuse for why I came back without the money or the fan. "That's everything I have. Now what did the warden say?"

He stuffs away the coins. "He said no prisoners from Tulan have been admitted in the last month."

With that, he slams the gate shut.

His words settle over me like heavy chains. Chains that will keep me bound to the Ogdens. Blindly, I trudge back up the streets, pushing angrily against the crowd of people making their way to Eleanor Square. I drop onto a bench next to the fountain of King Fennrick, open my satchel and yank Mister Travers's book from it. Of all the things my mother could have left me, there *has* to be some reason why she chose this dusty old history book.

I flip through the dog-eared pages. Just like I've done a hundred times in the last two weeks, whenever I was out of sight of the Ogdens. I'm searching. For what, I don't know. A sign from my mother, maybe. Something to tell me who she was and who she might have been—who *I* might have been—if she hadn't given me up. The only memory I have of my mother is a vague, hazy image of a kind-faced woman, her curly red hair tickling me as she sang a lullaby. Or at least, I've always assumed she was my mother.

I settle on a page and begin reading:

The Legend of the Split Opals weighed heavily on Eleanor in her final years. Indeed, she called for her physicians often and said she was haunted by nightmares. She claimed that in these dreams she saw who would eventually cause the Opal Split. "Me," she was said to have confessed. "She looked just like me."

I stop reading at the sound of Serena's voice, coming from a nearby bench. A rose bush sits between the benches, shielding us from view of each other. I can barely make out her words. Something about a fan and a new dress, I think.

I slam the book shut. For Eleanor's sake, what more could she possibly want? Slippers made of pure gold? Hair ribbons blessed by the Masked Princess herself?

"I don't care about a silly fan," she says.

"You could've fooled me," comes Cordon's teasing voice. "I think your mother's not the only fine actress in the family."

"Yes." Serena laughs. "But worthings or not, Mother would never send her away, not as long as she thinks I have need of her."

Their voices are drowned out by children splashing in the fountain. I lean into the rose bush—nearly getting stung on the ear by an irritated honeybee—and strain to hear them. My stomach tightens. Why are Serena and Cordon resting together on a bench?

"We'll have to tell them soon," Serena is saying. "We can't wait forever."

Cordon is silent for a moment. "You're right. But let me tell Elara first."

Fed up with being able to only hear half of what they're saying, I stand up and step out from around the rose bush. "Tell me what?"

But when I see Cordon and Serena's clasped hands, the meaning of their words becomes all too clear. Small details click into place: the growing distance between Cordon and me, his insistence that Serena has changed. . . .

I am a blind fool.

The shock in their faces mirrors my own. "You two? You're . . . *together*? How long?" I sputter at them.

Cordon jumps up. "Not long, Elara. And I wanted to tell you—Serena told me from the beginning I needed to say something."

Serena rises and nods. "Yes, Elara. I was unkind to you when we were children, and I'm sorry for that. But I swear I—"

"Do you love her?" I ask Cordon, ignoring Serena.

Cordon grabs my hand, his eyes pleading. "I'm so sorry, Elara. I didn't mean for it to happen, but . . ." He says a bunch of words, of how they ran into each other one day and suddenly things between them were just . . . different.

"But . . . I thought you loved *me*?" My words come out plaintive, and I hate myself for it.

"When we were children, I did love you. As much as you'll let anyone love you. But sometimes I'm not sure I even know you, Elara. I need someone who will tell me how she really feels, someone who will let me in. Someone who will let me love her."

I nod blindly because I understand. I am not like other girls. I am broken. I am not normal.

"But I still remember the promise I made to you," Cordon is

saying. "And Serena and I have been trying to figure out a way to—"

"What?" His words rip me out of my reverie. "You *told* her? You told her of your promise?" I look at Serena. She does nothing to hide the pity in her eyes. How pathetic I must seem to her. All this time while I've wondered why Cordon hasn't asked me to marry him, they've been meeting secretly and discussing me. As though I'm a problem the two of them have to solve.

"Once we're married, you can come live with us," Serena says. "You don't have to stay with my parents. I know my mother can be—"

"I would *never* be your maid," I hiss at her.

Cordon pales. "That's not what she meant." He looks at Serena. "Right?"

Serena pauses before she nods. "Right."

"Not as our maid," Cordon continues. "You could be— well, I don't know what, exactly, but *not* our maid."

"How kind of you," I say.

A thousand knives stab at my heart, and I envision the pain as a small, ugly box—one that I crush with a mallet. Then I imagine stuffing the broken box somewhere deep within me where I won't have to feel it.

Tears are prickling my eyes. But I refuse to let them see. "I hope you'll be very happy together." I manage to choke out the words.

And then I run.

CHAPTER 11

WILHA

 uards flank either side of my family and the ten
Guardians as we travel the narrow underground tunnel which connects the Opal Palace to the Galandrian Courthouse in Eleanor Square. The palace is full of such passageways. Centuries ago my ancestors decided it would be safer for royalty to travel secretly underground and they built several tunnels connecting the palace to key sites in Allegria.

Lit torches line the passageway, casting dim shadows on the stone walls, and I shudder at thinking of all the stone and packed earth above us.

Lord Murcendor falls back at my side and puts an arm on my shoulder. "Just a few more minutes, and we will reach the courthouse. Remember, the guards will enter first, then the Guardians, then Andrei, and then you and your father."

"Why does Wilha get to enter last with Father?" comes my brother's petulant voice from behind. "I am the future king of Galandria, not her." I glance backward and see Andrei's mouth pursed in displeasure.

My father either does not hear Andrei or chooses to ignore him. He is laughing and jesting with Lord Quinlan while Lord Royce walks quietly behind them. Besides a good feast, my father loves nothing more than a grand entrance and a captive audience.

"Hush, Master Andrei." Lord Murcendor drops farther back, drawing even with Andrei. "Your father has an important speech to deliver and Princess Wilha is needed. When you are king of Galandria, you can make your own decisions."

Lord Murcendor, who has taken it upon himself to pay Andrei the attention my father does not, is the one person my brother listens to. Andrei quiets down and says, "Sorry, sir."

"Don't apologize," Lord Murcendor answers. "Royalty should never apologize." He drops his voice and says something else, and Andrei whispers in return.

Patric, who has been walking at my other side this whole time, takes the opportunity to whisper, "What does he mean by that, that you are needed in the king's speech?" He glances around. "Apart from your father, everyone seems unusually grave. We are announcing a peace treaty, after all."

I smile faintly. "A treaty with your enemy is not always cause for celebration."

Now I wish I had told Patric the terms of the treaty. Because this moment will be the one that punctuates all the others, dividing our time together into the *before* and the *after*.

"Whatever happens," I whisper to him, "know that these last few months have been the best of my life."

"What exactly is that supposed to mean?" he says. But thankfully, Lord Murcendor falls back into step with me, preventing us from speaking further.

When our procession reaches a dead end, a guard holds up his torch and inspects the stone wall. My ancestors marked the entrance and exit to each passageway by a small opal inlaid in the wall. The tunnels, and the methods of opening them, are known only to my family, the Guardians, and a select number of the palace guards.

"Here it is," he mutters and presses on the opal. The wall slides back, sending a wave of fresh air into the passageway, and my anxiety recedes slightly as I step into a small hallway in the Galandrian Courthouse.

The guards extinguish their torches and we silently walk up the hallway and to the double doors that open out to Eleanor Square.

The Clock Tower starts to toll and somewhere outside the royal trumpeters begin to play. When they finish, a guard addresses my father. "Your Majesty, it's time."

The doors open out to Eleanor Square and sunlight falls upon our faces. With one last glance at Patric, I step outside.

CHAPTER 12

ELARA

My satchel slams against my hip as I flee, and I hear Cordon running after me, calling my name. I push through the crowd and pass Gunther, the man from the orphanage, who is heading toward the inn.

"Elara!" he calls out. "I must speak with you."

"Not now!" I shout back.

Behind me, Cordon continues to call after me and I let myself get carried along by the crowd into Eleanor Square. Rose petals fall from the rooftops, and palace guards are stationed along the edge of the square. Trumpets begin to sound and I steal a glance backward. Cordon is scanning the crowd, still looking for me. I elbow my way toward the courthouse, hoping to put as much distance between us as possible. I'll hide in the crowd while the king gives his speech and slip away afterward.

With a final ringing crescendo, the trumpets cease and the doors to the courthouse open. Soldiers file out and surround the steps. The Guardians come next, clad in emerald green robes. I pay them little mind, though, as we all wait to see the royal family. Crown Prince Andrei comes out next, followed by King Fennrick, who wears an ornate crown bristling with opals atop his head. And finally, Princess

Wilhamina emerges from the courthouse.

Like the rest of the crowd, I gasp in awe. Her mask and dress, adorned with more jewels than I can begin to count, glitter in the sunlight. A thick necklace made of jeweled keys hangs around her neck. As she steps forward to take her place next to her father, several people raise their fans to cover their eyes.

"Please, Masked Princess!" The man next to me holds a gaunt little boy over his head. "My son is ill. Only look at him, and he shall be healed!"

"Healed?" shouts a haggard woman with stringy white hair. "The princess can heal no one. A curse is what she is! Raise your fans! Protect yourself from the Masked Princess!" She holds her fan over her face and continues railing against the princess until two palace guards appear and drag her away.

I cast a look back into the crowd. I can see Cordon, but he hasn't located me yet. I push forward, until I'm standing behind several Maskrens who are lined up only a few feet away from the row of soldiers.

Silence falls over the crowd as King Fennrick raises his hands. "Citizens of Galandria!" he says, "It is my great honor to celebrate the sixteenth birthday of Princess Wilhamina with you in our esteemed capital, the illustrious city of Allegria! To all of you who have journeyed many miles, I bid you welcome and I thank you, for it does me great honor.

"Today I come to you with the most joyous news. For months you have been hearing of an impending war with Kyrenica. Yet I say to you this day, fear not! For I have secured peace for our great kingdom. King Ezebo and I have pledged our mutual determination to avoid an escalation in hostilities. As a symbol of our goodwill, King Ezebo has pledged his son, and I have pledged my daughter—your own Princess Wilhamina—in a commitment of holy matrimony. Now the House of Andewyn and the House of Strassburg, at odds with each other for a century, shall be bound together for all time!"

I look around and see many shocked faces. "The princess should never have to marry a Kyrenican dog!" shouts a woman nearby. But most people in the crowd don't hear her as they erupt into cheers, drowning out the king. My attention strays from him to Princess Wilhamina. Her shoulders quake and I wonder if she is happy over her betrothal. Or has love been unkind to both of us today?

I'm still wondering when I hear a whizzing sound above my head, and something small and red lodges into the banner hanging above King Fennrick.

It's not until a red arrow strikes the palace guard in front of the king that I understand what is happening.

"It's an attack!" a guard shouts.

His cry is followed by the screams of hundreds of terrified citizens trampling each other as they attempt to flee the packed square. Not too far off I hear the sound of an apple cart being upended and crashing onto the cobblestone street. The palace guards quickly form a wall and cover the Andewyns, pinning them to the ground. A guard is screaming that they need to get the royal family back into the courthouse.

More arrows fly toward the Andewyns. While everyone panics around me, I am frozen where I stand. Through a gap in between the guards I see the Masked Princess. Her jeweled mask is hanging askew, exposing half her profile. Instinctively, I begin raising a hand to cover my eyes, but stop when it strikes me that her face, feared by so many in our kingdom, reminds me of—

"*Elara!*"

It's Cordon's voice I hear. But when I turn, it's Gunther from the orphanage I see. His steps are determined as he advances toward me. The fear that's kept me from running away must have done something to my vision as well. Because when Gunther removes a sword from beneath his cloak, I get a glimpse of what looks to be the uniform of a palace guard.

An arrow lands at my feet. I stare down at it and blink stupidly. Are the attackers aiming for me?

"*Elara—LOOK OUT!*"

Pain explodes in my head, and the ground rises up to meet me. The last thing I see before blackness closes in is Gunther's pale, pockmarked face, and his aloof brown eyes, staring into my own.

CHAPTER 13

WILHA

"*G*et them up! Get the royal family back into the court-house!" screams a guard.

Arrows fall like angry red raindrops. Like the rest of my family, I am pinned to the ground by guards. Their shields are up, hoping to deflect the arrows. I moan, feeling like the side of my ankle has just been scraped against the stone steps.

"Don't move." Patric's breath is hot against my neck. The second the first arrow struck, he was at my side and covering me with his shield.

"The arrows are coming from the Clock Tower! Get someone up there!"

I feel the unfamiliar sensation of air directly on my face. In the confusion, my mask must have come untied, and no one seems to have noticed. I straighten it quickly. Through a gap in the guards I see people fleeing Eleanor Square. At the foot of the courthouse steps, several Maskrens and guards lie dead. Not too far away a guard is punching a boy with dirty blond hair. Nearby lies a peasant girl who seems to have fainted.

"Wilha," Patric says, "you need to get up. We're moving you back into the courthouse."

He helps me to my feet and I wince. The pain in my ankle seems to be getting worse. Arrows continue to fall as guards surround me, and we move swiftly up the steps, away from the screams of the crowd, and into the courthouse.

Inside, several guards crouch over my father. He is on the ground, writhing in agony. Blood spurts from an arrow embedded in the side of his cheek.

"Someone call for the king's physician!" screams Lord Royce.

Two guards sweep from the room, back down the hall-way leading to the secret passageway. I lean on Patric, dizziness washing over me as I stare at my father. "Will he be all right?" I call out to the guards.

Patric grabs my arm and checks me for wounds. "I'm fine," I say, yanking my arm away. "Help the others."

Two Guardians are on the ground. One is unmoving and the other is crawling on his hands and knees, spitting blood. Blood seems to be everywhere. Near my ankle, a scarlet river runs down the white marble floor.

"Lord Quinlan," Patric says, "Are you all right? There's blood on your hands."

Lord Quinlan stares at his hands as though they belong to someone else. "I don't think this is my . . ."

His words are drowned out by the sound of someone falling to the floor.

"Another Guardian has been hit!"

The pain in my ankle grows. I must have scraped it hard on the stone steps. I walk unsteadily toward Andrei to see how he is doing.

"Are you all right, Andrei?"

Andrei, paler than usual, looks at me with his clear blue eyes. "If father dies today does that mean I will be king?"

"Father is not going to die." I reach out my hand, but he sidesteps me.

"But if he *does* die," he insists, "that means I get to be king. Right, Wilha?"

"Yes, Andrei," I say quietly. "If Father dies, you will be king."

Andrei nods. "Excellent."

I turn away, nauseous from my brother's matter-of-fact tone and my father's anguished moans. I hear Lord Murcedor and Lord Quinlan shouting at each other. "I thought your men checked every building in the square!" Lord Murcendor rages.

"They did! Multiple times! No one could have gotten into the Clock Tower without them knowing."

"So you're saying your men just welcomed Kyrenican assassins into our city with open arms?"

"We don't know where those arrows came from!"

"Don't we? What other kingdom dyes their arrows red and wants to get their hands on Galandria's wealth?"

"It wasn't the Kyrenicans!" Lord Quinlan shouts back at him. "You know who wanted the king dead—and you assured us he and his men were taken care of! If someone is to be held responsible for this, it should be you!"

Lord Quinlan rushes over to my father, who appears to be going in and out of consciousness. "Your Majesty! I swear we checked the Clock Tower. You know I protect you as though you are my brother. You and I were boys together!"

"Lord Murcendor, Lord Quinlan, hold your tongues!" Lord Royce admonishes them and glances at me. "You are upsetting the princess."

Patric comes over. "Princess, you're pale. Come sit down." He tugs at my arm, but I don't move. My eyes are drawn to the red trickle by my ankle.

"Princess? Wilha"—I feel Patric shaking me—"Are you all right?"

Just as Patric lifts the hem of my dress and shouts, "The princess has been hurt!" The weight of Lord Murcendor's words sink in.

If he is right, if Kyrenica is behind the attack, then that means the Strassburgs, my future in-laws, have just tried to assassinate me.

CHAPTER 14

ELARA

A strange clanking sound awakens me. Darkness meets my eyes and my head throbs. I remember Cordon screaming my name, and red arrows flying toward the royal family. Was I struck by an arrow? But a quick hand to the back of the head tells me no. The ache is from a lump on my scalp.

A fire hangs in the dark sky. At first I assume I'm lying in Eleanor Square, and that the sun is setting. Or maybe it's rising? Yet my eyes don't adjust in the surrounding darkness, and the ground beneath me feels soft, like hay. When I take a deep breath and my lungs fill with air that is both dank and musty, I realize I'm indoors. But how did I get here? And where is my satchel?

I roll over—and promptly fall to the floor. I sit up and my head starts pounding. Panic rises in my chest. "Cordon? Cordon are you there!"

"You shouldn't scream." A faint, hoarse voice echoes from behind me. "They will only hit you harder."

"Who's there? Where am I?" I call, but the darkness swallows my words.

"We're in the place where it all started," answers the voice. "And the place where it all ends."

"What?" I stand up shakily and move toward the voice. "Where are we?" I say again. I stare at the faint orange glow and realize it's not the sun, but the last flickering embers of a mounted torch. I take a few more steps, and cold metal brushes my hand. Bars. I'm being kept in a cell?

In Eleanor Square I remember guards screaming. I remember Cordon telling me to watch out. But there was something else, wasn't there? Before the world went dark, I had seen something. What was it?

In the dim torchlight, I see someone huddled in the cell next to mine. And when my eyes adjust, I realize it's someone I know.

"Mister Travers?"

He is slumped against the bars and his clothes are torn. I crouch down to get a better look at his face. His cheeks, once full, are now sunken. Dry blood crusts his face and his hands, and purple bruises shadow his glazed eyes. "Are you a ghost?" he whispers.

"It's me, Mister Travers. It's Elara." I give him a small shake and then touch his forehead. He's burning up.

"Elara?" he says dreamily. "Lord Finley wasn't sure where she was, but we knew if we watched him close enough, we'd eventually figure out where he hid her." His eyes flutter closed.

"Lord who? What are you talking about?" He's not making any sense. If we are being kept in cells, are we in Allegria's prison, despite what the guard told me earlier about Mister Travers not being here? But why am *I* here?

"I failed her," he says and begins to weep. "The guards are coming for me. The order has been signed. They only kept me alive this long so I would tell them where the others are. And to my everlasting shame, I told them." He weeps harder.

The sound of clanking metal and jingling keys followed by rough laughter makes me jump. Flickering torchlight appears in the distance. This may be my last chance to talk to him.

"Mister Travers, listen to me!" I shout, as he weeps louder. "You haven't failed me. I'm right here. You did find me, remember? You said you knew my mother. Who was she?"

The clanking grows louder. It seems to penetrate Mister Travers's delirium. He stops weeping and his eyes clear. "Elara?" He glances in the direction of the brightening torchlight, and grasps my hand tightly. "Whatever you do, don't trust the Guardians."

"I don't understand. What are you—"

The door to Mister Travers's cell opens and two guards step in and seize him. Just before they drag him away he shouts, "Don't trust the Guardians! The king's secret has poisoned them!"

CHAPTER 15

WILHA

I sit by my father's bedside and hope he will awaken. His face is pale and his breathing is labored. An arrow only grazed my ankle. Although it bled a lot, it is already healing. But my father has not been so fortunate. His physician was able to successfully remove the arrow from his cheek, but he has lapsed into a fevered unconsciousness. If I listen carefully, I can hear the cries of the people echoing from the palace gates, as the city waits to hear the fate of their injured king.

Eight Maskrens, four palace guards, and two Guardians have died in the assassination attempt. The masquerade ball has been canceled. Sir Reinhold has sworn an oath that, despite appearances, Kyrenica had nothing to do with the attack and that they have every intention of honoring the treaty. King Ezebo himself has sent pigeons carrying messages reaffirming his commitment to the treaty.

As I sit here and wait, the Guardian Council is gathered for an emergency session to determine Galandria's response, as well as my future.

I take my father's slackened hand. The physician did a remarkable job, but the wound has puckered into an angry welt. For the rest of his life, however long or short it is, my father will bear a jagged scar upon his cheek.

What will he do when he awakens and sees his new face? Will King Fennrick the Handsome dare to appear in public? Or will he, too, wear a mask?

A firm knock hits the door and it opens. The remaining members of the Guardian Council file into the room.

"Has the council reached a decision?" I ask.

"We have," answers Lord Royce.

I need not listen to his long, formal explanation. From the seething anger I read in Lord Murcendor and Lord Quinlan's expressions, and the way the other Guardians look everywhere but in my eyes, I know the answer.

". . . The council is inclined to believe that the assassination attempt was perpetrated by men still loyal to Lord Finley, not the Kyrenicans, and so we will move forward with the treaty," Lord Royce finishes.

I nod. No one has spoken to me directly about Lord Finley, one of my father's former Guardians, but I have heard servants whispering of his treachery. Many of them attended his execution.

"Lord Finley's men were disorganized and stupid," Lord Murcendor interjects. "I have no doubt the Kyrenicans were behind the attack."

"Your views on this matter have already been heard, and were overruled." Lord Royce stares impassively at Lord Murcendor. "You will forgive me, but no one in this room

believes you can be objective when it comes to the princess."
Lord Murcendor glares at him, but says nothing.

I offer the Guardians no protest, no indication that, in deciding to send me to Kyrenica, it feels as though they have just signed the order for my execution. Instead I nod and offer them my thanks for their quick handling of the matter.

One by one the Guardians begin bowing themselves from the room, and I try to still my shaking hands.

Behind me a throat clears. I turn around again and see that Lord Murcendor, Lord Quinlan, and Lord Royce remain in the room. Lord Murcendor pulls a chair close and sits down next to me. "They are fools," he says, casting a furious look at Lord Royce. "Mark my words, if we send her to Kyrenica, only treachery and loss can come of it."

"The king himself ordered the betrothal," Lord Quinlan says. "I would like nothing more than to declare war on the Kyrenicans, but we must move forward." He turns to me. "The council has ordered me to oversee security arrangements as you travel to Kyrenica, and I have a plan in place to insure your safety."

I glance over at Lord Murcendor. Judging from his scowl, whatever this plan is, I know he does not approve of it.

"What is it?" I ask.

At this, Lord Quinlan glances at Lord Murcendor.

"Leave us," Lord Murcendor says to the guards stationed at my father's bedside.

After Lord Royce has closed the door behind them, Lord Murcendor continues. "The plan is only known to Lord Quinlan, myself, and Lord Royce," he says carefully. "It is not something known to the rest of the Guardians, nor to anyone else." He pauses, before adding, "Do you ever wonder why you have been made to wear the mask?"

"Of course," I answer, startled at the change in subject. "I recall asking you many times when I was a child."

"You are not a child anymore, Wilha." The look he gives me appears to be an invitation, one that has never before been extended.

I whisper the words and my voice carries the question. "Why have I been made to wear the mask?"

In response, he glances at Lord Royce and Lord Quinlan. Lord Royce says, "It is time."

Lord Murcendor nods and turns to me. "A long time ago, the three of us—as well as Lord Finley—had to make a difficult decision. One that we kept from the other Guardians. Indeed, we concealed it from the whole world." He pauses, glancing again at my father.

And then Lord Murcendor begins to tell me a tale so unbelievable, I have no doubt it is true.

CHAPTER 16

ELARA

What is the king's secret?

I spend my days in darkness. I never see Mister Travers again and I am left alone pondering his words.

My days fall into a hazy routine. In the morning (or what I assume is morning), a guard appears and brings me a bowl of broth that faintly tastes of onions. A few hours later I am given stale bread and small hunks of moldy cheese.

The fear of being taken to wherever Mister Travers has been sent to fades after the first few days and is replaced by several other concerns. Small creatures skittering around and biting at my feet. Fleas that seem delighted with my blood. The unimaginable cold of the cell, and a deep, gnawing hunger.

At first I tell myself this is nothing. There were mice and fleas in Ogden Manor. And I know what it is to be hungry. But the guards begin to withhold water as well as food. My throat rots, and I'm not always sure if I am waking or sleeping. Mistress Ogden appears to me often, whispering, *"Worthless . . . Unwanted . . . Unlovable . . ."*

On what I believe is my second or third week here, a guard carrying a torch enters my cell. I feel his foul breath on my face. "Someone wishes to speak with you." Rough arms close in around me. A bag smelling of grain is yanked over my head and all is black again. The guard shoves something into my back as we walk, and I suck in gasping, grain-smelling breaths. A stitch pierces my side, and all I want to do is sit back down.

We continue walking for what seems like miles, and the air around me begins to change. It feels lighter and less damp. I hear the creak of a door opening and then closing. The guard shoves me forward and says, "As you requested."

A deep voice replies, "Thank you, Wolfram. You may go." Wolfram grunts and the door shuts again. Soft footsteps approach.

The bag is jerked off my head and sunlight scorches my eyes. I hear sharp gasps around me, but I can't see anything. Tears stream down my cheeks, and I raise my arm to cover my face.

"Give her a moment," says the voice.

When my eyes begin to adjust, I see that I'm in a circular room. The late afternoon sunlight streams in through high windows and a large crystal chandelier with several lit candles hangs from the ceiling. Carved into the walls are ten marble thrones with plush pastel cushions. Three of the thrones are occupied, and as the men's faces come into focus I do a double take, for I know one of them.

"Mister Blackwell?" My voice is dry and raspy from lack of water.

The men ignore me. The two I don't recognize stare at me in a kind of awe.

I look at Mister Blackwell. "What is going on?"

"Lord Murcendor," says one of the men I don't recognize. He's bald with severe-looking eyes and wears several rings and necklaces. "Make introductions."

Mister Blackwell casts a dark look at the bald man, and I shake my head in confusion. *What did he just call him?*

"I wasn't aware I took orders from you, Lord Quinlan," Mister Blackwell says.

The bald man—Lord Quinlan—flushes and his eyes narrow. "Make introductions, *please*," he says.

"Perhaps we should start by telling the girl where she is," says the third man in an annoyed tone. He is barrel chested and has thick, gray hair and an equally thick gray beard. He looks less polished than the other two. His face is tough and tanned and grooved, like weathered wood. He stares back at me with impassive blue eyes.

"Indeed you're right, Lord Royce," says Lord Quinlan. He turns to address me. "You are in the Guardians' Chambers in the Opal Palace."

For the first time it dawns on me that all three men are wearing thick emerald green robes. I remember seeing the Guardians wearing them in Eleanor Square. My stomach clenches as I remember, too, Mister Travers's feverish words.

"What do you want with me?" I murmur, glancing from Lord Quinlan to Mister Blackwell. "Why am I here?"

"You are here because in some sense, you belong here," says Mister Blackwell. "You are not an orphan as you have been led to believe, and I am not Mister Blackwell, nor do I work for the orphanage. I am Lord Murcendor, Guardian of the Opal Mines." He pauses. "And you, quite simply, are the daughter of King Fennrick."

The three Guardians look at me, but I stare back at them, unmoved. I don't know what game these men are playing, but I don't believe it.

"You're mad," I say.

"Am I?" Mister Blackwell—or Lord Murcendor—says. "Have you ever wondered *why* the Royal Orphanage paid for your care all these years? Do you really think such an arrangement was made for every orphan in Galandria? Do you have any idea how difficult it was to find a family desperate enough to accept you and the money, and too stupid to ever question it?"

His words stop me short, and blackness creeps at the edges of my vision. Everything seems to fade away, except for Mister Blackwell, sitting on a marble throne and draped in a Guardian's robe.

Don't trust the Guardians. The king's secret has poisoned them.

"But that can't be," I say. "I remember my mother. She was a villager with red hair. She used to sing to me—"

"What you remember," he interjects, "is the wet nurse we placed you with until I located a family to take you. The Ogdens."

I swallow and open my mouth to protest, but nothing

comes out. Because his words make sense. The arrangement with the Ogdens *is* unusual, isn't it? Why had I never thought to question it?

Am I the king's secret?

I am the daughter of King Fennrick, I try the words out in my mind, but they don't seem to fit. Yet I can't help remembering every evil word Mistress Ogden said about my mother, all the dirty names she called her. Was my mother such a woman? A woman who thought her life had changed for the better when she caught the king's eye, only to be cast aside later, after she had served her purpose?

But why wasn't I allowed to stay with her? Why the wet nurse? Why couldn't the treasury have paid my own mother to care for me somewhere in obscurity? Was it because she knew the king's shameful secret was considered a threat? Is she even alive now?

"Did you kill her?" I ask, swaying slightly.

"I am afraid you will have to be more specific," Lord Murcendor says.

"My mother. After she gave birth, did you kill her? Because you were afraid one day she'd proclaim her daughter the bastard child of King Fennrick the Handsome?"

The Guardians glance at each other, seemingly perplexed. "You misunderstand," Lord Quinlan answers. "Your mother was Queen Astrid. It is pure royal blood that flows through your veins."

I am poised to argue. If I am a princess, why was I given to the Ogdens? Why haven't I grown up in the Opal Palace?

Before I can ask them this, Lord Murcendor rises and knocks on a door behind him. "You may come in now."

The door opens, and a golden statue enters the room.

CHAPTER 17

WILHA

The Guardians bow as I enter the room. The girl across the room remains standing. I read the confusion in her eyes and realize they have not told her. Lord Murcendor's kindness in telling me a couple weeks ago, and giving me time to understand and accept it (in so far as that can be possible) has not been extended to her.

The girl glances from me to the Guardians. She is dirty and her hair is matted. Deep purple circles hang under her eyes and flea bites dot her arms. Covered in all that grime, it is almost too hard to believe she is who they say she is. Almost, but not quite.

"Your Highness," Lord Murcendor says, bowing again. "You may proceed."

All my life I have waited for this invitation. All those nights when I stared into my looking glass, I longed for the day when I could do this one small thing, and know truly, beyond a shadow of a doubt, that I could hurt no one.

I reach behind my head and untie the mask. With shaking hands I remove it.

There are several sharp inhalations and the girl's face whitens.

Lord Murcendor introduces us. He says the words. He

gives her the explanation she probably never suspected, but the one I have searched for my whole life.

The girl's face twists in disgust. Her rejection is sharp like an arrow.

And for the briefest of seconds, I want to put the mask back on.

CHAPTER 18

ELARA

I am staring at my own face. Except not quite.

The girl standing before me has my exact features, but with slight differences. Her skin reminds me of cream and roses. The way she carries herself is different. As though her shoulders and waist are tied to an invisible post, forcing her to stand straight. She wears a gold dress and her necklace of keys make a tinkling melodic sound as she steps forward. And in her hands she carries the jeweled mask she just removed.

The Guardians, except for Lord Murcendor, stare at us in awe.

"So alike," Lord Quinlan murmurs. "For so many years I have wondered."

"For sixteen years, we have all wondered," answers Lord Royce.

"Elara, may I introduce Princess Wilhamina Andewyn." Lord Murcendor pauses, and adds, "Your twin sister."

"That's imposs—" I begin, but stop as the memory I've been searching for finally surfaces. In Eleanor Square, just before I was knocked unconscious, I had seen Princess Wilhamina's mask come undone. And it had occurred to me that her face reminded me of another.

My own.

I can't tear my eyes away from her. Our height, our green eyes, our brown hair—we're identical. But this girl, this other me, she's quaking. As though our stares are too much for her to bear.

Lord Quinlan says to me, "There is a stool behind you." To Princess Wilhamina he says, "If you would care to sit down as well, Your Highness."

Princess Wilhamina looks quickly at Lord Murcendor, who nods, before she settles herself on a marble throne across from where I take a seat on the stool. Seeing a girl with my face huddled on a throne makes my neck prickle.

Lord Quinlan saunters to the middle of the room with a grand smile on his face. He circles around, taking his time, clearly enjoying the moment.

"Where to begin?" he says. "When it was discovered that Queen Astrid had given birth to twins, the king summoned four of the Guardians: myself, Lord Murcendor, Lord Royce, and another to witness the occasion. When we arrived, the king was almost mad with grief. The last time twins were born to the ruling Galandrian monarch was a century ago, with the birth of Rowan and Aislinn Andewyn. Back then, it was simply assumed that the older twin would rule, and that the line of succession would continue on peacefully. No one could have foreseen that Aislinn Andewyn—the Great Betrayer—would become a bitter woman. Bitter enough to betray her own sister and cause the splitting of our kingdom, thereby bringing about the fulfillment of the Legend of the Split Opals.

"But this time, the king had the advantage of his own family history. There was much unrest in Galandria in those days. Many feared revolution, just as they do now. And another set of twins could be seen as yet another premonition. Another split of a great and glorious kingdom by two heirs both bent on ruling.

"The king feared, and the three of us agreed, that if the birth of twins was announced, factions would immediately develop, supporting one girl over another, with the likely result one day being civil war. And so, the decision was made: There would be only one child born that day. Only one recognized princess of Galandria. And if the queen could conceive another child, the princess was to be removed from the line of succession. With neither of the twins knowing about the existence of the other, and neither of them in line to rule, it was thought the kingdom would be safe."

I sit there numbly as Lord Quinlan explains how the midwife was sent abroad, and how one of the twins— myself—was smuggled out of the castle to be raised anonymously by a wet nurse until they could locate a suitable home. How Lord Murcendor was appointed to watch over her and keep her location a secret.

"Wait a minute," I interrupt. "How did you decide?"

"Decide what?"

"How did you decide which twin would go and which would stay?" I need to hear him say it.

Lord Quinlan's eyes meet mine. "Birth order. Princess Wilhamina was born seven minutes earlier than you."

I nod. So when my father looked upon the second twin, he didn't see her. He didn't see *me*. He saw another Aislinn Andewyn. An act of treachery a century before I was born stole my future.

"So you decided to hand me over to an anonymous family to be treated as their servant?" I address my words to Mister Black—to Lord Murcendor.

Lord Murcendor stares at me from his marble throne. "It was better than the alternative."

"Which was?"

"Seclusion," Lord Murcendor says and rises from his throne. He stands in the center of the room, facing Lord Quinlan, who glowers back at him, seemingly unhappy to have someone steal his thunder.

"We could not have you wandering around the castle. And so we considered, when you were old enough, transferring you to a remote location and forging a mask to conceal your face," Lord Murcendor begins. "Yet it was thought by the king that such a mask would create a mystique. And the king and queen wanted the chance to know their younger daughter. So a second decision was made: Wilha would wear a mask. And if the queen was able to bear another child, not only would

Wilha be removed from the line of succession, she would also marry a foreign suitor and be sent away. And in turn, you were to be brought to the Opal Palace. Though the king could never tell you of your true parentage, he would arrange for you to be given a life here in Allegria. As no one would have ever seen the princess's face, it was thought you could safely reside in Allegria after Wilhamina left the kingdom."

I glance over at Princess Wilhamina. Her face has drained of color. Is this new information to her, too?

"The King was eager to reclaim you," Lord Murcendor continues, "and so Gunther was tasked with making sure you were safely brought to the Opal Palace and—"

"You call a blow to the back of the head being safe?" I snap.

"The attack in Eleanor Square forced his hand," Lord Murcendor replies impatiently. "Admittedly, he became overzealous." He turns to Lord Quinlan and Lord Royce. "And he has been dealt with."

The two Guardians nod at him, but my stomach clenches. What does that mean, Gunther's been "dealt with"? And how exactly do they plan to "deal" with me?

"Why tell me this now?" I ask.

"The attack on the royal family has changed everything. And now we have a proposition for you. Your sister is to leave very shortly for Kyrenica." Lord Murcendor pauses, and says, "We need you to serve as the princess's decoy on the journey to Kyrenica."

"Her decoy?" I choke out, stunned.

Lord Murcendor nods. "Sir Reinhold, the Kyrenican ambassador, has had several meetings with Princess Wilhamina. He has returned to Korynth, Kyrenica's capital, and will no doubt want to welcome the princess upon her arrival. He would recognize an imposter immediately, even if she wore Wilha's mask. But a twin sister whose hair, build, and voice is virtually identical is a different matter."

I stare at him while he speaks, but I don't really hear him. All I hear is that they believe Wilhamina, the twin that's been given everything, may be in danger, and they will do everything in their power to protect her.

The rage that's been bubbling in my heart now floods my veins. Where were these Guardians, so concerned with Wilha's well-being, all those years when Mistress abused me? Where were they all those nights I had to fend off drunken men in the Draughts?

And if King Fennrick is so eager to "reclaim me"—like I am nothing more than a piece of property he can annex or cut loose at will—then where is he now? If I have been missed for sixteen years, shouldn't I have been welcomed back with open arms? Instead, I've been thrown into a cell and denied food and water. Were they hoping to starve me into submission?

I look at Princess Wilhamina huddling on her marble throne, and a thought occurs to me. When the door opened and she walked into the room, I saw no guards standing in the hall behind her.

"What do you say?" Lord Murcendor asks when he has finished speaking. "Will you protect your sister?"

She is not my sister, I almost blurt out. I won't risk my life for her, this paler, pampered version of me. But if I refuse, what will become of me? The Guardians have already proven my life means nothing to them.

No, I will not entrust my fate to them. I have one chance, and I must use it well.

Quickly, I bottle my rage, and stopper it with a look of tired resignation. With as much grace as I can muster, I rise to my feet and step forward toward Princess Wilhamina. I lift my skirt, as though I'm about to sink into a curtsy—and then I make a mad dash for the door.

By the time Lord Murcendor yells for the guards, I'm already through the door. The hall beyond isn't narrow and deserted as I had hoped, but wide and circular, with white stone statues lining the back walls. Several guards lounge nearby, their expressions startled as I streak past them.

"Get her!" comes Wolfram's voice.

My movements are jerky, and my breathing comes in ragged gasps. After so many days in a cell my muscles are already cramping. But adrenaline fills my veins and I push forward, fleeing the hall. The sound of heavy footsteps and clanking metal follows behind me. If I doubted the

Guardians' words, I know now they were telling the truth. The white columned hallways, the crystal chandeliers, the gilded walls and the arched windows—this can only be the Opal Palace.

I round a corner and rush down a narrower corridor. When I turn another corner, I enter a large hall and realize I'm running straight for a golden throne.

I pull up short when several guards, who had been standing in front of a tall statue, unsheathe their swords and start running after me. Suddenly, I'm pushed from behind, and for a moment, I'm flying forward. I hit the stone floor with a *thud* and a guard lands on top of me. "I've got her!" Wolfram shouts. "Run like that again, and I'll gut you like a pig," he says to me.

My lip has split on the hard floor, and I taste blood in my mouth as the guards yank me to my feet. When I look up, I see I'm standing in front of a statue of Eleanor the Great. She holds two large, colorful opals in her hands.

The circle of guards around me parts for Lord Murcendor; his dark eyes are glowering. "Take her back to her cell," he commands. "And be careful with this one. She is not right in the head and has an unhealthy obsession with Princess Wilhamina. Pay no attention to whatever lies she may tell you."

CHAPTER 19

WILHA

*L*ord Murcendor returns to the Guardians' Chambers and dismisses me. "I would like for you to wait in your room. Lord Quinlan, Lord Royce, and I need to speak privately." He motions to my mask. "We will also need you to put that back on."

I obey and tie the mask back on my face. I leave the room, but as soon as the door closes behind me, I sink to the ground. Lord Murcendor told me only of Elara's existence. He said nothing of my father's plan to bring her to Allegria once I had left the kingdom. I bring a shaking hand to my mask.

All this time, has my father been counting the years until he could marry me off and be reunited with my sister? Did he ever wonder if he had made a mistake, if he should have sent me away and kept her instead? Given how quickly he has intended to hand me over to the Kyrenicans, I assume he must.

I think back to Rinna, the person I loved most when I was a child. Once she saw my face, did my father decide it was better if she—like the midwife before her—was sent abroad, so she couldn't one day identify Elara?

On the other side of the door I hear the low rumble of the Guardians' voices. No doubt they expect me to obey Lord Murcendor's orders and return to my room. All these years, the Guardians and my father have always required my obedience, and I have always given it.

Yet what if this time I didn't?

I rise and approach a maid passing through the hall. "Do you know where I can find Patric, the palace guard? I need to speak to him about our training sessions," I add hastily in case she says something to the Guardians.

"He's usually standing guard at the western turret this time of night," she answers, and hurries away, looking relieved to get away from me.

I see no one as I make my way down the corridor and up the staircase spiraling to the top of the turret. When I find Patric, he is staring out the window. For a moment I study him silently. His face is shadowed and his jaw is set in a firm line as he watches the sun set over the kingdom. My stomach lurches. I haven't seen him since the attack. I sent word to him that I was not ready to train because of my ankle. But in truth, I have been too scared to face him.

"So this is where you spend your nights," I say as I walk over to him.

Patric jumps and draws his sword, but sheaths it when he sees me. "What are you doing up here?"

"I have just come from a meeting with the Guardians, and I thought well . . . I just wanted to see you," I finish lamely.

"A meeting discussing plans to depart to your future husband's country?" The coldness in his voice is unmistakable.

"Yes," I answer, aware that I cannot tell him the full truth. "I should have told you the terms of the peace treaty. I am sorry."

"That's it? That's your apology?" he says. "Do you have any idea how it felt, hearing of your betrothal? Don't you think that was something I might want to hear from you, Wilha, and not from your father, as if I was just another guard?"

"I know I should have told you, but I was afraid," I answer, and my voice sounds desperate. "I didn't want our time together to end. And it doesn't have to, not yet. Lord Quinlan is seeking guards for the journey. You could volunteer and—"

"Volunteer?" Patric looks as though I have slapped him. "You want me to escort you to your husband's country? Would you like me to witness your wedding, as well? Shall I stay long enough to watch you give birth to his child?"

"No, that is not what I meant!" I reach for his arm, but he draws back. "I just . . . I wish things could be different."

"Don't you think I wish things were different, too?" he answers, his green eyes blazing. "That I could untie your mask and see the girl who—" He turns away and grips the edge of the window.

I step closer to him and take a deep breath. "You could untie my mask. If you want to . . ."

At this, he seems to forget his anger and turns to look at me, surprised. "It is forbidden. You know this."

"No one has to know. For once we are alone, and I would never tell anyone. None of the rumors are true—"

"I have *never* believed the rumors—"

"—and I promise, no harm will come to you." I place my hand on his and he tenses. "Please? I have to go to Kyrenica. Neither of us can change that. But before I go, I want you to look at me." I take his hand and place it on my mask. "Please? I want you to see me. Just this once, before I have to leave."

His hand moves up and tangles in my hair. I read the temptation in his eyes. But just as quickly as it came over him, his expression hardens and he drops his arm. "Let your new husband look at you. I will not."

He turns away and looks out the window. When he speaks again, his voice is hollow. "I cannot see you anymore. If you wish to continue your training, I will assign someone else for your remaining time in Galandria."

I wait, hoping he will turn back and tell me he has changed his mind, and that he really does want to see me. When he does not, I pull a gold ribbon from my hair and place it next to him on the window sill. "Something to remember me by," I say quietly. "If you care to, that is."

Before I descend the stairs, I look back at him one last time. Patric is still looking out over the city. The ribbon next to him stirs in the breeze like it is unwanted and already forgotten.

CHAPTER 20

ELARA

*S*even minutes sealed my fate. Seven minutes sentenced me to a life with the Ogdens. Seven minutes separated me from the life I could have had. The life I *would* have had if I had been born first.

I spend a dark night in my cell, trying to sort out my thoughts. It seems that I've always been viewed as a disposable daughter. Hidden away, when my existence was judged as too much of an inconvenience. And now that they feel their precious Wilhamina is in danger, they see me as nothing more than a body to take the arrows for her.

In the morning, I awaken to the sound of my cell door clanking open and Wolfram thrusting a mug at me.

"Breakfast," he grunts and leaves, slamming the cell door behind him.

I slurp down the broth hungrily and tell myself it won't be long until he returns with bread and cheese. But hours pass, and no one comes. I think of the last thing I ate that wasn't stale or moldy. The apple tart I hastily gobbled on my way to the prison . . . how many days ago was that?

That day in Eleanor Square, Cordon had been calling out for me to be careful. When Gunther struck me and carried me away, did Cordon try to stop him? Or did he turn away, happy that he and Serena's problem—*What to do with Elara?*—had been solved?

After what seems like almost a full day later, Wolfram finally opens my cell again. "Get up," he says.

Like yesterday, a bag is dropped over my head and I am led through a series of twisting halls. Only this time the air seems to grow darker and thicker with each turn. Finally we come to a stop and a voice that I recognize as Lord Murcedor's dismisses Wolfram.

The bag is yanked off my head and I instinctively raise my hand to shield my eyes. But it's unnecessary because I'm in a dark room lit by only a single candle sitting on a wooden table. Lord Murcendor and Lord Quinlan sit at the table with a large feast spread out before them.

"Please, join us," Lord Quinlan says, sipping from a golden goblet inlaid with opals. He gestures to an empty chair.

I look from Lord Quinlan, the candlelight glinting off the jewels he wears, and into Lord Murcendor's dark gaze. "Where is the other Guardian?"

"Lord Royce is the Guardian of Trade and has business to attend to." Lord Murcendor inclines his head to the empty seat. "Sit down."

I take an unsteady step forward. My head swims at the smell of roast lamb and my stomach growls.

"Hungry?" Lord Quinlan says.

"What is this place?" I ask, ignoring him.

"This is where we take those accused of treason," Lord Murcendor replies.

"Treason? How is it I'm accused of treason?" I ask as I sink into the empty chair in front of the two Guardians. Now I'm a traitor, as well as the Masked Princess's twin sister?

Lord Murcendor fills a goblet and pushes it toward me. "Drink," he commands. "You are in no danger here."

I suspect I am in the most danger of my life. I wouldn't put it past either of them to poison me right here. But if they truly want to send me to Kyrenica, then they wouldn't hurt me. Not yet, anyway. Not while they still need me.

I gulp the wine. It tastes bitter and I nearly spit it out. I wish they would offer me water.

From across the table Lord Murcendor watches me with his dark eyes. "I have something for you." From under the table he produces a brown satchel. *My* satchel.

"I believe you will find everything in order," he says, handing it to me.

I open the satchel, hardly daring to breathe. Inside, just as I hoped, is my mother's book. And so is my dagger.

I reach in and slowly tighten my hand around it and look up. Lord Murcendor has a dagger of his own, and it's pointed at my neck. "Your property was returned to you as a gesture of goodwill. But I would think carefully before you try anything foolish again."

I glance around the room and see there is only one exit.

No doubt Wolfram is just on the other side of the door. I release my grip.

"Tell me, the man you knew as Travers," Lord Quinlan says, "did he ever say anything to you of his purpose in locating you?"

Instantly I become stone. My face is a mask, as impenetrable as the one Princess Wilhamina wears. "Is Mister Travers not his real name?"

"No. It is not." Lord Quinlan looks at me suspiciously and says no more. He is waiting for an answer.

It's all I can do to keep my eyes from straying to my satchel. If they returned the book, then they must not realize it came from my mother. "He said nothing to me. I never had a reason to doubt that he was anything more than a schoolteacher," I lie, and tuck my satchel under my chair, safely out of sight.

"I find that hard to believe," Lord Quinlan says. "All those weeks in Tulan and he said nothing to you of his plans?"

I decide to give him a portion of the truth. "In the tavern, the day he was taken, he was talking crazy and said he had wanted to tell me something but that he had waited too long. He said something similar in the dungeon, before the guards took him away. But he was sick with fever by then, and I assumed he had gone mad."

"He was not mad, at least not completely," says Lord Quinlan. "Mister Travers was a spy working for Lord Finley."

He pauses and stares at me expectantly.

"I don't know who Lord Finley is or what he would want with me," I say, but I can't help remembering Mister Travers's words. *Lord Finley wasn't sure where she was, but we knew if we watched him close enough, we'd eventually figure out where he hid her.*

"Don't you? Lord Finley was a former Guardian. He was, in fact, the fourth Guardian who was summoned to the palace the day you and your sister were born. Over the years, it seems his devotion to the king died. He had been plotting to overthrow King Fennrick. What others outside this room do not know is that he did not plan on claiming the crown for himself, but for another."

"Who?" I say.

"You."

Me? The wine, combined with gnawing hunger and lack of sleep is making me dizzy. Lord Quinlan's features blur together, making him seem like a bejeweled slug.

"It makes sense, does it not?" he says. "Replacing one Andewyn with another? After all, it was out of fear that something very much like that would happen, which caused you to be sent away in the first place."

"What have you done with them?" I ask. "Where did you take Mister Travers and Lord Finley?"

"I took them here," Lord Murcendor speaks up. "I had a nice talk with Travers and Finley, and they both swore on their lives they hadn't had enough time to tell you of your true identity. Appropriate, as it was their lives we eventually took from them."

I feel nauseous, and not just from lack of food. I swallow back the bile rising to my throat.

"We had been under the impression we had captured all of Lord Finley's supporters," Lord Quinlan speaks up. "This of course, was before the assassination attempt in Eleanor Square."

At this, Lord Murcendor opens his mouth as if to disagree, and then seems to reconsider and closes it again.

"We know Lord Finley intended to place you on the throne," Lord Quinlan says. "What we don't know, is if you decided to join them."

"Absolutely not," I answer. "He never asked me to join him, and I never agreed to anything. I have no idea if some of Lord Finley's men were behind the attack. But I do know I had nothing to do with it."

"I see," Lord Quinlan says. He stands up, walks to the door, and opens it. Wolfram enters, holding a lit candle.

"Light them," Lord Quinlan commands.

Wolfram nods. He raises his candle and begins to light torches mounted along the room. As the light grows, pictures on the stone walls come into focus.

They are pictures of death. Death by strangulation. Death by hanging. Death by fire. A hundred paintings, rendering a hundred brutal deaths. What artist was commissioned to paint such scenes? I turn away, unable to continue looking.

Wolfram, finished with lighting the torches, exits the room.

Lord Quinlan looks at Lord Murcendor. "See that she is properly persuaded." And with that, he steps out.

Properly persuaded? I swallow thickly, thankful I haven't eaten anything yet. "Where did Lord Quinlan go?"

"He prefers to let others do his dirty work," Lord Murcendor says as he refills my goblet. "The king is currently unconscious. But if he awakens, how do you think he will feel when he discovers his long-lost daughter may have been working to depose him in order to see herself crowned queen?"

"I told you, I didn't know of Finley's plans."

"There is no way for us to know that. The only way is for you to prove your loyalty."

"Prove my loyalty?" My stomach roils as the meaning of his words becomes clear. "By posing as Wilha's decoy, you mean?"

He nods. "With the assassination attempt, there is great concern over the princess traveling to Kyrenica." He picks up an apple and begins slicing it with his dagger.

I take a small sip of wine, trying to stall for time. He starts eating the apple slices, and I look longingly at the feast. My mouth waters, and I wish he would invite me to eat. But

I shake myself. I know what he is trying to do, and I can't let myself become distracted. I need to stay alert. I saw the arrows flying toward the Andewyns myself. This is no small thing they are asking.

"Won't the king object?" I ask, trying to think of a way out of this. "If he wanted me back so badly—wouldn't he object to sending both his daughters to Kyrenica?"

"I think not. Sixteen years ago, the king and queen sent you into obscurity to protect the kingdom. If he were conscious enough to do so, I believe he would be the first to volunteer you now for this task." He sips his wine and continues. "There are two ways to look at this. One is that you were working with Lord Finley's men to assassinate your own family and attempted to flee when we brought you to the Guardians' Chambers for questioning. The other is that upon learning of your true identity, you immediately agreed to protect your sister in her time of need." He leans back in his chair. "Which scenario do you suppose will sit better with the king?"

"I know nothing about being a princess," I say.

"You can learn. I have watched the games you and the Lady Ogden have played. I am certain you can assume any role required of you. If you arrive safely in Kyrenica, you are to serve as the Masked Princess and Wilha will pose as your maid until it is determined that the Strassburgs mean no harm to your sister."

"But if Wilha serves as my maid," I say, thinking fast, "they will see her face. Won't they think it strange that my maid looks exactly like the Masked Princess?"

"Royalty rarely pays any attention to their servants. And you will be wearing the mask, which you are not to remove. They should have no indication of what the Masked Princess looks like. And your stay in Korynth will be short-lived. King Ezebo is planning a masquerade to formally introduce Wilha to Kyrenican society. Lord Quinlan, Lord Royce, and I have agreed to attend. Once we have seen for ourselves that the Strassburgs mean Wilha no harm, you two can switch back. Serve your sister, and when we return you to Galandria you will be given a new life, filled with more wealth than you could possibly imagine."

"You mean, you'll give me a new life, *if* I'm not assassinated on the road or in the Kyrenican Castle."

His lips curl. "Yes. *If.*"

I rack my brain frantically, searching for another reason to object. When I can't find one I say, "And what if I refuse?"

"You could," Lord Murcendor says, glancing around the room meaningfully, "but of course, Lord Quinlan and I would have to figure out what to do with you."

It's not much of a choice. Impersonate the princess, or die. Of course I will do it. But there is one thing I want in return. One thing I want so badly I'd escort Wilha not just to Kyrenica but across the Lonesome Sea and back again if I could obtain it. "I'll do it, on one condition."

Lord Murcendor seems amused by this. "I was not aware you were in a position to issue any conditions."

"What I'm asking for will cost you nothing."

"And that is?"

"My name. Before the king and queen sent me away, what did they name me?"

"They didn't," he answers flatly. "Your father handed you over to me and said that as far as he was concerned, only one child had been born that day."

"What?" It takes a moment for his words to register. "They didn't name me?" My chest is heavy, and I curse at myself when I feel wetness on my cheeks.

How could they have denied me the simple courtesy of a name?

"I will leave you to your meal," Lord Murcendor says and stands up. "When you are finished, Wolfram will escort you to your new room."

Several minutes later when I am finally myself enough to eat, I take a bite. But the rich, colorful food tastes rotten, and I spit it from my mouth.

PART TWO

*"And so she arose, knowing not
what the future held. Knowing only
that the time to act had come."*

ELEANOR OF ANDEWYN HOUSE:
GALANDRIA'S GREATEST QUEEN

CHAPTER 21

WILHA

I hold up my candle and look at my masks inside the glass cases. Each of them stares back at me. A silent, expectant audience. I press my thumb on the embedded opal, and the wall next to the cases slides away, revealing the passageway beyond. I swallow my fear, and step hesitantly inside.

The Guardians have decreed that Elara and I are to be kept separate while she is trained to be my decoy. Elara will be housed in the old servants' quarters near the armory until we leave for Kyrenica. And though I know I should follow their orders, tonight I cannot. Not when I know my very own twin is so near.

With a soft moan, the wall to the servants' quarters slides back. The room is windowless and smells musty and rank from disuse. Bunk beds line the far wall. Outside the door, I hear guards laughing. The only light from the room comes from several candles on a nightstand.

Elara sleeps in the lower bunk beside the nightstand. Her tangled hair spills over a grimy pillow. Her lip is swollen. Her hands are calloused, and her fingernails are rimmed with dirt. I watch as she scratches at a cluster of bites on her arm.

"Elara?"

Her eyes flutter open. She bolts upright, a dagger clasped in her raised hand.

I jump backward. "It is only me," I whisper. "Wilha."

She lowers the dagger and blinks. "Wilha?" she says thickly.

I nod, staring at the dagger. "That is what everyone calls me."

She rubs her eyes, which are red and puffy, and then looks to the door.

"The guards don't know I am here," I say.

"How did you get in?" she says, blinking again.

"Through a secret passageway. The palace is full of them."

We stare at each other. I am sure the curiosity in her eyes is reflected in my own. After a moment's thought, I decide to remove my mask so she can see my face.

"May I sit down?" I ask, gesturing to her bed.

She hesitates. "You're a princess, aren't you?" she answers finally. "I don't suppose you need permission."

I sit and she scoots backward, putting some distance between us. She leans against the wall and tucks her knees underneath the plain cotton shift she wears.

I look away from her. There is a pitcher of water and a clay pot of sweet-smelling salve on the nightstand.

"It's for the bites," she says, following my gaze.

"So they are treating you well here?"

She shrugs. "They kept me in a cell until last night. Today Lord Quinlan has brought me my meals. He says tomorrow I am to begin training to be . . . you."

Her face is inscrutable as she speaks. For so many years I studied other people's faces; I was trying to understand what about my own appearance was so different that it required the mask. Now, after so much careful observation, it has become easy to read others' expressions. But this girl, my very own sister, is unreadable.

"Why have you come?" she asks.

"I needed to know if it is true."

"If what's true?"

"The Guardians say you might have been involved in the . . ." I cannot finish. The idea that she could have been part of the assassination attempt leaves me nauseous.

She shakes her head. "It's not true. I had no idea who I was until you walked into that room."

Her face is still impassive, but her voice betrays more than a hint of bitterness. She crosses her arms over her knees, as though she is holding herself together, and I find I believe her. I do not see another Aislinn Andewyn, a younger twin determined to wear a crown. I see a shell-shocked girl, one who looks just like me. And one who, judging by the look of her, has not been well taken care of these last sixteen years.

"I never knew about you," I say suddenly. "If I had, I assure you I would have done something. I would have . . ." I stop myself. It is a meaningless promise. For all the deference the Guardians pay me it has never amounted to anything remotely resembling power.

It occurs to me that if Elara had not been born, I would not have been removed from the line of succession. I would have been raised to rule Galandria, as Andrei is now. The next statue to grace the Queen's Garden would have been my own.

But none of that seems to matter right now.

"I always wanted a sister," I whisper. "Have you?"

"I always wanted to find my family . . . ," she answers, and it looks like the admission costs her some effort. She glances around the room.

She doesn't finish her thought, but her meaning is clear. Whatever she expected to find, being accused of treason and locked inside this sour-smelling room is not it.

Her gaze travels from my silken night dress, to the plain cotton shift she wears. "Please don't come here again," she says.

She lies down and turns toward the wall, as though she has forgotten me already.

CHAPTER 22

ELARA

"*H*old still!"

Arianne, the king's impossible secretary, and the only person the three Guardians have told of my existence, attempts to drag a comb through my wet hair. She grunts and tugs as pain shoots up my scalp.

Early this morning Lord Quinlan introduced me to Arianne and said she would be assisting me with my training. So far that has meant the humiliation of bathing in front of her and hours of being plucked, pulled, buffed, and scrubbed until my skin is raw and red.

"Lord Quinlan must think I am a miracle worker," she grumbles. "Now pay attention. You will need to know about the Kyrenican royal family," she says, and launches into a vitriolic description of the Strassburgs.

Arianne is interrupted when a knock sounds at the door and Lord Quinlan enters the room. "Ah, Madame Arianne, I was just coming to check on your progress."

"Well, I don't know what you expect," Arianne snaps. "She has spent most of the morning complaining and has the manners of a pig."

"Oink, oink," I snort.

Lord Quinlan seems to suppress a grin and says, "Would

you mind terribly if I had a word alone with the girl?"

"Gladly." Arianne sniffs and heads for the door.

After she is gone Lord Quinlan says, "The council has decided to move up the date of the princess's departure, which means we only have a week to get you ready. You will need to listen carefully to Arianne. She will instruct you on a number of topics that you will find useful."

I very much doubt that, but I nod politely. "Is this why you came to see me?"

"No." He flicks his eyes over to the door, and lowers his voice. "I am here to suggest that there is yet another way you can prove your loyalty to the king." He moves further into the room, and the thick jeweled necklaces he wears sway back and forth.

"What are you talking about?" I ask as he circles the room, running his fingers over the furniture as though checking for dust.

"Your sister carries a reputation for being obedient and . . . not altogether competent." He turns back to me. "But you on the other hand, could prove quite useful. For a short time you will be living in the Kyrenican Castle, and have unprecedented access to the Strassburgs. And I would find it exceedingly . . . *helpful* if you could report back to me any information you may hear."

"What sort of information?" After my "chat" with Lord Murcendor, I am smart enough to know this isn't actually a request.

"Anything that strikes you as noteworthy. King Ezebo has sworn publicly he has no intention of attacking Galandria. But I should like to know what he says privately. Lord Royce has convinced the Guardian Council that there was simply not enough evidence to conclude that the Strassburgs were behind the assassination attempt. And though it pains me to admit it, he has a point. But," he smiles, "if you could obtain information proving that Ezebo does not plan to uphold the treaty, I would be most grateful."

"So you want me to spy?" I ask, sickened by the greedy look in his eyes. Doe he actually *want* Galandria and Kyrenica to go to war?

"I want you to be observant," he corrects. "If you happen upon any information that you find useful, I will expect you to pass it along. And in doing so, you will convince me, beyond a shadow of a doubt, that you can be trusted." He cocks his head. "Agreed?"

I suppress a shiver of revulsion and look him straight in the eye. "Agreed."

⚜

*I*t's difficult to contain my awe.

Arianne helped me change into a lavender gown—the finest I've ever seen—and led me through a passageway from the old servants' quarters to Wilha's closet. It is the same one, I assume, Wilha used to visit me a week ago.

I finger the lace of my sleeve as I look around. I knew Wilha had beautiful clothes, but being trapped for the last week in the old servants' quarters, which seemed only slightly better than some of the rooms in Ogden Manor, I couldn't have imagined this.

The room is bursting with gowns and jeweled dresses in fabrics so bright it makes my eyes hurt to stare at them. One whole wall is covered with glass cases containing hundreds of her masks. Dark cherry wood dressers line the other walls, which probably contain more jewels and shoes and other fine things. Strewn around the room are half-packed trunks swollen with even more dresses.

"Stop gawking and get a move on," Arianne says as the passageway slides shut behind us. She leads us out of the closet and into what I assume is Wilha's bedroom, where silky, gossamer fabric canopies a bed covered with thick velvet blankets. We walk into an adjoining sitting room full of finely crafted furniture where Wilha, Lord Murcendor, Lord Quinlan, and Lord Royce sit in gilded chairs. They rise when they see us.

"Stand side by side so we can get a look at the two of you," Lord Quinlan says. Wilha obeys and moves next to me. She is wearing a brown cloak, and in her hands she holds a gold-threaded mask.

While Arianne and the three Guardians squint at us, I continue looking around the room. It appears that this sitting room leads to several other rooms besides Wilha's bedroom.

"Are all these rooms just for you?" I whisper to Wilha.

Her cheeks flush. "Yes."

"Wilha doesn't have as many freckles on her nose," Lord Quinlan says, still squinting.

"That will hardly matter," Lord Royce points out. "Elara will be wearing the mask. I should think the nobles in attendance tonight will be quite fooled."

Tonight I am to attend a farewell dinner in the Opal Palace, where the noblemen and women will make several toasts in "my" honor. Arianne has made it clear I am not to speak to anyone, nor will anyone be given the opportunity to speak to me. Meanwhile, in just a few minutes, Wilha will leave with a convoy of guards to begin her journey to Kyrenica. They will travel through back roads in humble carriages disguised as peasants, with Wilha posing as a Maskren. It's an ingenious plan, really. For how can the princess be on the road when she is present at her farewell dinner?

And tonight if an assassin gets past the palace guards and into the feast? No matter. I'll be there to take the arrows for the beloved Princess Wilhamina.

Tomorrow I will leave, also posing as a Maskren, with another set of guards disguised as peasants. We will travel over the more well-worn roads leading from Allegria to Kyrenica. Then, just before we enter Korynth, our two processions will converge, and we'll make the final journey to the Kyrenican

Castle together, with me posing as the Masked Princess.

Lord Quinlan tilts his head. "We need to see what she looks like with the mask. Wilha, will you please escort Elara back to your closet to fetch a mask?"

Wilha looks at me uneasily. We haven't seen each other since the night she appeared in my room. More than once, as I tossed and turned on my bed in the servants' quarters, I've wondered where Wilha spends her nights. I guess now I know.

"Bring out the mask with the lavender colored opals," Arianne commands. "It will match the dress."

Wilha nods, turns, and starts walking over to the closet. With a sigh, I follow her.

The masks inside the glass cases glisten with gilt and opals and other jewels. The smallest looks as though it was made for an infant, and I recognize the jeweled one at the very end as the mask Wilha wore in Eleanor Square.

"So many masks," I murmur.

"New ones are given to me every year for my birthday." She turns to me, and adds, "Our birthday, I mean. Happy belated birthday by the way."

"What?" I say, startled.

"Happy belated birthday," she repeats. "We turned sixteen last month." She looks at me and frowns. "Did I say something wrong?"

"No, I just . . . you're the only person who has ever said that to me. The Ogdens didn't know the date of my birth, so we never celebrated it." Not that they would have celebrated it anyway.

"Oh." Wilha stares at me, perhaps seeing more than she expected to.

"How do you open the glass cases?" I ask, changing the subject.

Wilha removes her necklace of keys. "The key is here, see? The twentieth one, clockwise from the clasp. The one with the emeralds. If you look closely, you can see it is a bit more worn than the others." She opens the case, removes a mask, and hands it to me. She opens her mouth to say something, but Lord Murcendor coughs just then. Wilha takes it as a command and she turns and hastily exits the closet.

I run my fingers over the precious stones. Instead of seeing beautiful jewels, I can't help but see all the food this mask could purchase. It could have fed me well all those nights I went hungry at the Ogdens. Actually, the sale of this one mask alone could probably feed an entire village for several months.

Everyone is waiting for me, but I pause as I look again at Wilha's opulent chambers. Maybe it's a good thing no one has offered to let me visit King Fennrick, sick though he is. Because if I saw him, near death or not, I couldn't trust myself not to spit in his face.

CHAPTER 23

ELARA

*T*he mask is hot, heavy, and stifling. It limits my vision, and I can't help tugging on it as Arianne ties it on. Behind me, the Guardians stand silent as I stare at my new reflection in the hand mirror Wilha holds up. The mask is painted white with lavender colored opals feathering above the eyebrows and cheekbones, forming a swirling, flowering pattern. With the dress, the mask, and the necklace of keys hanging around my neck, I look exactly like Wilha.

"Stop fidgeting." Arianne grabs at my arm. "If you insist on acting like a dim-witted peasant, you'll be found out immediately."

"How can you put up with wearing this?" I say to Wilha, slapping Arianne's hand away.

She casts a fleeting look at the Guardians before answering. "I have never known anything else."

"Yes, but doesn't it bother you at all?"

"No," she says, "I suppose it does not."

She's a terrible liar, but I let it go and turn back to my own reflection.

"I think that's the best it's going to get," Arianne says with a defeated sigh. She wipes her hands as though washing me from them. "There is only so much I can do, particularly since you insisted on dismissing Vena."

"Vena wasn't discreet," Lord Murcendor answers.

"You have done an admirable job, Madame Arianne," Lord Royce says.

"Indeed," Lord Quinlan says grandly. "You have done us all a great kindness, and you shall be rewarded."

I glance at Lord Royce and catch him studying me with his ice blue eyes. He has accompanied Lord Quinlan on visits to my room, but said nothing. Of the three Guardians, Lord Royce is the most enigmatic. He lacks Lord Quinlan's pompousness and Lord Murcendor's zeal. Oftentimes, he seems to just blend into the background, like a piece of old furniture.

Lord Murcendor rises. "It is time to see the princess off." He eyes Lord Quinlan. "I trust you have selected only the best men to escort Wilha?"

"As Guardian of Defense," Lord Quinlan replies icily, "I have managed just fine." He turns to address Wilha and me, "Your guards are never to see your face, and you are to avoid contact with the villagers as much as possible."

Wilha glances at me before addressing Lord Quinlan, "And my father?"

At this, Lord Quinlan shifts uncomfortably. "He has given his approval of the plan. He sends you both his farewells and bids you a good journey. His health is improving, and when he feels stronger, he promises to write."

He promises to write? I can't help but feel a little sorry for Wilha. So King Fennrick the Handsome is now conscious enough to confer with his advisors, but has chosen not to say good-bye to either of his daughters? Not even the daughter he's known all these years?

"Thank you," she says stoically to Lord Quinlan. "Tell him I hope he recovers soon." She turns to me and nods. "See you in Korynth, Elara." She exits the room, followed by Lord Murcendor and Lord Quinlan. Arianne enters Wilha's closet, grumbling about needing to pack more gowns.

"I bid you a safe and good journey, Elara." Lord Royce's voice startles me. I had forgotten he was still there.

"Thank you, Lord Royce."

He turns to leave but stops and turns back. "Suppose Lord Finley's man *had* contacted you in time and told you of his plans? What would you have done?" His voice is casual and his blue eyes are impassive as he stares at me. But it's a dangerous question, and one Lord Murcendor and Lord Quinlan haven't thought to ask.

"I would have laughed and told him to cut back on the ale," I answer, which is true enough.

"Would you?" he asks. "If the opal crown was being offered to you?"

"I would have refused him," I say. "Galandria has done nothing for me. Let someone else rule this wretched kingdom."

Lord Royce nods and silently leaves. I blow out a breath, thankful to finally be alone. Thankful to soon be leaving the Opal Palace, and the Guardians' watchful eyes.

CHAPTER 24

WILHA

*O*ur procession bumps over the Kyrenican terrain and rattles to a stop at a patch of trees just outside of Korynth. I step out of my carriage and take a deep breath of air that bites and smells of salt—so different from the warmer, still air of Galandria. My hands are shaking. My heart flaps in my chest like a bird trying to escape its cage.

Miles behind me lies the kingdom I have known all my life. And here before me lies the kingdom I will one day rule as queen of Kyrenica. Upon my shoulders, I carry the expectations of two kingdoms.

I know little about Stefan Strassburg. But sitting in my father's court, I often glimpsed many a lord treat his wife as nothing more than a finely adorned possession. Is the crown prince such a man? Will he care to know me, or will he care only that with this treaty his kingdom has acquired the famous Masked Princess?

I pull a white handkerchief from my cloak pocket. Every night after dinner I have sat in my tent embroidering. On the left side of the handkerchief in gold thread is a curling, ornate *A* with the Andewyn coat of arms next to it. On the right side is an *S* with the Strassburg coat of arms. I suppose I intend it to be a present of sorts to the crown prince.

Yet at night when I sleep, I still dream of him locking me away in a crypt.

Behind me I hear the clomping of horses and the voice of Garwyn, the leader of my guards calling. "Your Highness? They're here."

I refold the handkerchief and tuck it back into my cloak. "Thank you, Garwyn."

The guards have been kind to me, but aloof. At night, after bringing dinner to my tent, they usually retreat to the campfire to whisper among themselves. They have not seemed all that eager to speak to me. Odd behavior, it seems, given that Lord Quinlan said they volunteered to accompany me to Korynth.

The arriving procession comes to a halt, and then Elara exits her carriage. As planned, she is dressed identically to me: a brown traveling cloak, black boots, and a gold-threaded mask. The only difference is that Elara carries a brown leather satchel.

"Did you have a good trip?" I ask.

She does not reply, but instead brushes past me with only the briefest of glances, before entering my carriage. I turn and follow her.

Our procession, which has grown significantly now that we have the carriages that traveled with Elara, starts up again. After I draw the curtains Elara unties her mask and tosses it aside. "I hate this thing. I don't know how you wore one all these years."

I nod, and after a moment's hesitation, untie mine as well. "How was your journey?" I ask.

"Bumpy," she answers curtly.

"And the farewell dinner, did they believe that you were . . . that you were me?"

"Why shouldn't they? I'm an excellent liar," she says. From the tone of her voice, I cannot tell if she is boasting—or bitter. "Besides," she adds, "Arianne wouldn't let me speak to anyone."

"Yes," I answer quietly, "she is often like that."

Elara turns and stares at the drawn curtains, and I cast about for something else to say. All these weeks on the road, staring out the window of my carriage, I have wondered so much about her. She grew up in a small village, not in Allegria, that much I have understood. I can't help but wonder what it was like, walking about with no guards before or behind her, no citizens screaming her name in either adoration or hatred.

"What was the family like—the ones who raised you, I mean?"

Elara tears her gaze from the curtains. "Is this an inquisition?"

"What? No, of course not."

"Then I don't feel we need to talk. Let's just get to the castle."

"Okay . . . but I shall spend my life here in Kyrenica. I don't imagine I will return to Galandria that often, maybe ever. And you will only be in Korynth until the masquerade."

She stares back at me, not comprehending. "And?"

"Well, we only have a short amount of time together and . . . I mean, don't you want to get to know each other?"

Her eyes are hooded. "What I want has never mattered."

"I understand that, Elara. I really do. However differently we have been raised, I do understand that, at least. You cannot know what it was like, being forced to wear the mask."

"Forced?" A sardonic smile twists at her lips. "So they held you down and strapped the mask to your face every day, is that it?"

"Well, no," I say, frowning, "But—"

"Did they starve you? Threaten to throw you in the dungeon? Lock you in your chambers?"

"No, of course not. But there were so many rumors. Of my ugliness. Of a curse. Even some people in the palace believed them."

"Some people are idiots," she snaps. "So what? You're not blind, and you own a mirror. Obviously you must have known there was nothing wrong with your face."

I am speechless. Her life may have been harsher, yet for all her smugness she cannot know what it was like, to endure the constant rumors.

"You are the daughter of the king," Elara continues, her eyes now intent on mine. "And the sister of the crown prince. You could have refused to wear the mask."

"It is not that simple," I insist. "Our family—"

"I don't have a family," she snaps. "Or a name," she adds softly.

"What?" I lean forward. Then a thought occurs to me. "Who named you Elara? Did our parents—"

"I'm tired," she interrupts. "I want to be alone. Tell the driver to stop so you can find another carriage."

"But Lord Quinlan said we were to travel together until we reached the castle. The guards were given orders."

"Lord Quinlan is a pompous fool," Elara says. She turns away and shouts, "Driver, stop the carriage!"

The carriage slows, but doesn't stop.

"I'm sorry, Your Highness," comes the driver's voice. "But Lord Quinlan said—"

"I don't care what Lord Quinlan said," she interrupts. "I am Princess Wilhamina Andewyn, Daughter of King Fennrick the Handsome. And for your sake you had better stop this carriage, before I take off my mask and look upon the one who dares to defy me!"

The carriage stops so fast I am thrown backward, and I stare in wonder at Elara.

"That was amazing," I say. "I have never spoken like that to anyone in my life."

She gives me a withering look "Maybe if you had, your father wouldn't have tossed you out of the kingdom."

My hands tremble as I hastily tie on my mask. When I step outside, a guard appears to assist me. "Please take me to another carriage. We should like to travel separately."

Confusion marks the guard's face and I can guess what he

is thinking. Is the girl he's looking at the decoy, or the princess?

"Find another place for her," Elara calls. The guard mumbles his assent, and when he turns back to me, the confusion is gone.

It is clear he has decided I am the decoy, while the voice inside the carriage can only belong to royalty.

CHAPTER 25

ELARA

I am being unkind to Wilha. Cruel, even. But I can't look at her, at the girl who was given everything. I know the best I can do, before I say something truly unforgiveable, is to get away from her.

After she's gone and the carriage has started up again, I settle back into the plush cushions. My nerves are brittle and need only a spark to light them. For the last two weeks as we've traveled, the guards halted every time they heard so much as the snap of a twig and seemed to ready themselves, as if preparing for an attack.

But did they grip their swords just a little more carelessly? Did they ask themselves that, since I am not the Masked Princess, but merely a decoy, if I was worth risking their lives for? And if so, during those moments when they kept watch in the forest, did it occur to them that they could just run away?

Aislinn Andewyn will forever be known as the Great Betrayer. For the first time, I find myself sympathizing with her. What would it be like to grow up in the shadow of your older twin? To be treated all your life as a second copy, when one was all that was ever wanted or needed?

I reach under my seat and find my satchel. I open it and

pull out some of the items I've stolen. Several nights after the guards have fallen asleep I've rifled through Wilha's trunks. I have carefully selected the smallest items I could find that won't be missed. Opal earrings, a tiny opal ring, several worthings from a bag intended to purchase foodstuffs in case the guards were unable to hunt up enough food.

I have decided I won't stay in Korynth until Lord Murcendor, Lord Quinlan, and Lord Royce arrive. Despite their promises of a new life in Allegria, I don't trust them. Once I have done their bidding, what is to prevent them from disposing of me on the road back to Galandria? A quiet death, for someone they suspect is a threat to the monarchy.

Even if their offer is genuine, why would I want to return to Allegria, where I'll always be under their watchful eyes? And really, will Galandria ever be safe for me? Lord Finley may have been caught, but are there others who know of my existence? Others searching for the lost Andewyn daughter? Men who are eager to place me on the throne, beholden to their cause? What would they do if they found me?

I don't intend to find out. Once we reach the Kyrenican Castle, Wilha is on her own.

CHAPTER 26

WILHA

When the carriage comes to a halt before a stone manor that is set into a hill, I call out to the driver. "Why are we stopping?"

"We're here," comes his muffled reply.

"Here, where?"

"The Kyrenican Castle."

A guard wearing a breastplate bearing the Strassburg coat of arms waves us through a wrought-iron gate. I study the manor as our procession crosses a small courtyard. It is made of gray stone and is smaller than the estates of Allegrian nobility. *This* is where the Kyrenican royal family lives?

"Now what?" I hear one guard ask another. "Do we bang on the door until they let us in?"

But it doesn't take long before a flustered servant emerges from the castle and inquires who we are. His cheeks redden when Garwyn answers.

"We were not expecting you for another three weeks. The king and queen will be so angry to not have been here to receive you. They are attending an engagement in the city. The crown prince is not even in residence."

"Then perhaps you should send a messenger to tell the king and queen of our arrival," Garwyn replies. "In the meantime, I am sure they wouldn't like to hear you have made the Masked Princess wait outside their door."

Garwyn's words snap him into action. He hurries over to Elara's carriage and bows to her. Garwyn extends his hand and she emerges.

"The princess needs to rest from her journey. Could you show her to her chambers while my men see to the horses?"

"Of course," says the servant. He bows to Elara again, and they both head up the stone steps that lead up to the castle's main entrance.

"Smell that?" mutters one of the guards standing by my carriage. "Smells like dogs, don't it?"

"Silence, Moran," Garwyn says, glancing in my direction. "There will be none of that." He gives him a meaningful look. Something passes between them, but I don't understand what. Moran immediately quiets down though, and begins unloading trunks.

Garwyn pokes his head into my carriage and stares for a moment. I think he is trying to figure out if I am me or the decoy. "I believe you should also be journeying with the other girl to the princess's chambers," he says tactfully.

Accompanied by Garwyn, I scramble up the steps just as the servant is ushering Elara through a dim foyer lined with scarlet tapestries. He pales when he sees me and stares back and forth between Elara and me, no doubt confused by our identical cloaks and gold-threaded masks.

"I'm sure you can understand the princess's need to travel with a security escort," Garwyn says. "If you will show them to their room both the princess and her maid can change into proper attire."

"Of course." The servant leads us down several twisting corridors lined with lit sconces. Yet there are few windows, making everything seem dark and dim.

"Here we are," he says, stopping before a door and opening it.

As we enter, I see that my new chambers are made up of three small rooms. The first is a sitting room with plush red velvet chairs and a large fireplace. The second room is a bedroom for me, and next to it is a smaller bedroom for my maid.

Before long, the Galandrian guards enter carrying trunk after trunk into the sitting room. Garwyn places several velvet boxes containing my masks on my bed. Elara specifically directs one guard to return to the carriage and fetch her satchel. Another servant comes in, lights some candles, and gets a fire going in the sitting room. She stares in awe at Elara and me, almost setting her sleeve on fire.

The trunks begin to pile up and spill out from each room, forming a haphazard maze.

"I don't know where you expect us to put all your things," Elara says once the guards and servants have left and we are alone.

I nod. "I didn't expect the castle to be so small."

Elara looks at me wide-eyed. "You think this is small? A person could easily get lost in this place."

"Yes, of course," I say immediately, reading her incredulity and remembering that we have grown up in very different places.

Elara disappears into my bedroom and closes the door behind her. I assume she has gone to change into the Masked Princess's costume, so I untie my gold-threaded mask and sink into an armchair next to the fire.

These three small rooms may be where I spend the rest of my life. One day I may very well die in these chambers, an aged queen. And as death draws near, will I be able to say I enjoyed anything of my life here?

I try to find comfort with the thought that Elara will at least be the Masked Princess for a few weeks, and I will have time to watch the Strassburgs unnoticed.

But all the voices of my childhood come rushing back. My father declaring that the Strassburgs are not to be trusted. Lord Murcendor railing against the Kyrenicans. All the fear and loathing I have been taught to feel for the Strassburgs rises up, making my heart pound harder.

Before I let my worrying get the better of me, I rise from the armchair and open the door to my new bedroom. Elara has removed her mask, but she has not changed out of her traveling clothes and into the Masked Princess's finery. Next to the velvet boxes, a pile of my things are laid out on the bed along with several worthings and a brown leather book I don't recognize.

"What are you doing?" I ask.

"I'm leaving." Her voice is curt, and she begins stuffing the items into her satchel.

"Leaving? But you are not supposed to leave until it is safe."

"We've arrived in Kyrenica. You're safe and alive." She spreads her hands wide. "Congratulations. Welcome to your new fairy tale."

"But—"

She holds up a pair of opal earrings. "I'm taking these, all right? I doubt they mean all that much to you, but they'll fetch me a nice price." She stops and scrutinizes me. Her eyes stray to the velvet boxes lying on the bed, and she seems to soften slightly. "You don't have to wear the mask just because they say you do. Tell the crown prince you refuse to be treated like a puppet."

Puppet? At this, a spark kindles in my chest. I force myself to find the right words, to let her know she cannot join the long line of people who have presumed to tell me how to carry the weight of being the Masked Princess. Not when it turns out she is the reason I have been sent away.

"I can't stay here," she says before I can speak. "I know I said I would. But I can't. All I'll ever be to the Guardians is a threat. I have to leave now before—"

She breaks off at a sudden commotion in the castle corridor. There are muffled sounds of shouting and rushing footsteps, followed by a loud *click* in the sitting room.

We glance uneasily at each other. "What was that?" Elara says and leaves the satchel on the bed. I follow her into the sitting room, but nothing seems to be amiss.

Elara turns about the room. "I know I heard something."

I nod. I heard it too. But it did not sound like someone entering the room, it sounded more as though . . .

The strength leaves my legs, and I fall into an armchair. "They have locked us in."

"Locked us in?" She hurries to the door, and finding that it is indeed locked, calls out, "What is the meaning of this? Why is the door locked?'

"The commander of the Kyrenican guard has ordered your room to remain locked for the time being," says an unfamiliar voice though the door.

"That makes no sense," Elara calls out. "I demand an explanation. You can't lock me in here without my consent." She turns to me and lowers her voice. "Can they?"

"King Ezebo can do whatever he pleases," I say, staring into the fire. "He could execute me if he wished it, and no one could stop him."

"He doesn't want you dead," she says dispassionately. "He wants to put you on display for all the world to see."

"What a comforting thought," I whisper. Yet is this not my

nightmare, come to life? That the crown prince would decide it was better if he locked me away?

Elara turns back to me. "Check your room. See if you can find a key to the door."

I return to the bedroom and search the drawers of a small writing desk. When I don't find a key, I sit on the bed and look around the room. The walls of my new life seem to be closing in around me already. When they unlock the door, what will become of me?

Elara appears in the doorway. "Did you find a key?"

When I do not answer she rolls her eyes and rifles through the drawers of the writing desk. After she finishes she goes to the maid's room to continue her search.

I cannot help but think of my great-great-grandmother, Queen Rowan. She was once a prisoner in this castle as well. When she learned the Kyrenicans had decided to execute her, was she in this very same room?

My eyes fix on a tiny smudge on the wall across from the bed. The smudge seems to shine when it catches the light, and I remember that the same family who built the Opal Palace—*my* family—also built this castle. So many underground tunnels connect the Opal Palace to different locations in Allegria. Would my ancestors have insisted on a similar construction for what was once their seaside estate?

Because Queen Rowan the Brave didn't die in this castle. When the executioner came for her in the morning, she was gone.

I stand up and walk toward the wall with the smudge. I feel a wave of relief when I realize it is not a smudge at all, but a small opal embedded in the stone wall.

I press on the stone for several seconds and with a groan the wall slides back, revealing a dark tunnel. This must be how Queen Rowan escaped, or if not down this exact tunnel, then one just like it. I grab a candle on the writing desk with unsteady hands. I see Elara's satchel and pick it up. How exactly did she plan to use my jewelry to support herself? Hesitantly, I step into the open corridor. Cobwebs brush my face, like wispy, welcoming hands beckoning me down the hall my ancestors once traveled. I hold up my candle, and find the opal embedded on the other side of the tunnel.

"Wilha, did you find—" Elara strides into the room and stops short when she sees me in the tunnel. Her eyes widen. "What are you doing?"

"Please," I say. "I just need a little time. I will come back, I promise."

The door in the sitting room opens and a man calls out, asking to speak to the Masked Princess.

"Get your mask on and get out of there," Elara hisses and glances quickly over her shoulder. "Stop being a coward." She waits, expecting me to obey. The word "coward" hangs between us like a royal pronouncement.

My gaze slides from Elara to the masks lying on the bed.

If she is so much braver than I am, let her face the guards. I press on the embedded opal, and just before the wall slides back into place, I hear the guard calling again for the Masked Princess. For the first time ever, I do not answer the summons.

If Elara thinks my life is such a fairy tale, then she is welcome to it.

CHAPTER 27

ELARA

"*W*ait!"

I cross the room and pound on the stone wall. How did Wilha manage to find a passageway? Frantically, my hands push and prod at the wall, but it won't yield to my touch.

"Come away from there," orders a voice. A guard seizes my arm and spins me around. He stares at my dirty boots and traveling dress and his eyes narrow. "Where is she? What have you done with the Masked Princess?"

A second Kyrenican guard enters the room. "Don't touch her you fool! Do you wish to hang? She's the princess's maid."

"Once we find the Masked Princess, she can get another maid." He tightens his grip on my arm. "Tell us where she is."

I'm not sure where Wilha went or if she is coming back, but it doesn't require a tremendous amount of intelligence to understand that a missing servant is less troublesome than a missing princess.

"She is right here," I say.

"Where? We've searched the chambers. You are the only one here."

"Exactly." I yank my arm away. "I sent my maid to fetch something from my carriage almost an hour ago. *I* am the

Masked Princess, and you have interrupted me while I was changing. If you would kindly hand me my mask, you will find it is on the bed."

"You're cracked. Fine princess, you are," he says, eyeing my traveling clothes. But the color drains from his face when the second guard picks up the gold-threaded mask and hands it to me.

"You don't look like a princess, anyway," the first guard says.

"And what do you suppose she should look like?" I inquire in a cold voice, tying on the mask. "You think because you haven't dropped dead yet that I cannot be the Masked Princess?" His hand tenses and flexes, and I wonder if he wants to cover his eyes. Or strike me. "What do you suppose," I continue, rubbing my arm where he grabbed me, "is the penalty for injuring a member of the royal family? In Galandria we execute those who would hurt us. In any event, you have come at the right moment. My maid never returned. She seems to be missing, as well as a satchel filled with my jewels"—I tell the first lie I can think of—"I suggest that instead of manhandling me, you search the castle. If you find my maid, then maybe I won't tell the king of your incompetence."

The guards glance uneasily at each other. "Yes, Your Highness." They bow and quickly leave the room.

And I smile at how easy that was.

CHAPTER 28

WILHA

The candle I hold seems small and insufficient compared to the deep darkness of the tunnel. I grip the strap of Elara's satchel and fight a wave of panic. I close my eyes and imagine the passageway is lit with a golden glow, and every female ancestor of mine who has ever traveled this tunnel stands at either side urging me forward, away from the Strassburgs and toward whatever lies at the end of this path.

I stretch my hand out, walk several steps, and stop when my fingers close over something long and thin. I let out half a scream before I realize it is just a torch and not someone's arm. Of course, the passageway is probably lined with torches.

But if the passageway is known to the Kyrenicans, then lighting the torches will surely give me away, so I let the faint glow of my candle light the way. At the sound of something small skittering near my feet, I jump and drop the satchel. It opens and several opals spill out. Hastily, I pick everything up and continue on. I pass several doors at either side of the tunnel. I don't open any of them, as they probably lead to other rooms in the castle. I decide I will follow the tunnel until I reach whatever final destination my ancestors planned.

The candle burns low. Hot wax drips down my hand, and I stifle a cry of pain. Lower and lower the candle burns as I fumble forward, until the wick drowns in its own wax, extinguishing what little light there is.

Hours seem to pass, though I know it can only be minutes, and I begin to think I will never escape the darkness—until I walk straight into a stone wall. I set down the candle and put out my hands, searching for the opal that will open the door. After several more minutes, I finally feel a point in the wall that feels smoother than the others and press on it.

The door gives way with much creaking and moaning, and I trip and tumble into a pile of sand. Coughing and spitting, I stand and brush myself off. I am in a shallow cave, and I hear the sound of rushing water. The air is sharp and cold, and besides the sand, I taste salt on my tongue. To my right, late afternoon sunlight beckons. I find the embedded opal on the other side of the wall and press down, and the door groans shut.

I cautiously step out of the cave, but come to a halt. I am perched on a small ledge on a mossy cliff side. Spread out before me is the ocean. A single large rock rises up in the water, moss covering it like an emerald gown. Down below, the shore is strewn with tall, jagged rocks, and whitened wood. Several hundred yards up appears to be Korynth's seaport.

I look down, searching for a path to get to the beach below. Hidden under a layer of slippery moss is a steep stone staircase, which cuts through the cliff and leads down between two tall boulders to the beach. Cautiously, I make my way downward, trying not to focus on the jagged rocks below.

When my feet touch the sand, I walk up the shore—almost as if in a trance—toward the docks, both amazed and horrified by my actions. I expect to hear the heavy footsteps of soldiers rushing behind to capture me. Yet no soldiers come and the sailors at the docks pay no attention to me.

A salty wind whips my hair. I tilt my head toward the sun and feel my cheeks, hidden all my life behind masks, beginning to burn.

For the first time ever, I am outside and alone, free of palace walls.

But as the sun sinks beyond the horizon and shadows creep across the docks, I ask myself:

Can I exist in a world without walls?

CHAPTER 29

ELARA

*I*f I don't find Wilha soon, I may well be executed.

The lie I told about the missing maid has bought me time, but how much? How long before someone suspects it's not the maid who has gone missing, but the princess herself?

I've been stuck in Wilha's chambers the entire night, but she hasn't returned. The only person I've seen at all is a timid maid who visited to tell me that the search of the castle had ended, and my missing servant hadn't been found.

"King Ezebo has returned, and I have been asked to tell you that you need to remain in your chambers this evening. He's entertaining a large party of nobles who have come to stay a few nights at the castle, and doesn't yet wish to announce your presence in the city. Tomorrow he promises to receive you properly," she finished, before quickly leaving.

As the evening has given way to night I've passed the hours sitting in front of the fire or clawing at the wall in Wilha's room, trying to gain entrance to the passageway, and wishing I'd paid more attention to how Arianne opened the tunnel in the Opal Palace.

Wilha may not have gone far. For all I know, she's been stuck on the other side this whole time trying to get back in. I put my ear to the wall and knock softly. I don't hear anything, but then again, the wall seems thick.

Wilha opened the passageway seemingly without too much difficulty. There has to be a way in, something I'm not seeing. . . .

She pressed something to make the wall slide back, I remember suddenly. Something lower to the ground. I crouch down on my hands and knees, pressing my fingers to the wall. After several minutes, I spot a small smooth stone—is it an opal?

I press it and the wall slides back, revealing the passageway. Once my eyes adjust to the darkness, I see a row of mounted torches. Quickly, I stride back to the sitting room. I stick a piece of kindling into the fire until it ignites, then carry it back to Wilha's bedroom and light the first few torches.

I'm about to step into the passageway when I pause. I don't know where the tunnel leads. I only know I need to find Wilha, or get out of this castle—preferably both. But if I'm caught, it will attract no small amount of attention if I'm dressed as the Masked Princess. Quickly, I untie my gold-threaded mask and throw on my cloak, thankful that I still haven't changed out of my traveling clothes.

I remove the first torch from its mount and decide to leave the passageway open. The tunnel is so dark; I want the candlelight from Wilha's room—dim though it is—to guide me.

I flip up the hood of my cloak and move deeper into the tunnel. It's not long before I come to a door, but I pass it quickly. Wilha had been in such a hurry, I don't think she would have taken the first exit offered to her. After a few more minutes of walking, the torchlight glints off of something small on the ground. I crouch down and see it's a small opal earring, one that I had stuffed into my satchel. The earring is lying next to a door. Did Wilha exit the passageway here?

I search around and find another opal in the wall and press on it. The wall slides back. I'm greeted with more darkness and see that I'm staring at the back of a floor-length tapestry. I extinguish my torch, leave it in the passageway, and step out from around the tapestry. It appears as though I'm in a small receiving room of sorts. I cross the room quickly and cautiously open the first door I see, but draw back immediately.

A boy who looks to be a few years older than me is exiting another room just across the corridor. As noiselessly as possible, I hurry back to the tapestry. After several minutes, I decide he didn't see me, and venture out again.

The corridor is deserted. The only light comes from several flickering sconces lining the walls. If Wilha came this way, where would she go? I look over to the door the boy exited, thinking that maybe she wouldn't have wanted to be so exposed in the hallway. I cross the corridor and grasp the door handle, which is shaped like a gargoyle, and I'm about to push it open when—

"What do you think you're doing?"

I jump and turn around. At the end of the hall is the boy. His hand is on the hilt of his sword, which hangs at his waist.

"I *said*, what are you doing?" He walks a few steps closer, passing into the glow of sconced candlelight. He is tall and tanned with golden blond hair and a strong jaw. But despite his good looks, his hair is disheveled and his clothes are dusty and dirty. All in all, it looks to me like he's a squire in need of a bath. A really long one. When he gets closer he draws his sword and points it at me.

Don't panic, I tell myself. I loosen my shoulders.

"You can put that down," I say, in a breathless but bubbly voice. "I promise not to hurt you."

A hint of a smile plays on his lips. "Thank you for assuring me," he says and turns serious again. "I am wondering, though, why you are sneaking around. This corridor is part of the Strassburgs' private rooms. It is off limits to most of the palace staff."

"Maybe you could help me then," I say, thinking fast. "My lady and I only arrived at the castle tonight, and she has sent me to the kitchen—a healthy appetite, she has—and I've been wandering around trying to find it."

"Who is your lady?" he asks, looking suspicious.

"Um, the spoiled one."

At this, he grins and sheaths his sword. "Most of them are."

"So do you know where the kitchen is?" I repeat, feeling I have no choice but to embrace my lie.

"I do. I will take you there now."

"No, that's quite all right. You don't have to accompany me. If you point me in the right direction, I'll be on my way."

"It is not a bother. And besides," he adds with a pointed look, "that way I can make sure you get where you need to go."

He sets off down the corridor, and I have to run to keep up with his long strides.

"Are you a servant here?"

"In a manner of speaking," he replies. "I have only just arrived."

When we reach the kitchen, he offers me a seat at a small wooden table next to a fireplace, where embers glow the color of a fiery sunset.

"This is where Cook takes her meals. I will stoke the fire and find some food."

"Won't we get in trouble?" I ask, though I'm not worried about a scolding from the kitchen staff. Wandering around the castle with a servant—a servant who's seen my face— seems like a dangerous game. And I still need to find Wilha.

"No one else is up at this hour," he answers. "And I am one of her favorites." He closes a cupboard and brings me a bowl of soup. "There is not much left. This is all I can offer your lady."

"That's all right."

"Are you sure you are not the one who is hungry?" he asks, after my stomach growls.

"I'm, well . . . yes, I'm a little hungry, actually," I admit. "I found I couldn't eat much of what was served at dinner."

"And what was that?"

"Tuna eyes," I say. The maid brought dinner to me when she informed me the search of the castle had finished. And while I was thankful for the meal, a meal someone else cooked, and served in a portion larger than I ever would have received at Ogden Manor, I couldn't bring myself to try it. Not with those wiggly black eyes staring up at me. I ended up disposing of the food in the fire after the maid left.

"Ah, tuna eyes. Yes, I think I would be tempted to skip dinner as well." He laughs a deep, throaty laugh, and I feel myself beginning to relax more. He pushes the bowl of soup toward me. "Eat. There is still enough left for your lady." He stares at me expectantly. My stomach rumbles again, and I decide there's no harm in it.

While I sip the soup, which is a rich, fragrant broth tasting of onions and mushrooms, he adds wood to the fire. Then he leaves and returns with a tray for "my lady" as well as a plate of plum tarts. "I also found these. I think Cook was hiding them. Would you like some?" He grins and offers me a tart.

I accept the pastry, and we eat in silence. When I'm full, I settle back into my chair. The fire and the food have me feeling drowsy, and perhaps a little bit reckless. I should return to my chambers, I know. Or pretend to, anyway, and keep searching for Wilha.

But when I look into the squire's liquid brown eyes, I find myself exhaling deeply, as though I've been holding my breath for a long time. Since the day I woke up in the Opal Palace's dungeon, in fact. I want to pretend I am just a servant, not a princess. Or, it's the princess role that's the pretense—isn't it?—because I've been a servant all my life. Though somehow, I guess I am both. A servant princess.

My thoughts are confused and hazy, and I'm slightly startled when the squire says, "You speak with an accent. Where are you from?"

I'm at least alert enough to know that question can only get me into trouble, so I turn it back on him.

"You first. You said you've only just arrived. Where did you come from?"

"I was sailing, actually."

"Really? What was it like, sailing on a ship? One day I'd like to travel across the Lonesome Sea." *Maybe one day very soon, after I find a way out of this castle.*

Because it looks as though tonight I won't be leaving or finding Wilha.

"What, you? You hardly look strong enough to survive a voyage on the sea."

"I'll have you know I am capable of surviving a good many unpleasant things," I say, thinking of my years with the Ogdens. "More than you, probably."

"Oh really?" He smiles slyly. "Let us have a contest, then.

The person who has survived the most grievous thing shall win this last plum tart. You first."

"All right," I say, warming to the game. "One time I—" But I find I can't say what I want to. The fire and the food have gotten me to drop my guard, and I almost begin to tell him of the night I spent shivering in the barn, hoping I wouldn't freeze to death. But I never even told Cordon about that night. Instead I say, "One time I decided to run away from home. I climbed the tallest tree in my village, but found once night came that I'd changed my mind, yet I was too scared to climb down in the dark. I spent the entire night stuck in the tree, staring at the stars."

"A night staring at the stars, contemplating the heavens and all their mysteries? That does not seem nearly so grievous." He grabs the plum tart off the plate. "You will have to do better than that."

I give a slight laugh and nod, though I purposely didn't tell him the truly grievous part. The thrashing I received from Mistress Ogden the next morning when I finally roused up enough courage to climb down and return to Ogden Manor the next morning.

"All right. Once I was walking in the forest, on my way to the Dra—to an inn—and I nearly walked right into a grizzly bear," I say, which is actually true. I just don't tell him it was a very small cub that must have gotten separated from its mother.

"A grizzly bear! And how did you live to tell the tale?"

"I stared him down, and he went running away."

"Stared him down?" He opens his eyes wide. "With what? The sheer force of your beauty?"

"Yes. That was it, exactly." I roll my eyes. "No, you fool—I had a shiny dagger, and I shoved it in his face and roared as loud as I could."

"You roared at a grizzly bear?" He throws back his head and laughs, and has to catch himself from tipping over in his chair. "But that does not seem so bad either," he says when he stops laughing. "It sounds to me like the bear was more scared than you were."

"This is true." I pause, and think for a moment. "All right, I have it. Once I had to listen to a two-hour lecture from a woman on the appropriate use of cutlery." I don't say that woman was Arianne, or that it was part of my training to become the Masked Princess.

"Horror of horrors!" He places his hand on his chest. "Your lady must be truly terrible, to subject you like that. Yet I can do you one better. Once I had to listen to a discussion for *three* hours on the appropriate way to hook a fish."

"*Three* hours? I don't believe it!"

"Oh yes, you will find the men in Korynth are quite serious about their fish."

We laugh, and I find myself wanting to say something more. Something real. "I once spent *four* hours scrubbing out a skirt for a noblegirl. She dirtied it on purpose so I wouldn't be able to attend the dance being held in our village that night. Her mother was quite harsh, and I knew what would happen if I returned the dress still stained."

"Harsh?" His smile vanishes. "What do you mean?"

"Oh," I wave breezily, "aren't all rich people harsh with their servants?"

"No, not all of them." He leans forward. "The lady you work for now, is she kind?"

"Oh, um, yes, of course," I say, caught off guard by the concern in his eyes. "She is very kind."

"I am glad," he says and hands me the plum tart. "And now I think you have won."

Wordlessly, I accept the tart and stuff it into my mouth. An unfamiliar feeling crawls its way into my belly, and it's a moment before I recognize it for what it is. Shame. As usual I have said too much, so I decide to leave the truth behind. It's easier and far less painful to slip back into my lies. "I'm so glad my lady sent me." I lounge back in my seat. "Now tell me, if you could go anywhere or do anything right this minute, what would it be?"

"I would be talking to a beautiful girl in the king of Kyrenica's kitchen, and wondering what she was *really* doing out of bed in the middle of the night." His eyes study me, as though he can't make up his mind if he should have me questioned, so I rise and quickly make up an excuse about needing to get back to "my lady."

"She'll have my head if I'm gone any longer." I turn to go.

"I think you have forgotten something." He gestures to the tray sitting on the table, and his eyes narrow. "That *is* why you were sneaking around the castle, wasn't it? To get her a snack?"

"Yes, of course." I grab the tray and turn away.

He stands up. "I will accompany you."

"No! I mean, she may be kind, but she's also strict, and it is quite late after all. If she sees me with you, she might get the wrong idea. Please," I add in my most desperate voice, "I can't afford to be dismissed from her service."

"A fair point," he acknowledges. "But," he sharpens his gaze, "I shall be patrolling tonight, and I expect no more late night activity from you."

I nod. "Of course."

Before he can change his mind, I turn away again and stride from the kitchen. I travel back to the room with the tapestry and enter the passageway. If I'm not mistaken, I hear the faint echo of footsteps from far down the corridor. Quickly, I close the passageway. Once I've hurried back up the tunnel, the faint candlelight from Wilha's bedroom is a welcome beacon. I pour the broth out into the fire, and I place the tray and the empty bowl inside the passageway and close it, certain no one will miss a few of the king's dishes.

It's only later, when I'm crawling into bed, that I realize the squire never told me his name.

CHAPTER 30

WILHA

*T*he next morning I awaken groggily, stiff and numb with cold, to the sound of seagulls and pounding surf. At first I wonder why my mattress feels so hard, why my covers are so rough. But I remember the abandoned tarp on the docks I hid under last night and wake up to the full horror of what I have done. I have walked out of the castle as though the life the Kyrenicans presented me with is nothing more than a new dress I do not care to purchase. Not the fulfillment of a treaty preventing war between two kingdoms all too eager to believe the worst of each other.

Cautiously, I peek out from under the tarp that covers me. It looks to be midmorning judging by the bright sun. Several ships have just come into port, their white sails billowing in the breeze, and sailors haggle with shopkeepers over the price of their wares. No one seems to be looking my way, and so I quickly slip out from my hiding place and stumble to a nearby bench. My cheeks are hot, not from sunburn, but from shame.

Last night I could not bring myself to return to the castle, but neither could I work up the courage to journey into the city. Instead I lingered at the docks for hours, frozen in indecision, until it was clear I would need a place to spend the evening. I glimpsed the tarp in a neglected portion of the docks, and hid under it for hours (just like the coward Elara believes I am) until sometime in the middle of the night, I must have fallen asleep.

I look over to the cliffs, and the stone steps that are hidden under the moss. Fleeing the castle and leaving Elara to face my own fate is the most selfish act I have ever committed, and I know I have to come to my senses.

Yet is this really how I want my adventure to end? I imagine my ancestor's stone faces in the Queen's Garden, and the disapproval I have always read in their eyes. Do I want to come creeping back to the castle, defeated and dirty, without so much as having walked the streets of the city?

No doubt Elara was all too happy to tell the Kyrenican guards of my cowardice. At any moment I am sure soldiers will be storming the streets looking for me. In the meantime, is it selfish to want to continue my charade for just a little longer?

I replace the image of my stone ancestors with another. I imagine myself, years from now as a middle-aged queen, looking into my daughter's face and saying, *"Yes, it is true when I was younger people thought me incompetent and fearful. But once upon a time, I changed their minds. For I did something truly and wonderfully mad. . . ."*

I stand up. Yes, that is the story I want to one day tell. After all, the soldiers should be here any moment.

*B*ut they never come. For hours I walk through the crowded streets, marveling at how they smell of salt, sweat, and fish. Everywhere I look I see new construction, evidence of a younger, thriving kingdom. The older buildings are made of wood and are tall and narrow. Their roofs bottleneck into chimneys, reminding me of giant wooden wine bottles. Clotheslines are strung up high across the streets, and women lean out of second- and third-story windows, calling out greetings to one another as they hang laundry to dry.

The streets are packed with sailors, traders, and townspeople, and I force myself not to flinch when they brush past me. From an inn called the Sleeping Dragon wafts the warm smell of fresh bread. My mouth waters, and I realize I have not had anything to eat or drink since just before we reached Korynth yesterday.

I follow the smell into the inn, where a fire roars in a large hearth. Most of the wooden tables in the room are empty, and what few customers there are seem bleary and only half-awake. A boy about my age, who is thin with a mop of flyaway brown hair, is polishing the bar with a rag. "Can I help you, miss?" he asks when he sees me.

"That bread smells wonderful."

"We buy it from the bakery next door," he says, flashing a

crooked smile. "Would you like some?"

"Yes, please." As I speak, I realize I am swaying.

He frowns. "Why don't you take a seat and I'll bring some out?"

Feeling lightheaded, I nod and find a seat near the fire. I stretch my hands out to warm myself, and then lean back into my chair, nearly dozing off to the low hum of nearby conversations. But my ears prick up when I hear someone mention Galandria.

"You're sure, Anton?"

"Positive. He spoke with a Galandrian accent. Said he just arrived in town yesterday and needed men for a job. Jaromil—I think we should consider it."

Cautiously, I turn my head and look over. Two men are sitting at a nearby table, holding goblets. The first one, whom I take to be Anton, is young and thin, while the second— Jaromil—is older with a belly so round he looks to be with child. Yet both of them have tanned faces and leathery skin, as though they've spent most of their lives outdoors. Are they sailors?

"I'm not working with a barbarian."

"I told him as much at first—but he said his master would be willing to pay us more money than our scruples could possibly be worth."

"To do what, exactly?"

"Not sure. Said his master had something planned for the

masquerade ball for the Masked Princess."

At this, I feel my hands growing numb again, despite the warmth from the fire.

"Is his master a Galandrian or a Kyrenican?"

"Didn't say. Didn't *want* to say, it seemed like. He just said King Ezebo—"

Jaromil curses. "King Ezebo is a traitor, to bring an Andewyn into our land. If I caught sight of the Masked Princess, you can bet I'd wring the little freak's barbaric neck." He spits onto the ground. "All right, I'll hear the man out. Where did he say to meet?"

"Tomorrow morning, just after dawn, on the beach."

"All right," Jaromil says again. "And don't worry, Anton. I never had that many scruples to begin with." They laugh and clink goblets.

I stare into the fire, my heart racing, hoping they won't realize their voices have carried. Of course I should have understood that, just as many Galandrians hate the Strassburgs, so too, it must be that many Kyrenicans hate the Andewyns—hate *me*. I remind myself they could not possibly recognize me. Today, my own uncovered face is a mask.

It sounds like these two men, Anton and Jaromil, are being hired to do something, something that has to do with the masquerade. But what?

The boy returns with several slices of bread and a cup of water. "That'll be two klarents, please."

"Oh, yes, of course," I say, startled. I start to reach into Elara's satchel, but freeze. I don't have any klarents, the Kyrenican currency, only worthings and opals. And with Jaromil and Anton sitting so close, that is not something I want anyone discovering.

"I—I do not have any klarents." I stand up to leave, though it is everything I can do not to snatch up the bread and water. "I will go. I am sorry to have bothered you," I take care to shorten my vowels, as the Kyrenicans do, all too aware of my accent, and that Anton and Jaromil are staring at me with interest.

"No, no," the boy says. "You don't have to leave." He calls over his shoulder. "Victor, can you come here?"

"What is it, James?" A burly and grizzled old man approaches. The boy James whispers something to Victor, who looks at me.

"I see," Victor says when James finishes.

Victor takes a seat next to me and crosses his arms over his massive chest. "When was the last time you ate?" he says gruffly.

"Um, yesterday," I say.

"You've only just arrived in Korynth, haven't you?"

"Yes," I answer.

He nods, as though he expected this, and says, "I know who you are."

CHAPTER 31

ELARA

When I wake up the next morning, Wilha is still gone. The bed in the maid's room is empty, and the covers are undisturbed. I had hoped she would return after I'd fallen asleep and decided to spend the night here.

The stone floor is cold on my bare feet. I've used up all my firewood, so I sink down into an armchair, grumbling to myself. Where could Wilha have gone, and more importantly, when will she be back? How dare she leave me here in this castle?

But you were going to leave her. Even though you'd promised to stay with her.

The voice comes from somewhere deep within, and I quickly dismiss it. I rise and pull a blue gown out from one of her trunks and set to work removing the opals stitched into the bodice. Since Wilha stole my satchel, I'm going to steal more of her jewels, and use them to get as far away from this dank place as I can.

I'm not wasting another night on a half-cocked search for Wilha. Tonight I'm leaving, whether or not she comes back.

Although, I smile in spite of myself. Last night wasn't a complete waste.

When I've finished removing the jewels, I stuff the dress

down at the bottom of the trunk where it won't be found. I open another trunk filled with Wilha's clothes and run my hands over the silken dresses, preparing myself to face the day as the Masked Princess. What does a princess wear when she is going to be received by her future in-laws? Arianne never instructed me on that.

After I've changed into a pastel green gown, which takes several minutes longer than it should, I open the velvet boxes and settle on a pale green mask encrusted with diamonds and pale-colored opals.

A soft knock sounds at my door. "Your Highness?" comes a timid female voice. "Is it safe to come in?"

Safe?

"Are you wearing your mask, Your Highness?" she clarifies.

"Oh, just a minute," I say and quickly tie on the mask. I hate how it restricts my vision and remind myself not to fidget with it in front of anyone. "Okay, I'm decent," I call out, but stop. *You are royalty speaking to a maid, you idiot. Act like it.* "I mean . . . you may come in."

A girl carrying a tray of bread, berries, and cream enters with an apologetic look on her face.

"I am sorry, Your Highness," she says, curtsying. "I was supposed to visit your chambers early this morning, so that when you woke up you would have food and a fire going in here, but"—she glances up at my mask before looking away quickly, and her cheeks flush—"that is . . . none of the servants were sure . . . I mean, we've been told you must wear the mask at all times, and we weren't sure if you slept in one," she finishes in a rush, clearly uncomfortable.

"Um . . ." I don't have the first clue if Wilha wears a mask while she sleeps. "How about this?" I say. "When I have retired to my bedroom, I will shut the door to the sitting room. And you can enter in the morning without worrying."

She nods, and when she continues to linger, looking uncomfortable, I ask, "Is everything all right?"

"The king will be calling for you later today and, well, I thought you may want to know the buttons on the back of your dress are crooked. If you want, I could fix them?"

"Yes, thank you," I say, realizing that of course Wilha must have had a maid to help her get dressed.

"King Ezebo is going to appoint another maid for you," she says after fixing my dress. "And well, if you'll have me I just wanted to tell you it would be an honor to serve you." She flushes and looks down.

I'm tempted to tell her I don't need a maid, that I'm quite capable of taking care of myself, but I doubt that's something Wilha would have said. Instead I ask, "What is your name?"

"Milly," she answers, still looking at the floor.

"Well then, Milly, I accept."

Milly smiles and curtsies, and then brings in more wood to start a fire in the hearth. After she leaves I sit in an armchair to warm myself, but pretty soon I become aware of whispers and giggles in the corridor outside. I cross the room and lean my head against the door, and hear the hushed voice of a young girl.

"You knock."

"No. *You* knock."

"No, Leandra. *You*."

"Ruby, you are the one who wanted to come here in the first place."

The first girl's voice lowers to barely a whisper. "Do you think she is really ugly?"

I open the door. Two young girls with surprised looks on their faces straighten up quickly and apologize. The older one has pensive, serious-looking green eyes, and the younger one has reddish-blonde hair and freckles. The bottom of her dress is torn.

"Hello," says the younger one, "I am Princess Ruby." She smiles, revealing two very large front teeth.

"We are sorry to disturb you," says the older one. "I am Princess Leandra. I tried to stop Ruby from coming here, but she insisted."

Ruby closes the door behind her. "We're supposed to be in lessons," she says conspiratorially. "But we're not!"

"Really? Well, why don't you come in and sit down?" I lead them deeper into the sitting room and motion to the armchairs. What did Arianne say about Leandra and Ruby, the crown prince's two siblings? *Dogs in training*, that's how she described them. At the time, I hadn't given it much thought. Arianne, puckered prune that she is, didn't seem to have a kind word for anyone. But staring at Leandra and Ruby now, her words seem particularly cruel. Ruby can't be more than seven, and it seems unfair to label her or Leandra a dog, just because they are Kyrenican.

"We mustn't stay long," Leandra says with a frown, "or we will be in trouble."

"We heard Father say you were the most glamorous lady in the world, and that if you married our brother, it would bring Kyrenica much glory," Ruby exclaims as she plops onto a plushy velvet cushion.

"Ruby, hush!" Leandra scolds. "That is not all he said," she assures me. "He said he was thrilled a peace agreement could be reached, and that your marriage to our brother would save countless lives." She recites the words formally, as though she has memorized them by heart.

But they stop me cold, nevertheless. They remind me there's a purpose to this betrothal, to avoid a war that many thought was inevitable. I am reminded, too, that I promised Lord Quinlan I would try to find out if Ezebo was serious about maintaining peace.

Something that just might play in my favor if it's discovered that I'm not Wilha, and I have to appeal to the Guardians for help.

"Is your father happy with the peace treaty, then?" I ask Leandra carefully.

"Of course, why shouldn't he be?" Leandra frowns.

Ruby and Leandra move to dismiss themselves, saying that their father should be calling for me soon.

After they leave, I take several deep breaths as I prepare myself to face a king.

CHAPTER 32

WILHA

Victor stares at me. Anton and Jaromil stare at me. Suddenly, I am more aware than ever that I am roaming around Korynth without any guards, without any protection whatsoever. If Kyrenican soldiers entered the inn now, I think I might run to them in relief.

"I know who you are," Victor repeats.

"Who?" I grab Elara's satchel, getting ready to run.

"One of them kids from the villages, thinking finding a job in the city will feed your family."

Relief washes over me and I relax my grip. "Yes," I answer, well aware that Anton and Jaromil are still listening. "I am from Tyran," I add, more grateful than I have ever been for Lord Murcendor, and the fact that he insisted I study geography. Tyran is a village just on the Kyrenican side of the border. Like most Kyrenicans, the villagers in Tyran shorten their vowels, yet they speak slightly more formally, making their accent not quite Kyrenican, yet not quite Galandrian either.

"Most families are smart enough to send their sons," Victor continues. "More jobs for sons."

"Are there jobs for daughters?" I ask. I do not want to lie outright. Yet the truth obviously will not do.

"For tough ones there are." He looks me up and down

skeptically. "Are you strong enough to haul crates of fish?"

I shake my head.

"Can you bake loaves of bread? Mix potions? Make cheese or brew ale?" he says, as I continue shaking my head. "Well then, what can you do?" he asks in exasperation.

What *can* I do? After all these years of feeling useless as a princess, capable of nothing more than dazzling crowds, not because of any great wit or beauty I possess, but because of the mystique of the Masked Princess, it seems I am useless as a person, too. Have I learned anything worthwhile in the sixteen years of my life? Any skills others may find helpful besides sitting in a chair and—

"Embroidery," I say suddenly. "I am really good at embroidery."

"You mean that fancy kind of sewing all those noblegirls do?" He seems to consider this. "It's not often we get someone with those talents down here." He stands up. "Follow me."

"I—" I almost tell him I am not looking for a job, but after another quick glance at Anton and Jaromil, I decide to play along. I follow him over to the bar, where he grabs a tarnished silver key off a peg board and hands it to me.

"What's your name?" he asks.

"My name is Will—" I stop abruptly, because I can't very well tell him my real name.

"Will? That's an odd name for a girl."

"I think my father wished I was a boy," I answer quickly. "Though, oftentimes he called me Willie."

He nods. "Nice to meet you, Willie. I'm Victor." He starts up a staircase behind the bar, and gestures for me to follow him.

"Where are we going?"

"I've got a room for you. Mind, you'll pay me for it, once you get a job." He stops at a door. "Before I show you in though, I want you to understand something. The streets are no place for a girl like yourself. But this inn ain't no palace, either."

He pauses for me to consider this, and I cannot help thinking that no matter how rough the inn is, I doubt I will be locked inside like a prisoner.

"Lots of questionable characters come in here," he continues, "and you're to be cautious. Understand?"

I nod, and he unlocks the door. Inside the room is a bed, a small desk, and an even smaller bedside table. "It's not much, but it should help you for now." He looks at me critically. "You look like you could use a good long rest. I'll have James bring you up some food. Tomorrow, I'll take you to get a job at Galina's."

"Who is Galina?" I ask.

"A seamstress, one of the best in the city." Before he leaves, he tells me to lock the door behind him. I do, and then lie down on the bed, touched by Victor's kindness, and sad I will have to disappoint him. Tomorrow morning, if the soldiers do not come for me, I will have to leave. I have a cliff to climb and a life to return to.

CHAPTER 33

ELARA

Words are power.

The right words, said in the right tone of voice, can bring a man to his knees. They can make him fall in love with you. *"Say the right words,"* Mistress Ogden once told me, *"and it will get you what you want."*

And right now, as a guard leads me to the great hall to be received by King Ezebo, I want just one thing: to avoid detection, and execution.

I haven't been able to get Leandra's words out of my mind. *"He said your marriage to our brother would save countless lives. . . ."*

For a moment the walls of the castle corridor fade away, and I am back in Eleanor Square. I see King Fennrick just before the attack, addressing the crowd and announcing the peace treaty between Galandria and Kyrenica. I hear the ringing applause—as joyous as wedding bells—and the relieved shouts of the people, thankful that peace had been achieved. It's incredible how much hangs on this marriage. Not just Wilha's happiness, but the destiny of two kingdoms.

If I leave the castle before Wilha returns, it will look as though the Masked Princess has simply vanished. I have no doubt King Ezebo and the Guardians in Galandria will each accuse the other of deception. With the likely result being war.

I know little about Wilha. She seemed to follow whatever order was given to her. I have to believe if she gave her word that she would come back, then she means to keep it. In the meantime, I promised to play the role of the Masked Princess until the masquerade. I also promised to find out what I could about King Ezebo, and if he intends to honor the peace treaty. True, these were promises I never had any intention of keeping, but that's beside the point now.

The guard leads me through an arched hallway and to a set of ornately carved wooden double doors, where a second guard waits.

"The king and queen will see you now, Your Highness." He bows.

I take a deep, steadying breath. The berries and cream I ate earlier roil in my stomach. It's with a little loathing that I ask myself what Mistress Ogden would do if she were here in my place. She certainly wouldn't cower before a challenge like this. She would instead relish the chance to impersonate royalty. My fear begins to melts away, and a new resolve steadies me.

I smooth my skirts and straighten my mask. *Chin up, shoulders back*, I remind myself. *And keep your mouth shut as much as you possibly can.*

The large, carved wooden doors open and the guard beckons me inside.

Let the show begin.

⚜

The great hall is poorly lit. The silver chandeliers above are void of candles, and the majority of the light in the room comes from a large fireplace along one wall. The room is covered in dark wood paneling, and portraits that I assume are of the Strassburg family line the walls. To my right, a long staircase curves up to a balcony overhead.

At the end of the hall on a dais are two wooden, high-backed thrones. A plump man with graying hair sits on one. Next to him sits an elegant-looking woman clad in a scarlet gown. Standing in front of the dais is a short man with oily hair and a pug nose dressed in scarlet robes, and he bows before me.

"And so you come at last to our humble kingdom, Your Highness! Soon the entire city will know of the Masked Princess's arrival," he says. "You look well, just as you did in Allegria. Truly, the very air of Kyrenica seems to agree with you."

I have a brief moment of panic before I understand this must be the Kyrenican ambassador who met with Wilha. What did Arianne say his name was?

"Thank you . . . Sir Reinhold," I answer, remembering his name just in time.

Sir Reinhold grins and with a flourish of his hand, says, "King Ezebo, Queen Genevieve, may I present Princess Wilhamina Andewyn of Galandria."

They both stare at me expectantly. I think back to Arianne's lessons and wish I had paid more attention. Am I supposed to curtsy or kneel before them? After being attacked by one of their guards and locked inside my room, I don't particularly feel like doing either. I remind myself of Wilha's impeccable manners and curtsy, but almost tip over from the weight of her mask and dress. I straighten up quickly and hope they didn't notice.

I soften my voice. "It is a pleasure to meet you. . . . I am at your service," I say, for added measure.

Queen Genevieve beams, but King Ezebo wears a disgruntled expression. "This is scandalous," he says.

"I beg your pardon, Your Majesty?"

"To arrive unannounced," Ezebo continues, as though I haven't spoken, "it is unheard of. We had no pigeons, no word of your earlier arrival. Does Galandria expect us to stand for such a disgrace?"

"My father's advisors judged it to be safer if I left Galandria earlier than expected and traveled anonymously," I say, just as Arianne instructed.

Ezebo is red-faced with his lips pursed in a petulant frown. This is something I didn't expect. I expected a cunning monarch, not a king having a temper tantrum. I've learned well how to handle Mister Ogden when he was in one of his foul moods. I know what to say to a man to calm him down and shut him up. But does Wilha? My guess is not, so I say nothing.

"Had we known you were coming," he continues, "plans would have been made to receive you properly."

Properly? Did they require advance notice *not* to lock me in Wilha's chambers all night? I doubt shy Wilha would demand to know why she was left to rot in a locked room the moment she entered the castle. But *I* want to know. Something isn't right here, and I wonder if Lord Quinlan is right to doubt King Ezebo's intentions.

"If Your Majesty pleases, I wonder if you could tell me why I was locked in my chambers?" I keep my voice soft and my eyes downcast.

Ezebo sighs. "The door was locked for your own protection. After unloading your trunks, your guards were given orders to report to the head of my palace guard. Yet one of them—Moran, I am told is his name—was found stealing from the jewels your father sent ahead as payment into our treasury." He pauses, and when I say nothing, continues, "And when he was discovered, instead of submitting to my men and explaining himself, he fought back and has now escaped, along with the jewels that now belong to me. Your chambers were locked and guarded while my men searched the castle attempting to locate him. The same precautions were taken for the princesses Leandra and Ruby. And I have been told that your maid has also stolen jewels from you. Strange, is it not?"

"Not so strange," I say, telling the first lie I think of. "I saw Moran and my maid giving eyes at each other. I had meant to ask her what her intentions were with him, and now I find that I was remiss in not doing so earlier. Her mother is quite strict, and would not have allowed her to marry a soldier. Perhaps they saw their opportunity to begin a new life together and have taken it." Under no circumstances do I want King Ezebo dwelling on the missing "maid."

King Ezebo stares at me indignantly. "Regardless, your procession has arrived unannounced, and your people have stolen from me. This is *not* how I imagined our first meeting. Sir Reinhold questioned another of your guards. . . ." He pauses and looks at Sir Reinhold.

"Garwyn," Sir Reinhold supplies.

"Yes—Garwyn—and found his answers unsatisfactory. Therefore, I have dismissed him and the rest of your guards and commanded them to locate Moran, your missing maid, and the jewels, and not to return to the castle until they have done so."

I pause. "You mean, none of my guards are now here in the castle?"

"Your guards were at my disposal," Ezebo retorts, "and they will be welcomed back as soon as they locate Moran, the jewels—and your maid."

I can detect no falsehood in Ezebo's words. It's possible that he's telling the truth. Maybe Wilha's guard really *did* get caught stealing and Ezebo has sent the others after him. Then again, perhaps Ezebo is a practiced liar and is merely playing a role, as I am.

Somewhere in all of this lies the truth, hidden though it is. But what I do know is if it is discovered that Wilha herself is missing, *I'll* be under suspicion. If Ezebo is willing to lock me in a room just for my "protection" what would he do to me if he believed I'd harmed the Masked Princess?

I don't know the answer to that. But I think I do know how Wilha would respond to Ezebo's words. "I apologize on behalf of my guards, as well as my maid," I say, looking downward. "Their behavior is truly scandalous."

Ezebo grunts. "If your father's advisors had bothered to do a better job selecting—"

"Ezebo, that's enough." Queen Genevieve stands. "This is no way to treat your future daughter-in-law. She nearly lost her father and she has said good-bye to her homeland, all in the same month. That is a lot to throw at a girl. Remember what a wreck I was the day I arrived in Korynth?"

Ezebo looks away from me and smiles at Genevieve. Something warm passes between them; a spark of affection I never once saw between Mister and Mistress Ogden. Then Genevieve gives him a stern look and Ezebo sighs.

"I must ask for your forgiveness, Princess. Your entourage

has caused quite an uproar. We have eagerly looked forward to meeting you for several weeks, and now I fear we have given you a poor first impression."

"Yes," Genevieve says, with another look at Ezebo. "And to make up for that I must ask you to join me, the princesses Leandra and Ruby, and Ezebo's mother, the dowager queen, for tea tomorrow."

"Of course, Your Majesty."

Genevieve smiles and then both the king and queen look expectantly at Sir Reinhold, who clears his throat.

"There was one other thing," he says. "King Ezebo means to start a new Kyrenican tradition. We have heard of the crowds that your sessions on the balcony of the Opal Palace brought to Allegria. King Ezebo would like to see Korynth similarly honored. He requests that you appear on the eastern balcony of the castle each night at sunset before whatever crowd has assembled." He pauses, waiting for my response.

It's a spectacularly stupid idea, and I'm sorely tempted to tell him so. I remember the Andewyns standing on the steps of the courthouse, rose petals raining from the rooftops. Right before the arrows flew.

Of course, if it's true the Kyrenicans had nothing to do with the attack, then making appearances on the balcony shouldn't be a problem. How did Sir Reinhold describe Wilha to Ezebo and Genevieve? Shy and soft-spoken, with an easily malleable will? I remind myself to be cautious.

I remind myself to be Wilha.

"That is a lovely idea, Your Majesty. I am at your command."

"Excellent. Sir Reinhold will see you back to your chambers. Later, we will be having dinner with several noble families and we will ask you to join us." King Ezebo beams and nods, and Sir Reinhold takes my arm. Clearly, I'm being dismissed.

As Sir Reinhold escorts me back to my chambers, I can only hope that Wilha returns soon, before the guards locate her.

That is, if Ezebo actually sent them after her.

CHAPTER 34

WILHA

*D*awn comes, but the soldiers still have not. I throw back the thin cotton blanket I slept under and pull Elara's satchel out from under the mattress. I upend my pillowcase, where I have hidden the opals, Elara's dagger, and her book about Eleanor the Great, and begin repacking the satchel.

I awoke from my nap yesterday to the loud sounds of music and drunken carousing coming from downstairs. After I ate the dinner James brought up, I spent the rest of the night in my room reading of all the great deeds my ancestor had done. Each word felt like a sentence being pronounced, a judgment of my own cowardice. For I doubt Eleanor the Great would have run away from her own life, as I have done.

Downstairs, the inn is messy, but quiet. James is near the fireplace, sweeping up broken glass. "It's a bit early to be going to Galina's, isn't it?" His eyes are tired and his brown flyaway hair sticks up in all directions.

"I'm . . ." I try to think of something to say, but nothing comes to me.

"Oh, I see." His eyes flick to Elara's satchel. "You're leaving."

"Yes. I mean, no . . . I am going . . . to take a walk on the beach." I will, after all, have to walk down the beach before locating the staircase leading up the cliff. I do not relish that climb.

"Right then," he says, looking as though he does not believe me. "Wait here just a moment." He exits through the door to the kitchen, and when he returns a moment later he holds up a sack stuffed with a loaf of bread and a roll of cheese.

"Walks make people hungry," he says simply, pressing the sack into my hands.

Something catches in my throat. I have received many gifts before, oftentimes from the richest men in Galandria. But rarely have I received something that was offered solely because someone saw I had a need for it.

"I don't know what to say."

"Thank you is always good," he says and flashes his crooked smile. "It's too bad, really. You would have been the prettiest tenant Victor's ever had."

"Thank you," I say, swallowing. I tell James good-bye and step outside, before I can change my mind.

The streets smell like wood smoke, and the city is quiet except for the sound of seagulls screeching overhead. It must have rained late in the night, because the streets look like puddled mirrors. When I look down I see my grim, maskless reflection staring back. What will happen when I return to the castle? Will I be received as a missing princess? Or as an escaped prisoner?

While I walk I nibble on the bread and cheese, shivering under my thin cloak. How can it be this cold in the summer?

When I reach the docks, I head toward the beach and see the cliffs rising up in the distance, but quickly stop. Anton and Jaromil suddenly emerge from behind a cluster of large rocks. They seem to be talking to someone else; someone still hidden behind the rocks. I crane my neck, trying to see who it is they are speaking with, and my heart quickens. I remember they were seeing about a job, something to do with the masquerade. What type of job requires so much secrecy?

I jump when I feel a hand on my shoulder.

"It's all right, it's just me," Victor says with a concerned look on his face. "Didn't you hear me, Willie? I was calling your name."

"Um, no, I did not." I glance back over my shoulder. Anton and Jaromil are still there. They appear to be listening carefully to whoever is behind the rock. "I had thought to take a walk early this morning."

"I always fancy a good walk in the morning, myself," Victor says. "And Rowan's Rock is as good a place as any."

"Yes, and—" I break off as his words register. "Rowan's Rock?"

Victor nods. "It's the big rock over there, the one rising up in the ocean," he clarifies. "It was named after Rowan the Brave, the Galandrian queen. She had been condemned to death nearly a century ago, and yet, the night before her execution, she was spotted on this beach near that rock. The next day it was discovered she'd vanished from the castle.

Legend says you can still see her sometimes, weeping for the kingdom she lost." He offers me a burly arm. "Galina gets an early start, and I'm almost through here. Had to purchase fish for tonight's dinner at the inn. Shall we head over to her shop now?"

I hesitate, trying to think of good excuse to tell him no, and look over at Anton and Jaromil one last time. They have turned to face the docks where Victor and I stand, and seem to be staring at something in the distance. For a brief moment, I am certain they are looking at me.

"That would be lovely," I say quickly, deciding that I will have to climb the cliff later. As we set off toward the city, I tell myself I'm being ridiculous, that of course they were not looking at me.

I also tell myself that the numbness I feel spreading through my chest is simply from the cold.

CHAPTER 35

WILHA

A small bell jingles when Victor pushes open the door to Galina's dress shop. Shelves containing bolts of lace and brightly colored fabrics line the room. A mirror sits in the corner. Upon a large claw-footed wooden desk are silver boxes of shiny buttons and glass jars filled with thread. Several girls about my age are seated on light green velvet couches. Each of them are busy stitching.

"Is Galina around?" Victor asks.

A girl with hair the color of spun gold stands. "Hi, Victor!" She glances at me and smiles. "Have another one for us, do you? Galina!" she calls to the back of the shop, "Victor's here again!" She turns back to me. "I'm Kyra."

"I am—Willie," I answer, almost forgetting my new name, and a couple of the other girls laugh quietly.

I glance over at them, and am surprised to read the distaste in their eyes. Some of the girls are openly staring at my stained traveling cloak and dirty boots. It reminds me of the way the ladies at court stared at the peasants who came to the Opal Palace to see me wave from the balcony.

An older woman with white hair tied up in a severe bun emerges from a back room. Her eyes glance from me to Victor. "I don't need another mouth to feed," she says flatly.

"Galina, this is Willie," Victor says. "She says she knows embroidery well."

"I don't have a place for her to sleep," Galina says, unmoved. "I gave the only bed I had to the girl you brought me last week."

"I've already given her a room at the Sleeping Dragon. Will you give her a job?" Victor smiles and raises his eyebrows, and despite his massive size and gruff manner, he looks charming, like an old, grizzled prince.

"Oh honestly, Victor. How many more strays do you intend to take in?" Galina glowers at him, and then sighs and turns to me. "Do you have any samples?"

"Samples?" I ask, confused.

"Of your work," she says, tight-lipped. "If I am to hire you, I must know you have the appropriate skills." She casts Victor a furious look, and I read the dismissal in her eyes when she turns back to me. It is a look I saw often from Arianne and Vena.

Suddenly, I am not standing here simply because I did not wish to be left alone on a beach with Anton and Jaromil. I *want* this job. Once I return to the Kyrenican Castle, any adventure I may have hoped to find will fade and will be replaced by the demands of royal life, and people like Arianne and Vena, who see me as nothing more than useless and fearful.

I left the castle on my own accord. I will return to it

when I have found a story to hang on to during the lonely days and years that are sure to follow. I see the image again, of me telling my daughter my story. The one only *I* know.

"Here." I hastily pull the handkerchief I had been sewing on the journey to Kyrenica from my cloak and hand it to Galina.

Victor and I wait while she examines the stitching. "The technique here is excellent," she says.

"Thank you," I answer, and as I stare at the dresses the other girls are working on I realize my skills far surpass theirs. This is unsurprising, I suppose, given all the practice I have had over the years. There was little else to do in the Opal Palace when I was not waving from a balcony or attending a royal engagement.

"These are the Andewyn and Strassburg coat of arms," Galina says, looking up.

"Yes," I answer quickly. "I intended it as a wedding present to the Masked Princess. I hear she is due to arrive in the city soon."

"We really could use more help," Kyra says. "You were just saying so yesterday."

Galina nods and it is settled. She motions to the girls and they shift around on the couches, making a place for me. After inviting me to dine with him and James tonight at the Sleeping Dragon, Victor leaves, and Galina hands me a needle and a spool of thread.

"Now then," she says, "King Ezebo has planned a masquerade in the Masked Princess's honor, and orders are already pouring in from ladies who are attending. I need someone to assist me with the embroidery on their dresses. Can you do that?"

Galina stares at me expectantly, and something deep in my chest seems to detach and float up and out of my mouth in a laugh.

"Yes," I gasp amid everyone's curious stares, "I can stitch dresses for the princess's masquerade."

CHAPTER 36

ELARA

*T*hankfully my head is still attached to my neck. Somehow I've managed to survive my first two days in the Kyrenican Castle. The dinner with the Kyrenican nobles went all right—I think. The ladies complimented my mask and dress excessively. Of course, they also seemed positively gleeful when I knocked over a wine glass.

After dinner, Leandra and Ruby escorted me back to my room. It seems I am expected to stay in my chambers when I'm not visiting with the Strassburgs or attending an engagement. I had planned on exploring the passageway after everyone retired for the evening, but after a day of pretending, I was exhausted and fell asleep.

I was still tired when I woke up this morning. Wilha asked for time. How much does she expect me to give her? When I put my mask on today—a pale lemon-colored one with yellow fire opals that matches one of Wilha's yellow gowns—it felt heavier than ever.

As Milly helps me get ready for tea with Queen Genevieve, my thoughts turn to the squire. I have watched the comings and goings of the servants, but haven't spot-ted him again. Has he left the castle? Our conversation in the kitchen was the only part of the last two days that I've actually enjoyed.

"Oh, I nearly forgot," Milly says, fastening a ribbon in my hair. "You received pigeons."

"Pigeons?" I repeat, snapping out of my reverie. What is she talking about?

"Carrier pigeons?" Milly frowns. "Letters from the Opal Palace?"

"Oh yes, of course," I say hastily. "I'm sorry Milly. I'm feeling a bit dull today."

I press my nails into the palm of my hand and command myself to stop thinking about the squire and *concentrate*. I can't forget, not even for a moment, where I am. And who I'm supposed to be.

Milly hands me two folded pieces of parchment, and tells me that the princesses Leandra and Ruby will come and fetch me for tea. After she excuses herself, I move to the sitting room and settle myself on an armchair. I take off my mask and blow out a breath.

I open the first letter. It's carefully worded, and very, *very* interesting. It's from a soldier named Patric. I gather he was training Wilha to defend herself, which surprises me. I read his message several times over. I think I read, too, what he is so carefully trying *not* to say, and I'm surprised again. I wouldn't have thought Wilha capable of what I suspect I see in this letter.

I open the second letter and it is from Lord Quinlan.

Your Highness,

I hope you reached Kyrenica safely. Lord Royce, Lord

Murcendor, and I expect to arrive in Korynth shortly before the masquerade and look forward to meeting with King Ezebo. Please remind your maid of her duty to you and to us.

His words, too, are carefully worded, yet I understand the meaning of the last line:

Guard the princess. Find out what you can about Ezebo, and if he intends to honor the treaty.

A knock sounds at the door. "Come in," I say absently, still holding the letter. Since I was received by Ezebo and Genevieve yesterday I've heard nothing to indicate that they are anything less than extremely pleased about the treaty. So what does Lord Quinlan expect me to do? Break into Ezebo's—

The door opens and a scream echoes.

"Wilha, your mask!" Leandra says with a hand raised to her eyes, looking ready to faint. Behind her, Ruby stares at me wide-eyed.

I quickly snatch up my mask and tie it on, cursing my own idiocy.

"You're not supposed to take it off!" Leandra cries. "No one is ever supposed to see your face!"

"I know," I say, rushing over and leading her to an armchair. "I was thoughtless. I'm sorry."

Ruby tugs at my skirt. "Wilha, are we cursed now?" she asks in a hushed voice. "Will we die?"

Leandra gives a frightened whimper and hides her head in her hands.

I crouch down until I'm level with Ruby. "No," I reassure her firmly. "You will both be fine, I promise. No one in this room is cursed, not even me. It's just a rumor, and not a very nice one."

"I don't understand," Ruby says. Her eyes search my mask, but I think she's seeing beyond it, imagining my face. "You are not very ugly."

"Does that mean I'm only a little ugly?" I ask, and I see Leandra, color returning to her cheeks, suppress a grin.

"No," Ruby says, seeming to be thinking hard. "But if you are not cursed, and you are not really ugly, then why do you have to wear the mask?"

I decide to tell Ruby a small truth, one I'm sure Wilha herself would agree with. "Because of all the things my father, King Fennrick the Handsome, has valued in this world, his daughter's happiness is not one of them."

⧉

"*Y*ou are different than I expected," Leandra says as we make our way to Genevieve's chambers. Now that she has gotten over her fright, she's resumed her usual formal air.

"Oh? How so?" I keep my voice casual and my eyes fixed on Ruby, who has skipped ahead of us.

"I did not think you would be so bold. In the report Sir Reinhold sent us he said you were proper above all else."

"Really?" At this, my stomach tightens. "What else did the report say?"

"Only what is expected when considering a betrothal. Was a similar report not given to you of my brother?"

"If such a report exists, I wasn't allowed to read it," I say carefully. "But I am curious to know what yours said of me." *Tell me everything,* I want to say. *Everything you might know about Wilha that I don't.*

Leandra's lips suppress a grin. "It said you hate potatoes."

"Yes, I do," I reply automatically, surprised that Wilha and I actually have something in common. Mistress Ogden made me peel so many, I've lost my taste for them.

Leandra looks troubled. "But I was merely poking fun. The report actually said you complimented the potato stew you ate in the ambassador's presence. He suggested we serve it here in the castle." She shrugs. "I only thought it was funny he mentioned it."

I force a laugh. "Of course. I was merely joking as well."

Leandra nods, yet from the way she stares, I'm not quite sure she believes me.

I rush ahead to break some of the tension and join Ruby, who leads me out on a balcony overlooking the city. "Father says crowds will gather outside the castle gates to see you tomorrow night. Can I go out with you Wilha, please?"

Leandra catches up to us and says we must move along or we'll be late. As we make another turn, two men wearing scarlet robes are exiting a room halfway down the corridor. With a start, I realize I recognize this hallway, and that door. It's the one with the gargoyle door handle. The same door the squire caught me trying to open two nights ago.

"The plans are coming along," the first one says.

"I agree," says the second man, shutting the door behind him. "I will tell the king—"

Upon seeing us, both men quickly stop talking. "I hardly think the northern wing is fit for foreigners," the first man says to Leandra, with a pointed glance at me.

"Of course." Leandra, flushing, grabs my arm and hurries me away. When we have turned the corner I ask, "Those men are your father's advisors, aren't they? What were they discussing?" But she just shakes her head and replies that we mustn't keep her mother waiting.

She moves ahead, but I can't help look back and wonder what was in that room that Ezebo's advisors—and the squire—don't want me to see.

We turn down a few more corridors. Voices carry from the room Leandra marks as Queen Genevieve's chambers.

"I don't know why Ezebo thought he needed to fetch a wife for my grandson from the most barbaric kingdom in the world," comes an unpleasant female voice.

"Eudora, hush. She will arrive any minute," answers another voice, which I recognize as belonging to Queen Genevieve. She says something else but I don't hear what.

Eudora, Ezebo's mother, the dowager queen, has pleaded a headache the last two days, so I have yet to meet her. But I heard quite a bit about her from Arianne, who referred to her as the Great Viper.

We arrive at the door and Leandra hesitates before walking in, looking at me with a horrified expression. I put my hand on her shoulder to stop her. I want to hear this. And I want to catch them off guard.

"She cannot help being an Andewyn anymore than we can help being Strassburgs," Genevieve says.

"You are not a Strassburg by birth, Genevieve," Eudora snaps.

"Of course," Genevieve says. "But if we are to truly accept her into the family, we must see past her origins."

"Humph. Never trust a Galandrian. They will dazzle you with their wealth and then stab you in the back when you're not looking. As far as I am concerned they are all a bunch of—"

"Good afternoon," I say as I step inside. Next to me, Leandra's shoulders slump and Ruby skips ahead of us to give her mother a hug.

Genevieve gives me an apologetic look as she reaches down to Ruby. But Eudora, the dowager queen, looks at me with unkind and appraising blue eyes that see out of a small wrinkled face.

An awkward silence descends as we all look at each other. The only sound in the room comes from the crackling of the fire. The walls of the room are covered in red tapestries. Behind Genevieve and Eudora is a dining table made of dark cherry wood.

Eudora shoos away Ruby, who tries to hug her. "Your dress is stained," she snaps, and Ruby's face falls. "Genevieve, how many times do I have to tell you to take a firmer hand with your daughter?" Eudora looks me up and down, staring everywhere but in my eyes. "She has small hips," she remarks to Genevieve, as though I'm not in the room. "It is a good thing we were able to secure so much from the Galandrian treasury. With hips like those, I doubt my grandson will be able to get any sons from her."

Eudora's leering stare feels dirtier than any I've ever received from men at the Draughts. Great Viper, indeed. For once, Arianne's assessment seems to have been right on target.

"Have the barbarians in Galandria taught you nothing?" she snaps, her eyes taking in my dress distastefully. "You don't wear your finest gown to afternoon tea."

"This is hardly my finest gown." The words are out of my mouth before I can stop them. It's only then that I notice Genevieve and Eudora, as well as Leandra and Ruby, are wearing dresses in muted shades.

Eudora's cheeks seem to swell. "How dare you—"

"Eudora, I don't think she meant anything by it—" Genevieve begins.

"Nonsense, Genevieve. I know when I am being insulted,

and I won't have it. Not in my own home. And certainly not by a barbarian."

I open my mouth, but quickly bite back the tart reply rising to my lips. And though I'm clenching my hands so hard my nails bite into my palms, I force myself to say, "I'm sorry," in a demure, soft voice. "I wasn't quite sure what the Kyrenican expectations were for afternoon tea."

"Apology accepted," Genevieve cuts in before Eudora can speak. "Shall we sit down?" she says with forced pleasantness, and everyone makes their way to the table.

I had thought "tea" meant sitting down for, well, a cup of tea and maybe a few slices of bread. That is what passed for tea at the Ogdens. But apparently royalty has a different standard. Platters of fruit, cheeses, olives, and bread are spread out on the table before us. Several forks and knives frame either side of the plate in front of me. Really, why do the wealthy require so many utensils just to eat a single meal?

Probably because they never have to wash their own dishes.

Genevieve and everyone else seem to be staring at me expectantly. I'm not sure what to do, so I say, "What smells so good?"

"Ah," Genevieve says approvingly, "that is the scarlet tea. It is a Kyrenican specialty. I believe I may have fallen in love with it before I did with the king." She smiles at me, ignoring a sharp look from Eudora, and signals to a maid hovering in the corner. "Please pour the princess a cup of scarlet tea."

The maid complies. When I raise the cup to my lips, I smell cinnamon and peppery spices. As I sip, I feel myself growing warm all over. "This is the best tea I've ever had in my life," I say honestly.

As we make small talk and dine, I find that eating while wearing the mask is tricky, just as it was last night. When Genevieve or Eudora asks me a question, I try to think of what Wilha would say and give soft, demure answers. This seems to go well until Genevieve asks me what subject I most enjoyed studying with my tutors.

"History is my favorite," I answer truthfully, because I have no idea what Wilha's answer would be.

"Is it?" Eudora says. "You are aware that my late husband was the grandson of King Bronson the Liberator? Oh, but I forget," she adds with a wicked smile after I nod, "Galandrians have another name for him, do they not? Tell me, what is it?"

Her eyebrows rise as though daring me. Maybe I should take Arianne's advice, which suddenly comes back to me in full force. *Be pleasant at all times. Smile, even in the face of unkindness, for you are to be above it all. Feign ignorance if you must.*

But I can't do that, no matter how much Arianne's words nag at me. I won't declare myself ignorant of my own history, not when there were so many days I had to beg Mistress Ogden to let me attend school.

"Bronson the Butcher," I proclaim. "So named because of

all the Galandrians he slaughtered."

"Hold your tongue, girl," Eudora snaps, seemingly shocked that I dared to speak the truth. "In this country, Bronson Strassburg is considered a war hero, not to mention our founding king."

"Interesting," I say coolly. "Because in *my* country he's considered a murderer."

Shortly after this the tea ends, and I am escorted back to my room by an unsmiling Leandra.

She is careful, I notice, to avoid the northern wing.

CHAPTER 37

WILHA

*S*ince I received the job yesterday in the dress shop, I have been comforted by the sound of rustling silk and the rhythmic, methodical puncture of needle through fabric. It is the first thing that has seemed familiar since our procession reached Korynth, and slowly, some of the knots in my stomach have begun to untie.

Yet not all of them. As I have stitched in the dress shop, not attempting to return to the castle, I have wondered at the goings on inside the castle. While I hide, what has become of Elara?

Word that the Masked Princess has arrived in Korynth officially reaches the dress shop late afternoon via a noblewoman named Alvirah who needs alterations to the gown she intends to wear to the masquerade. She stands in front of a mirror while Kyra kneels before her, pinning her dress. "We dined with her and the royal family the night before last. Really, you would think that—ouch!" Alvirah looks down at Kyra, "Watch it."

My hands go still at her words. So instead of telling the soldiers I fled, Elara is still in the castle and pretending to be me.

Kyra stares up at Alvirah in awe, as though she herself were royalty. "You met the Masked Princess? What was she like?"

"Clumsy and dim-witted. She knocked over a wine glass and used the wrong fork at dinner. Really, why the world is so enamored of her I just don't understand." She plucks at her dress and frowns. "Anyway, the king has decided she will appear on the balcony every night at sunset. Why anyone would *want* to see her, when she is probably wretched-looking under that mask, is beyond me."

"But there are so many rumors," Kyra says. "Maybe it's not that she is ugly, maybe it's that she's beautiful."

"Ridiculous," Alvirah scoffs. "How can she be beautiful? She's a Galandrian."

"Did it seem like . . . she was being treated well?" I ask.

"Of course," Alvirah says. "The Strassburgs threw a feast for her, did they not? And the princesses Leandra and Ruby seem quite taken with her." She plucks at her dress again. "Galina, this hem is crooked, can you look at this? Your girls are not yet as precise as you are. . . ."

Galina bends down, and while they all examine Alvirah's dress I turn away, pretending to concentrate on the sapphire-colored gown I have been working on. Listening to them speak of the Masked Princess makes me feel oddly invisible, like I am a ghost haunting the room long after my death. But hearing that Elara is well, that no harm has come to her as a result of my disappearance, revives me. She is the reason why no soldiers have come for me. She must truly be the great pretender she boasted to be.

Or perhaps not, I think, shoving my needle through sapphire satin. Perhaps the Guardians could have stuck a mask on any girl's face and the Strassburgs would have been fooled. King Ezebo wanted his son to marry the Masked Princess, not necessarily Wilhamina Andewyn.

"Willie," Kyra says, "we should go tonight and stand outside the castle gates and wait for sunset to see the Masked Princess."

"Me?" I say, surprised. "You want me to go with you?"

"Of course." Kyra laughs. "Why not?"

"I—no reason," I reply. I can't tell her I'm not used to people enjoying my company.

"It will be cold tonight," Kyra continues, glancing at my thinner traveling dress. "Didn't you bring any other clothes with you to the city? Or a heavier cloak?"

I don't answer right away. I'm thinking of all the trunks that accompanied me to Korynth, but Kyra mistakes my hesitation for something else.

"Don't be embarrassed," she says. "Many people arrive in the city with very little." She turns to Galina. "Please, can we give her some dresses from the castoffs?" she asks, and Galina nods.

"Castoffs?" I ask.

"We have several cast aside dresses here—orders that were never claimed or dresses that were donated so we could practice our stitching." Kyra leads me to a back room and selects a couple of plain dresses in shades of black and gray. "These should be a fit." Both of the dresses are made of wool, much warmer than what I am wearing now.

"Thank you," I say and accept the dresses from Kyra gratefully. Perhaps I, and everyone else in my father's court, have been wrong about the Kyrenicans.

"Tonight after supper you must meet me at the Broken Statue. We'll go together to see the Masked Princess." Kyra smiles. "Okay?"

"Okay," I say, smiling back. "I will."

⚜

*I*t is not until later, during dinner with Victor and James, that it occurs to me I do not know where the Broken Statue is.

"It's near the castle," Victor answers, pushing away his plate of salmon. He stares hard at me and crosses his arms across his chest. "You just arrived in the city. You shouldn't be wandering around the streets like you were a couple days ago."

"Victor," James says lightly. "I don't think Willie appreciates you ordering her around."

The inn is busy tonight. Servers dash about the tables, bringing out food and refilling goblets. A man plays a lute while several ladies look on, gazing at him adoringly. Near the fireplace, two men are playing cards. And at the table next to them are Anton and Jaromil, who are surrounded by a group of rough-looking men. All of them are staring intently at Anton, who is talking.

All through dinner, I have wondered what they were discussing, and if it has anything to do with the masquerade. Or, my mouth goes dry, with the Masked Princess. Whatever job someone hired Anton and Jaromil to do, it is clear they have found others to help them.

My father is still recovering from the attack in Eleanor Square. But the men who tried to assassinate him—whoever they are—did they sit around an inn just like this, plotting while everyone around them went about their business?

"I'm just saying," Victor says, undeterred. "You young people think—"

He is interrupted by shouting. The men playing cards are accusing each other of cheating. One of them stands up and hurls his plate at the wall. It shatters and the pieces land on the ground, very close to Anton and Jaromil.

"They're going to brawl," James says, standing quickly.

"Not in my inn, they're not," Victor says, also standing.

"I'll fetch a broom and see to the broken plate," I say suddenly.

Anton, Jaromil, and their companions are deep in conversation as I come over and sweep near them, but their voices are lowered, making it impossible to hear what they are saying in the noisy inn. I edge closer.

"Why would we do such a thing?" says one man.

"Why not? I'd sell my own soul for the kind of money he says his master is offering."

"You already *have* sold your soul, Jaromil," says a third man, and the table erupts into loud guffaws.

"We'll need help at the docks that night. We'll need to recruit more men," Anton says once they've quieted down again. "If there's enough of us, we can get it done fast, before anyone can stop us. And we'll also—" He breaks off suddenly.

I hazard a glance over to the table, and see the men are looking at me.

"Taking you an awful long time to sweep up," Anton drawls. His hand shoots out and grabs my arm. "Hear anything useful?"

"What? No," I say, conscious that my voice sounds high-pitched.

Anton pulls me closer and whispers, "Want to know what my father said I should do with nosy girls?"

I don't answer. My breath is coming in ragged gasps; my heart feels ready to escape my chest.

"Take your hands off of her." James appears at the table with a determined look on his face.

"You going to make me, James?" Anton says and tightens his grip on my arm.

"If I have to." James stares at him, until finally Anton curses and releases my arm, sending me to the ground. "You and your friends need to leave," James says after he has helped me to my feet.

Anton scowls. For a moment I think he is going to punch James. But instead he finishes the rest of his ale and spits. "Fine. But tell your girl to mind her own business."

"Thank you," I whisper to James after they leave. I take a few deep breaths, and James escorts me back to our table, my heart still hammering; my cheeks warm at being called James's girl. I glance over at him. *Does* he have a girl? If so, I have not seen her.

"Nicely handled," Victor tells James after we sit down. To me, he says, "You need to be careful, Willie. Anton and Jaromil are regulars here, and are rarely up to any good."

"I overheard them talking," I say hesitantly. "Something about a job at the docks? On the night of the masquerade—something that a Galandrian needed help with," I say, careful, as I have been the last two days, to shorten my vowels, and sound more Kyrenican.

Victor considers this. "Could be working with a Galandrian trader."

"But I thought Kyrenica and Galandria do not trade with each other?" I say, surprised.

"Not officially, no—though that will soon change, with the new treaty. But a lot of illegal trading still occurs. It's a profitable business, for those willing to risk it."

I nod, and wonder if Lord Royce—the Guardian of

Trade—is aware of this. I relax a little. I suppose it makes sense; perhaps Anton and Jaromil and their companions intend to trade goods on the night of the masquerade, while the city is preoccupied.

Victor gestures about the noisy inn and resumes the earlier conversation. "The Masked Princess has just arrived in the city and already it's a circus. I'm surprised Galina didn't talk more sense into you girls. Go meet Kyra, if you must. You can watch the princess wave from the balcony, and then you come immediately back here."

James laughs. "Victor, Willie is your tenant, not your—" He breaks off, and the color drains from his face. "I mean"— he stammers—"I only meant that—"

"It's all right," Victor replies gruffly with a wave of his hand.

I look between the two of them, unsure what is going on. "I appreciate your concern," I say to Victor.

Victor nods. "James is right, though. I can't tell you what to do. But"—he looks pointedly at James—"as my employee, I can tell *you* to do whatever I want. If Willie is determined to see the princess then you will accompany her there and back."

I expect James to protest, but instead, he smiles at me and says, "I'd like that. Very much."

*O*utside the inn, the streets are festive and several groups of people laugh and jest as they head toward the castle. The city smells of fish, and a chilly, briny wind blows up the street.

"What was going on between you and Victor earlier?" I ask James as we walk. "Did you offend him somehow?"

James's smile fades. "No, but I'm a fool." He rakes his hand through his messy hair and continues. "Victor was a general for King Ezebo once, and as fierce as they come. Stories are still told about him to this day. But about ten years ago he returned from a border skirmish to find his wife and four girls dead. They'd gotten sick with the fever, see? That kind of loss, it changes a man, to lose his wife and daughters."

I nod, though I want to tell him that some men are not nearly so attached to their family. Some men *choose* to lose their daughters.

"And now, whenever he sees a girl by herself he tries to help her. He's gotten a bit of a reputation in the city for having a soft heart. It drives Galina and some of the other merchants mad."

The streets become more packed as we make our way toward the castle. When we push through a particularly crowded section, James places his hand on the small of my back and I flinch.

"I'm sorry," he says quickly, removing his hand. "I didn't mean—"

"I know," I answer just as quickly. "I only—"

I stop, because how can I explain? Except for the few times Patric and I held hands, few people have ever willingly touched me.

I am searching for something to say to ease the awkwardness that has sprung up between us, when James says, "Look, the broken statue is up there."

I follow his gaze and gasp. I had assumed "the Broken Statue" was an inn or a tavern. But now I see Kyra had been speaking literally.

Standing in the middle of the street rising up over the passersby is a white stone statue of my great-great-grandmother Rowan, much like the one that stands in the Queen's Garden in the Opal Palace. Except this statue is indeed broken. Queen Rowan's head lies on the ground before the rest of the statue's body, as though someone beheaded her.

"Willie? Are you okay?" James says.

I nod. I suppose to everyone else, the broken statue is just a monument, or a meeting place. But to me, it's a reminder of the bad blood between the Strassburgs and the Andewyns.

"Hi, Willie!" Kyra appears. Her eyes stray to James. "Have you bought candles yet?"

"Not yet," James answers. He turns to me. "I'll go and get ours." He points to a nearby vendor and leaves.

"Candles? For what?" I ask Kyra.

"To light at the castle gates, of course." She grins slyly. "So, you and James?"

I blink. "Me and James . . . *what?*"

Kyra rolls her eyes. "He walked you here and he's buying you candles? He likes you, Willie."

"No, you misunderstand," I say, although I can feel my cheeks coloring. "Victor told him to accompany me. He said he didn't want me walking alone."

"Yeah," Kyra says, a smile pulling at her lips. "I'm sure Victor had to twist his arm."

James returns and we set off. A large crowd has already gathered in front of the castle. James lights our candles from a woman standing nearby and soon the street glows with light.

Everywhere people are crying out, appealing to King Ezebo to let them see the Masked Princess.

"Look!" Kyra cries. "The doors to the balcony are opening."

Several guards bearing torches step out onto the balcony. After a moment—where it seems the whole world is holding its breath, the door opens again, and the Masked Princess—Elara—emerges.

I gasp. It's like looking at an image of the girl I once was. Can that really be only a few days ago? She wears a golden gown and one of my newer masks, the gilded one with the fire opals, which glows with streaks of red, orange, and yellow. With the torchlight glinting off her jewels and the sun setting behind the castle, dusting the sky in bright shades of orange and pink, she truly does seem unearthly.

So this is what it's like, I think, listening to the excited shouts of the people around me. This is what it's like to be on the other side of the balcony.

My eyes stray to the front of the gates, and that's when I see him:

Garwyn.

He is not watching Elara like everyone else; his eyes are sweeping over the crowd. Now that I look, so are two of the other guards I traveled with, though I have forgotten their names. Garwyn and his men are wearing street clothes, which seems odd. I distinctly remember hearing Lord Quinlan say they were to remain at the castle serving King Ezebo for as long as he saw fit, and then return immediately to Galandria.

Just then, a younger girl joins Elara on the balcony.

"Look, it's Princess Ruby," Kyra says.

The smaller girl steps in front of Elara and begins blowing kisses, and the crowd laughs and applauds.

"The Masked Princess seems to be getting on well with the royal family," Kyra remarks.

"Very well," I answer. Whatever Elara has said or done these last few days seems to have endeared her to the Strassburgs. She certainly doesn't look as though she is merely enduring pretending to be me.

A chill slides down my back and I shudder. What if she is doing more than just pretending and waiting for me to return? I know she wanted to find a new life. What if, in fleeing the castle, I handed her the opportunity she was looking for?

I glance at Garwyn. If I went to him proclaiming myself as the true Masked Princess, would he believe me? Or would Elara tell him *she* was the Masked Princess, and I was the decoy?

No, I cannot return to the castle yet. Not when I don't know Elara's plans. I will have to find a way to meet her face to face.

And the meeting will occur when *I* am ready. Not one moment before.

Elara and Princess Ruby wave one last time before turning away and disappearing inside the castle. The torchbearers follow behind them, and the crowd begins to dissipate. Garwyn turns away from the castle and heads up the street.

When I glance up at James, he is staring at me. "What did you think of the Masked Princess?" I ask.

"Why should I care about some Galandrian princess," he says, "when you are right here?"

Kyra, overhearing him, promptly says, "See you tomorrow, Willie," and gives me a meaningful look before she leaves.

It hits me then that James wants to be here—wants to be with me. Not the Masked Princess, but *me*. Is there anyone in my life who has ever preferred me over her? An image of Patric's face comes to mind, but I quickly push it away.

On the walk back to the Sleeping Dragon, James reaches for my hand.

And this time, I don't flinch.

CHAPTER 38

ELARA

The afternoon following my appearance on the balcony, I'm seated in Ezebo's study alone, wearing the mask and dress Ruby and Leandra picked out for me, and my hair is tied back in ribbons. Flames spark and crackle in the fireplace, but I still feel chilled. I tug at the mask on my face. It's sticky from the cold sweat pooling at my temples.

Word has come that the crown prince has returned, and is eager to meet his bride-to-be.

I jump at the sound of the door opening. But it's only a servant, carrying a silver tray with a pot, cups, and saucers.

"Thank you," I say, once he has settled the tray on the table and handed me a cup of warm scarlet tea. He nods, and bows himself from the room.

The cup and saucer rattle in my hands. After a few more sips I put the tea aside, and stand up and move to the fire, hoping to warm myself. I try to remember what Arianne said about the crown prince. . . . *Insolent and as common as dirt if you ask me. Served first with Kyrenica's navy, until Ezebo commanded him to return and attend to his royal duties. It's a shame he was never killed at sea. . . .*

The door opens and Ezebo enters. "Princess Wilhamina

Andewyn," he says, grinning, "May I present to you my son, His Royal Highness Crown Prince Stefan Strassburg." He steps back and a tall, grim-looking boy enters the room. For once, I am thankful for the mask and that it covers my face, hiding my shock.

Because Crown Prince Stefan is the squire.

"*You?* You're the prince?"

"I am," he says, sounding slightly annoyed. He looks different today. Much different than the carefree squire I laughed with in the kitchen. His appearance, though washed and cleaned from the last time I saw him, is much altered. There is no twinkle in his eye, no sense that he is in any way enjoying meeting his bride-to-be. Instead he stares at me, examining me the way I imagine a cattle owner might examine a newly acquired goat. One he regrets purchasing.

"And you only just arrived in Korynth today?" My voice is accusatory.

Stefan frowns. "I returned briefly a few days ago, but had to leave again to see to business in the countryside, so I felt it would be best to delay our meeting. At any rate . . . Princess Wilhamina, it is a pleasure to meet you." He dips his head slightly and stops. He seems to be waiting for something.

"Oh, um, it is nice to meet you, too." For a second, a strange look crosses his face and I wonder if he recognizes me, or if I've failed at some sort of royal formality. But then the look is gone, replaced by grim resignation.

"Well, then, I shall leave you two to get to know each other," Ezebo says, still grinning. "Tonight the two of you will participate in an engagement ceremony. And tomorrow, you will begin taking breakfast together privately. You will have plenty of time to get to know each other." With that, he strides away and exits the room.

Stefan and I sit down. His long legs bump up against the small table in front of us. He looks squashed in the small armchair. He pours himself a cup of scarlet tea and stares impatiently out the window, drumming his fingers on the armrest.

I can't help feeling slighted by his behavior. I may be wearing the mask, but does he really not recognize me?

He sighs and crosses his legs, as though the very act of being in the same room with me is torture.

"Are you unhappy to be here?" I ask.

He looks away from the window. "What makes you say that?"

"Because you look like you just swallowed a rotten fig," I snap, then remind myself I'm supposed to be Wilha. "I mean . . . are you not a fan of the tea?" I continue in a softer voice. "Or is the company not to your liking?"

"The tea is fine," he counters. "And you are quite observant. Yet I am at a serious disadvantage, am I not? You can see every emotion that plays on my face, but I can tell nothing of you." He leans forward. "Take off your mask."

I hesitate, considering this. What harm would there be in revealing my face to him, really? I could just say I was in search of a little adventure a few days ago and we could have a good laugh over it. If Wilha is to marry him, he'll have to see her face one day anyway . . . won't he?

But I can't abide the way he speaks to me, as though he already owns me—I mean, already owns Wilha.

"I am rather sure," I say coolly, "that your father would like for the mask to remain on."

"And *I* am rather sure that in a year's time you shall be my wife. Take off your mask. If we are to be married, I expect to know what I am getting."

"Really?" I say, my voice rising. "Well, it appears *I'm* getting a prince who possesses the manners of a child."

"Our marriage was arranged solely for the benefit of others. Manners have nothing to do with it. I say again, take off your mask."

"No."

"And why not?"

"Because we have met not five minutes ago, and you are already ordering me about. I will remind you that with this treaty between our kingdoms you secured a wife, *a person*, not a piece of property."

He leans back in his seat, looking at me. "My father's advisor said you were a difficult, fearful princess. That you hid under that mask, scared of your own shadow—"

"I am scared of nothing." *Careful*, I remind myself. *He's talking about Wilha. Not you.*

"Scared of nothing?" he sneers. "Prove it, then. Take off your mask. Surely you do not like being hidden?"

In that moment, I want nothing more. Where is the kindhearted squire who seemed genuinely interested in my stories? He's vanished, leaving a churlish prince in his place.

When I don't answer, he says, "I did not choose you, you know. My father and his advisors made it clear you were my only option for marriage. They said that to secure peace, an alliance must be made with Galandria."

"Does your father intend to keep the alliance?" I ask carefully, thinking of the locked door. I clearly heard Ezebo's advisors discussing plans of some sort. And ever since, my stomach has twisted with one thought: What if the room behind that locked door contains exactly what Lord Quinlan suspects: evidence that King Ezebo still plans to attack Galandria?

Stefan's eyes narrow. "I am sure he intends to keep the alliance just as much as *your* father intends to." He sighs. "But you must know how it is. A king makes a decree and lives rise or fall accordingly, with little thought to the individual hopes and futures that are altered or extinguished in its wake. Surely you can understand that."

I do understand, in so many ways. But I don't know what to say to him. "I'm . . . tired," I manage. "I would like to finish my tea in peace. And I won't remove the mask."

He stares at me a moment longer—almost as though he's disappointed—before nodding and saying, "We shall have many more teas together," and he stands and heads for the door. "A lifetime's worth, unfortunately."

When I'm sure he's gone, I walk as fast as I can back to my chambers without attracting curious stares from the servants. Once my door is firmly shut behind me, I remove Wilha's mask and take a few deep breaths.

It's time I started facing up to my situation. I am not a princess and never will be. And neither am I certain that Wilha will ever return to the castle. If I stay here much longer my neck is likely to end up in a Kyrenican noose. I'll wait until tonight after everyone has retired, and then I'm leaving. I've done the best I can for the Andewyns—so much better than they have ever done for me. Let the Strassburgs—and the world—make of the Masked Princess's disappearance what they will.

I refuse to sacrifice my life for a sister I've never known.

CHAPTER 39

WILHA

All my life, I have considered the Opal Palace my home. Yet as I watch the people in the Sleeping Dragon dance and clap while a few men near the fireplace play lutes, I wonder if I have been mistaken all these years.

James approaches the table where Kyra and I sit. "Would you care to dance?"

I start to protest but Kyra says, "She'd love to," and nudges me with her elbow until I stand up.

"I am not a very good dancer." This is only a half truth. I'm a decent dancer, when I dance a waltz or another formal dance. But the random spinning and whirling the Kyrenican townspeople seem to favor is foreign to me.

"That's all right," he says, grinning, "neither am I."

He leads me out onto the floor. He spins me one way, then another, and I struggle to keep up with him. He's a much better dancer than he let on. Another song starts up, and we keep going. Sweat springs to my temples and my heart beats in time to the music. We spin, we clap, we whirl; faster and faster, until I am dizzy with laughter.

And as I look at James's smiling face I realize this is what I longed for, all those dark nights when I gazed into the mirror, wondering what was so wrong with me. This is the one thing men value more than jewels and gold.

This is freedom.

I am alone in a foreign city. No royal secretaries to command my every move. No kings to decide my fate. For the first time ever, I am the master of my own destiny.

"Are you free to take a walk with me later?" James says, panting, as the song comes to an end.

"Yes, I am free," I answer

They are the truest, most beautiful words I have ever spoken.

"I have a few more orders to fill," James says as we walk back to the bar, "but then I'm sure Victor would let me slip outside for a moment to get some fresh air. Would you like that?" I nod, and he offers me his hand. "Come on. Why don't you help me, the work will go quicker that way."

He fills several goblets of ale and places them on a tray. "Can you take this upstairs to the room at the end of the hall? There are a company of merchants staying there tonight."

I take the tray and walk slowly up the stairs, the goblets wobbling precariously. When I reach the end of the hall I hear a voice from behind the door. "Bit of luck, wasn't it? Getting chased from the castle. It's given me more time."

"How many men have you recruited?"

I freeze, because I recognize that voice.

It belongs to Garwyn.

"More than enough. Don't you think, Anton?"

I nearly drop the tray when I hear Anton answer, "Yes,

we'll be ready. But Moran here says there's also a girl you're supposed to be searching for. Who is it?"

"A Galandrian, and no one for you to be concerned about," Garwyn snaps.

At that, my breath catches, and I grip the tray tightly to keep it from shaking. Quietly, I press my ear to the door.

"She's got them opals she stole," Moran is saying. "Wonder what they're worth."

My eyes stray down the hall to my own room, where those exact opals are still hidden in Elara's satchel, under my bed.

"Forget the jewels," Garwyn says. "We have our orders." He lowers his voice then, so I cannot hear what he says, and I lean against the wall for support.

I don't understand everything I have just heard, but if Moran is the one hiring Kyrenicans, perhaps I have been wrong this whole time. Perhaps Anton and Jaromil are not mixed up with some sort of illegal trading at all. Did Moran hire them to find me?

Either way, if they know about the stolen opals it must only be because Elara told them. Is that what has really been going on inside the castle? While privately the Strassburgs parade Elara out on the balcony, pretending to be me—have King Ezebo and Crown Prince Stefan quietly ordered my guards to hire men, instructing them to search the city and bring me back to the castle in time for the masquerade, like I am a wayward child who does not wish to go to her own party?

And once I am brought back to the castle, will I face a prince happy to see me safely returned? Or a man enraged that his future bride dared to run away from him in the first place?

Quietly, I bend down and place the tray by the door. I walk back toward my own room, torn between grabbing the satchel and declaring myself to Garwyn, or locking my door and hiding the rest of the night.

"Willie?" James appears beside me. He frowns and touches my cheek. "You look pale. Perhaps we should walk another night?"

I lean back against the wall. "I like you, James." I'm not sure if this is a good-bye. I'm not sure of anything right now.

"I really like you too, Willie." He takes my hands in his. "I like you quite a bit, in fact." He leans forward, until mere inches separate us.

At the end of the hall, the door opens and Garwyn, Moran, and Anton exit the room. By the time they pass us, James is kissing me, and I hear Garwyn's whispered voice: "Who is that girl?"

"The barman's nosy girlfriend," Anton replies. "And a Kyrenican, if that's what you're wondering."

They start down the stairs, and as James and I break apart I sag against the door, grateful that all they saw was a Kyrenican couple stealing a quiet moment together.

And whether I let James kiss me because I wanted him to, or because I did not want Garwyn to find me, I don't ask myself.

CHAPTER 40

ELARA

*A*fter my appearance on the balcony again, I see Stefan briefly. We attend a strange engagement ceremony in front of Ezebo and his advisors where Stefan places a thick bracelet made of pearls and rubies around my wrist.

"That's very lovely," I say quietly.

"You think so?" he whispers. "I find it to be quite hideous myself. It belonged to my aunt Rayna. She too was thought to be fearful and odd," he replies, and I have to fight the urge to rip off the bracelet and hurl it back at him.

Dinner is a small feast with a newly arrived party of nobles. Once I've had my share of smiling placidly I tell Stefan and Ezebo I wish to retire early. Ezebo bids me good night and reminds me that Stefan and I are to share a private breakfast the next morning.

"What do you think of my son?" he asks hopefully.

"I don't believe I have the words to describe just how I feel about him," I say, in what I hope is a sweet tone.

After I'm in my chambers and I've waved off Milly's offer to help me undress, I put on my servant clothes and begin filling a purse with the gems I ripped from Wilha's gowns. I leave her mask sitting on an armchair, since it's too conspicuous to sell. I almost take the bracelet off and leave it behind as well, but decide against it. If Stefan values it so little, I'll sell it the first chance I get. After I've stuffed the purse until it's bursting at the seams, I take the ribbons out of my hair and then sink into an armchair to warm myself in front of the fire.

And I wait.

Much later, long after the fire has died out, I grab a candle from my desk and press my finger to the hidden opal. The wall slides open, revealing the passageway, and I step into the dark tunnel. Tonight I'll travel it the entire way and hope that it takes me far away from the castle. But I hesitate. When I reach the spot I went through my first night here, the door with the gargoyle handle beckons.

What could it hurt, just to try opening the door? If there is valuable information inside, maybe I can use it to my advantage somehow. I hear Cordon's voice in my head, urging me to be cautious and not to go looking for trouble. To get out of the castle as fast as I can and run. But whatever is behind that locked door is something the Strassburgs obviously don't want me to see. So much so they haven't allowed me back down that corridor since the day I first had tea with Genevieve.

And that, more than anything else, convinces me I have to try to open it.

The castle corridor is empty, and I have my hand on the

gargoyle door handle when I hear muffled footsteps behind me, and a voice I know all too well. "Looking for something?"

You've got to be kidding me. I paste a pleasant smile on my face and turn around. Stefan is looking at me with a mixture of amusement and exasperation. A nice change, I think, from the way he glowered at me earlier.

"Just on my way to the kitchen for a snack," I say, affecting my breezy, whispering voice and hoping he won't recognize me. I'm careful not to curtsy, not to let on that I know he is actually the crown prince. "The cook served seafood again tonight and I couldn't eat it."

"And that requires you to be in this corridor, *how* exactly?" He steps forward. "Curious that I again find you standing beside this room. A room you know you are forbidden to enter."

"Curious, exactly! I can't stand it for anything. I hate it when other people keep secrets. I so wish I could see inside"— I clasp my hand to my chest in feigned enthusiasm—"and I thought I could bring back a juicy bit of gossip to my lady."

Immediately, I realize my mistake. As my hand rests against my chest the pearl and ruby bracelet clinks into view, glinting in the flickering candlelight.

Stefan's eyes stray to the bracelet, widening as shock, and then anger, twists his features. "It was you all along," he says.

"I'm—I'm afraid I don't know what you mean."

"Really?" His voice drips venom. "Or are you now about

to tell me that you stole that bracelet from the princess?"

"I didn't steal anything," I say, realizing my last chance to flee the castle is fading. "I saw the bracelet lying on the floor, and I picked it up. I intended to give it back, I did."

"Every word out of your mouth is a lie." He practically spits the words.

"I don't know what you're talking about."

"I am sure you do not. Shall we go to the Masked Princess's room, then, and you can tell her yourself. . . . You do not look so eager to go. Why is that? Perhaps because we both know we shall find the room empty?"

"Stefan, I can explain," I say, dropping my bubbly voice. "I'm sorry, I just—"

"You're sorry? For what? For being a liar and a traitor? Your lost servant girl act was quite convincing the other night. So much so I actually found myself wondering . . . that is to say, I fell for it completely."

"Stefan, I'm sorry. In all honesty I—"

"Honesty?" He scoffs. "Do you even know the word? You stand here, before a forbidden door, dressed in traveling clothes." He grabs my arm, and in the dim light I see the fury in his eyes. "Who were you going to meet?"

"What? I have no idea what you're talking about—"

"After you got whatever information you *think* is inside that room, what were you going to do? Pay someone to take it back to your father the king? Or were you going to flee back to Galandria entirely? Did the Andewyns ever have any intention of honoring the treaty, or are you only just now deciding that I do not suit you?"

"Please Stefan I—"

"Here, I'll show you." He removes a key, and unlocks the door. Then he wrenches it open and gestures me inside.

The room is strangely empty, save for a long wooden table in the middle. Stefan yanks me forward. "If you are so curious, look for yourself."

Strewn across the table are large parchments. I stare at them, trying to make sense of all the sketches I see. They seem to be plans for a building of some sort.

I look up. "I don't understand."

Stefan won't return my gaze. He stares at the table; the fight seems to have left him. "My father and I have been secretly meeting with our masons. Ground was just broken on a new castle—a new palace. It will be several years before it's completed, of course. But one day"—he grimaces—"one day you and I will live there together as husband and wife. My father has long wanted to build a palace in the country-side to show Kyrenica's emerging strength." He drops his voice, until it's no more than a whisper. "And we knew, after living so long in the Opal Palace, you would find our castle sandy and impoverished in comparison." He runs a hand through his hair and his eyes seem tired. "We had hoped to surprise you with the plans at the masquerade. That is why we tried to keep you from the northern wing."

He stares dejectedly at the plans, and I'm tempted to drop the pretense completely and tell him that this "sandy and impoverished" castle is the grandest place I've ever been. And that it's certainly better than the Opal Palace, where I was treated as little more than a piece of Andewyn property.

Before I can speak, he seizes my arm. "There, you have seen it." He ushers me toward the door.

"Stefan I—"

"Enough! Or I shall call the guards and tell them I suspect you of treason." He pulls me along after him down the corridor and swears when he discovers the guards outside my door are sleeping. "Up!" He yells at them. "My family does not pay you to sleep." They awaken and jump to their feet, their apologies fading as Stefan shoves me inside and closes the door behind us.

He stalks into the room, and blanches when he sees the mask sitting on an armchair. He picks it up and stares, as if enchanted.

"And to think," he murmurs softly, "I believed the rumors. I thought the mask was because you were not beautiful to look at . . . but why, then?" He stares at the mask a moment longer before shoving it into my hands. "Wear it at all times. For I do not wish to see your face ever again."

CHAPTER 41

ELARA

The next morning, after Milly escorts me to a small dining room near the kitchen, Cook pushes a covered plate in front of me. "The crown prince sends his regards, and wishes me to tell you he will be unable to join you this morning. Though he does hope you will enjoy your breakfast."

She lifts the lid, revealing a plate piled high with tuna eyes.

"His Highness told us this is your favorite Kyrenican dish and that you would quite like to have them for breakfast. We made sure to make extra."

I look at her hopeful face. "Thank you," I say. "Please be sure to convey my utmost gratitude to the crown prince and tell him that his, um, *kindness* won't be easily forgotten."

I pick up my fork and cut into the tuna eye, although I imagine it's Stefan's eye I'm gouging. I take a quick bite and force it down. "It's delicious," I say, ignoring my stomach's protests.

A servant enters the room. "Your Highness, His Majesty the king asks me to inform you that your father's advisors have arrived and are eager to see you. King Ezebo waits with them in the great hall."

He bows himself from the room, and I apologize to Cook

that I won't be able to continue the meal.

"Of course, Princess. Don't you worry, you shall have another plate of the delicacy tomorrow morning," she promises.

On the way to the great hall, my mind races. I had forgotten that the Guardians were due to arrive in Korynth today. By now they will have heard of the missing maid. If I'm supposed to be "proving my loyalty" by posing as Wilha, what will they say if I confess in private I'm not Wilha, but Elara? Will they really believe that shy Wilha, who seemed to be scared of her own shadow, actually plucked up the courage to escape the castle on her own? Or will they believe I'm the threat they have always suspected me to be? Another Aislinn Andewyn, willing to harm her sister to gain her own ends?

Inside the great hall, Ezebo and Genevieve are seated on their thrones. Stefan stands next to his mother. Lord Quinlan and Lord Royce are poised before them and they bow when I enter.

Lord Quinlan steps forward. He is wearing more rings and necklaces than all the Strassburgs combined. "Ah, Princess Wilhamina, what a pleasure it is to see you again. I was just telling King Ezebo here what a fine little room this is." He gestures vaguely about the great hall.

Next to Lord Quinlan, Lord Royce's weathered face is strained, as though he's trying not to roll his eyes. Ezebo is red-faced, and Stefan stares at Lord Quinlan with open hostility. Yet Lord Quinlan, who doesn't seem bothered by the effect his words are having on his hosts, continues, "I have always thought that Galandrians, used to so much grandeur, are a little *too* ornate when it comes to palace design."

"Ornate would be one way to describe it," Lord Royce speaks up. "Gallingly tacky would be another." Lord Royce's face is as impassive as ever when he turns to look at me. And yet I can't help but think he is giving me a message: *Fix this.*

"I am inclined to agree with Lord Royce," I say quickly. "I find this hall to be one of the most elegant I have ever seen, though of course you're not to be faulted, Lord Quinlan, as I believe it is only those with the most discerning of taste who can recognize it." I turn away from Lord Quinlan, and though I've never done so before, drop to my knees before Ezebo. "You sent for me, Your Majesty?"

Ezebo and Genevieve beam at me, and even Stefan manages a smirk.

"Princess Wilhamina, please rise," Ezebo says, his eyes twinkling. "Truly, your presence delights us all. I am sorry to intrude on your breakfast, and to keep Stefan from you but—"

"How was your breakfast?" Stefan interrupts, showing every one of his white teeth.

"Pungent," I answer. "And wonderfully quiet."

"Yes, well," Ezebo continues, shooting a confused look between me and Stefan, "at any rate, the queen, the crown prince, and I have had the, er . . . *pleasure*, of meeting with your father's advisors for the last hour and they have wonderful news for you."

Lord Quinlan bows and steps forward. "I am happy to report that your father is greatly improving. His physician is hopeful that he will soon be back to his old self."

"This is good news for us all," I say demurely, though I'm sorely tempted to ask Lord Quinlan why, if the king is supposedly feeling so much better, he hasn't bothered to write as he promised?

The doors open then, and Lord Murcendor and Sir Reinhold enter. Instantly, I regret my earlier brashness. Of everyone, Lord Murcendor—the only person who has known both Wilha and me—is the most likely to discover I'm not Wilha.

Lord Murcendor bows deeply. "Your Highness. It is a pleasure to see you again." He looks at me with bright eyes. But it's not a look of admiration.

It's a look of undisguised longing.

A shiver passes over me, and I tug at my mask. Arianne mentioned how good Lord Murcendor has been to Wilha. A father figure, it seems. But there is nothing parental in the way he stares at me now, and I wonder if Wilha hasn't mistaken his intentions all these years.

Maybe I'm not the only one who notices, because just as Lord Murcendor says, "Princess, I was wondering if I could have a word in private. . . ," Stefan steps forward and interrupts, "Father, did you not say that once Sir Reinhold finished inspecting Galandria's latest payment of opals, you wished Lord Murcendor to meet with your councilors to discuss the mining rights?"

"Yes, I did." Ezebo nods. "They are waiting even as we speak. Sir Reinhold, will you show Lord Murcendor the way?"

Lord Murcendor looks poised to argue, but then bows and leaves again with Sir Reinhold. "Another time," he says as he passes me. I nod, careful to keep my eyes down and my mouth shut.

When I glance back at the dais my eyes meet Stefan's and we share a look. He seems troubled as he glances from me to Lord Murcendor's retreating figure. I nod slightly, and hope that, behind my mask, he sees my gratitude.

Ezebo rises. "If you will excuse me, I have other matters I must see to." He turns to Lord Quinlan and Lord Royce. "Rooms have been prepared for the both of you, and someone will show you the way." He nods, clearly dismissing us.

After the doors to the great hall close behind us, Lord Quinlan drops his smile and turns a scrutinizing eye upon me. "Wilha?" he guesses.

I stare at him and decide I can't drop the charade. I have nothing valuable to offer him, no information that would prove useful. As far as I can tell, Ezebo has every intention of honoring the peace treaty, news that may not be too welcome, as it's seemed like Lord Quinlan may be a bit *too* eager for the treaty to break.

"Yes, Lord Quinlan?"

He frowns. "For a moment there I thought . . . but you . . . seem to be getting on well with those Kyrenicans?"

I avert my eyes and soften my voice. "Father told me it was my duty to treat them as family."

"Yes, well, of course. You father is right, as always." He resumes his confident air; clearly he has decided I must be Wilha. "Ezebo told me of the mishap with the guards. To tell you the truth, I am shocked by Moran's behavior. I was also told of your chamber maid running off." He glances around to make sure that no servants are in earshot and moves in closer. "Tell me truly, what happened?"

I keep my eyes downcast. "Elara stole jewels from me and fled at the first opportunity she had. I have no idea of her whereabouts."

He nods. "That is what I suspected." His brow furrows. "But this is a problem."

You're telling me. "It is unfortunate, yes."

Lord Quinlan sighs heavily. "It is too bad your sister didn't turn out to be more like you, Wilha."

At that, I have to stifle a snort. Lord Quinlan wishes I was more like Wilha? More easily controlled, is what he really means.

For the first time, I ask myself which girl got the better end of the deal sixteen years ago. I got the Ogdens, and Wilha got the mask. But I also had Cordon. Did Wilha have anyone at all?

"Ezebo has not heard from Garwyn, but I will send more of my men to search the city and see if we can locate her," Lord Quinlan says.

"Locate her, why?" I ask. "She escorted me here, and clearly the Strassburgs do not mean to harm me. It would seem that she has finished her duty and chosen to start a life somewhere else, rather than return to Galandria." I keep my voice soft. I'm not challenging him; I'm a polite princess, making a polite inquiry.

But this is what I've wondered: If I said thanks, but no thanks, to the Guardians' offer of a new life in Allegria, what would they do? Would I be allowed to find a new life anywhere else?

"Your father has ordered me to bring her back to the Opal Palace," he answers. "It is his decision what becomes of her."

Exactly as I thought. And if Fennrick and the Guardians once contemplated sending me into seclusion—my sole offense being that I had the misfortune of being Wilha's twin—what type of "new life" would they choose for me now, when they still suspect I may want to claim the opal crown for myself?

No, Galandria is not safe for me, and never will be.

"As you command," I say sweetly.

Lord Quinlan excuses himself, and I turn away to head back to my chambers.

"There was one other thing."

I jump slightly at the sound of Lord Royce's voice. I had nearly forgotten about him.

"Yes?" Unease claws at my belly. His ice blue eyes are watchful, far from the impassive gaze he wore before Ezebo and Genevieve.

"Your Father commissioned Master Welkin to design another one of his creations to congratulate you on your betrothal. He knows what a fan you are of his work. Lord Quinlan and I have brought it here to Korynth."

Master Welkin? Creations? The name sounds familiar, but I can't place it. Lord Royce watches me closely, a muscle twitching near his jaw. Was he not so easily convinced that I'm Wilha? Is it possible that he's testing me?

I curtsy. "If you write to my father the king, please tell him his gifts are always welcome."

I plead exhaustion then, and tell him I must return to my chambers. I don't know if Lord Royce was simply delivering a message from his king or something else entirely. But I decide that the best thing I can do is avoid the Guardians as much as possible before the masquerade.

CHAPTER 42

WILHA

*G*arwyn may be searching for me, but I am not ready to be found. If there is one thing I learned in the Opal Palace, it was how to content myself with a life lived behind walls. The walls of my room at the Sleeping Dragon may be far less grand than my chambers in the Opal Palace, but they serve my purpose, nevertheless.

"Are you sure you don't want to go to the castle tonight?" Kyra says as we close up the dress shop.

I nod. "And besides," I hold up the bundle I carry, "I told Galina I would finish this dress tonight at home."

"Oh, come on, Willie. You've been sewing for Galina for the past few nights. It's really not fair for her to give you so much work." She glances over her shoulder, to make sure Galina, who is still in the back room, doesn't hear us.

"I volunteered to do it. I will stop once the masquerade is over."

After I leave the shop, I hurry up the street. When I arrive at the Sleeping Dragon, I find Victor and ask him, just as I have done the past few nights, if he could bring dinner to my room. Then I'm up the stairs and locking my door behind me. I place the bundle on my bed and step over to the window. In the building across the street, a woman is leaning out of her window and removing laundry from a clothesline. She waves at me. I wave back and look down at the street. Many Kyrenicans—most of them carrying candles—make their way west toward the castle.

Garwyn and Moran left the Sleeping Dragon the night after I heard them talking, presumably to try other inns in the area. But ever since, I have jumped at the sound of the bell in the dress shop, certain Garwyn had found me, certain he had finally realized I was not just "the barman's nosy girlfriend." My neck has prickled with the feeling of someone watching me. Each time I have whirled around, only to find no one there.

Garwyn may not have seen me, but I have seen him. Two days ago, from the window of the dress shop I glimpsed him strolling up the street, his eyes intent on the passersby.

And he is not the only Galandrian I have seen. Indeed, from the window yesterday I was certain I glimpsed one of Lord Quinlan's men and wondered if the Guardians had arrived in Korynth. I received my answer today when I saw Lord Royce this morning, walking toward the docks with Sir Reinhold. Are they also searching for me? I think if I had seen Lord Murcendor on the street I would have declared myself to him, and he would have instructed me how to make things right. But I know little about Lord Royce, so I stayed hidden in the dress shop.

A knock sounds at the door, but when I open it, it's not Victor, but James standing in the doorway, holding a plate piled high with steamed clams. He places the tray on my desk and closes the door behind him.

"I shouldn't have kissed you, I'm sorry," he blurts out, before I have the chance to say anything.

"It was fine, really." My voice sounds unconvincing, even to me.

"It can't be fine. You've been avoiding me all week."

"I have not."

"You leave early for Galina's, and you've been staying there all hours. Then when you return, you spend all evening in your room, sewing."

"It cannot be avoided," I insist. "The masquerade is nearly here. There is hardly enough time to fill the orders we already have, and more are still coming in."

"Then why are you asking Victor to bring your meals to you, when you could just as easily ask me? You're avoiding me."

"Okay," I admit. "I may be avoiding you, just a little."

"I knew it." He rakes his hand through his hair. "I never should have kissed you. I'm a fool."

"You are not," I assure him. "It is only that, well . . . I had never been kissed before."

I have imagined my first kiss a hundred times over, but with Patric. Yet surrounded by all my guards, fantasies were all I could hope for. With James, it was all so quick. One minute I was torn between hiding or declaring myself to Garwyn, and the next, James's lips were pressing against mine.

James curses. "I'm sorry. It was impulsive and I . . ." He sighs. "And I want to do this right. Victor said I could have a free morning tomorrow. Would you . . . go on a picnic with me?"

It is such a simple thing, a boy inviting a girl to share a meal. And any girl could easily accept. Any girl who is not me.

"I am sorry, James. With the masquerade coming up I can't."

He nods, disappointment etched on his face. "Well, it was worth a try I guess," he says and begins to back out of the room. "I really am sorry, Willie."

"No, James there's no need to—" I begin, but he closes the door behind him.

I lock my door again and move to my desk, but find I cannot eat. I stand up and throw open my window, and a salty breeze wafts into the room. Glowing lanterns hang from the rooftops and excited laughter spirals up like sweet incense.

Down below, everyone seems to be having a wonderful time. Yet up here, I hide, just as silent and fearful as I was during the years I spent in the Opal Palace.

I unlock the door and exit my room. Downstairs, James is filling several mugs with ale. When he sees me, he gives me a hopeful smile.

"I don't suppose you've changed your mind?"

"I have," I answer. "I would love to go on a picnic with you."

I refuse to find Garwyn or any of the others and offer myself up to them. But neither will I continue to hide. If it's me they're searching for, let them come.

In the meantime, I intend to enjoy my waning days of freedom.

CHAPTER 43

ELARA

If I spend one more day in this castle, I'll go mad.

When was the last time I saw the outdoors or breathed fresh air, apart from my waving from the balcony? While Milly fastens ribbons in my hair, I tug at the mask I'm wearing. When was the last time I spoke with someone without wearing this wretched thing? I think back to the night I enjoyed a midnight snack with the squire—with Stefan, rather. I wouldn't admit it, not to anyone, but I miss the squire. It's too bad, really, because I liked *him*. Stefan, on the other hand, can take a flying leap.

"Milly, if I wanted to get a carriage to take me into the city, how would I go about it?"

"Not sure, Your Highness." Milly yawns as she fusses over my hair. "Think you'd have to speak to the king."

Under Stefan's orders, Milly has moved into my chambers, and both of us know it's because she's supposed to be keeping an eye on me. "Your Highness," she said the first night, "the crown prince could fire me if he thought I wasn't doing a good job."

I looked at her fretful gaze and remembered how fearful I was over displeasing Mistress Ogden, as she had the power to toss me out. "I promise Milly," I had said, "you won't get in trouble on my account."

So I have resolved not to explore the passageway, not to make any plans at all, until after the masquerade, when the Guardians are safely on their way back to Galandria.

"And where is the king right now?" I ask.

"He is with Lord Quinlan." Milly gets a sour expression on her face. "His latest complaint is that his chambers aren't warm enough."

I suppress a grin. Thankfully, I haven't seen the Guardians since they first arrived in Korynth a few days ago. Ezebo has sent Lord Royce and Lord Murcendor to meet with several of his advisors as part of the peace treaty. How Lord Quinlan occupies his time, I can't be sure. He seems to have little use for me, now that he is sure I'm Wilha—but I hear about him often enough from Milly. Apparently he's gaining quite a reputation among the servants.

"Would you like me to escort you to the king's study?" Milly asks.

"No," I answer quickly. I have no wish to see Lord Quinlan.

"I suppose you could ask the crown prince over breakfast this morning," Milly says, careful to keep her eyes averted. I think she must know "breakfast" consists of me sitting alone with only a plate of tuna eyes for company. Where Stefan eats, or how he spends his days, I don't know either. During dinner, he speaks to whatever nobles are joining us for dinner, and is careful to avoid being alone with me. And yet, I've watched as he has swept Ruby up in a hug, and proceeded to waltz her around the room. I've seen him stand up for Genevieve, when Eudora starts in on her. Clearly, he's capable of great kindness—just not to me.

Not that I care.

"We both know Stefan would probably say no, even if he did show up for breakfast," I answer quietly.

At this, Milly meets my gaze and nods. "He's being most unkind," she says in a low voice. "I am sure that if the king and queen realized they wouldn't stand for it."

Her words give me an idea. I give Milly a gracious smile and utter a polite response, and head for my bedroom.

From the writing desk, I pull out a quill and a piece of parchment. I sit quietly for several moments, contemplating a letter that is sufficiently Wilha-like, but still gets my point across.

"Milly," I call when I'm finished.

"Yes?" she says, appearing in the doorway.

I hold out the folded parchment. "Can you please take this to the queen?"

Milly raises an eyebrow, but says nothing. After she has left, I smile—really smile—for the first time in days.

Stefan is not the only one who can play dirty.

CHAPTER 44

WILHA

With a picnic basket in hand, James leads me to the beach near Rowan's Rock. He spreads out a blanket and gestures for me to sit.

The day is overcast and the tide is low. I glance over at the cliffs and the staircase that I know is hidden among the rocks and moss. I purposely turn away from it, determined not to let anything spoil the afternoon.

"I can tell you're getting sick of eating so much fish," James says once we are settled. "It's okay," he adds, when I start to protest. "I grow tired of it after a while, too." He opens the basket and removes several nonseafood items: olives, figs drizzled with honey, boiled eggs, and a roll of soft goat cheese.

We watch the ocean and eat silently, the only sound being the rhythmic lulling of the waves. I kick off the slippers I borrowed from Kyra and dig my toes into the cool sand.

James gives a sigh of contentment. "Summer is finally making an appearance."

"It is?" I ask, glancing up at the overcast sky.

"Well, I guess it's not as warm as your border village, but this is what summer in Korynth looks like. This far north, you'll be amazed when you see how cold the winters are. But don't worry," he adds quickly, mistaking my dismayed expression for concern. "I will make sure you have warm enough clothes."

"Thank you," I say, managing a smile, and James closes his eyes and tilts his head back. I'm not worried about winters in Korynth, cold though they might be. At the moment, I'm entertaining another thought altogether. When winter comes, where will I be? What if Garwyn and his men never find me? What if they conclude I have left the city and the search is called off?

I think of the way the girls in the dress shop have begun to stare at me. Many of them seem to like my stitching, and have asked about my techniques. When I answer their questions, their stares are intent, as though they have decided I am someone worth listening to.

My eyes focus on Rowan's Rock, which rises up out of the sea. Elegant in her mossy finery, it looks as though she wears an emerald gown, like one of Galandria's Guardians. If only Lord Murcendor were here right now to give me counsel.

James reaches for my hand, and I think, *What if I didn't return at all? What if I stayed here, forever?*

As if in answer, the peaceful silence is broken by the excited shouts of townspeople, who are crying out that the Strassburgs' carriage has been sighted.

The Masked Princess is inside, taking a tour of the city.

CHAPTER 45

ELARA

*G*enevieve's response is immediate. I, along with Leandra and Ruby, am to visit the city this very afternoon.

When we emerge from the castle, a large gilded carriage bearing red Kyrenican flags and the Strassburg family crest waits for us. Several soldiers are lounging nearby, and when they catch sight of the three of us they quickly form a line and stand at attention.

"Are all these guards really necessary?" I ask Leandra. "Couldn't we dismiss just a few of them?"

Leandra frowns. "Wilha be serious. No one in the royal family ever visits the city without guards."

"Well, can't we be just a *bit* less conspicuous? It would be nice to travel anonymously."

"That would defeat the purpose," Stefan says, suddenly appearing beside me and opening the door to the carriage. "After you, my lady." He holds out his hand and grins at a giggling Ruby.

"What exactly are you talking about?" I ask.

"The queen has decided that the people should get a better glimpse of their future queen. And"—he grimaces—"as I have only recently been reminded that it is my duty to protect you—till death do us part—I cannot abide anything less than overseeing double the amount of guards."

"So just to be clear . . . this means you're coming with us?" I ask. "Because you really, *really* don't have to."

"This is your own doing," he says tightly. "I have just spent the better part of the morning being thoroughly scolded by my mother. Did you really have to compare me to a neglectful jailor?"

His face is flushed with indignation and I almost succeed at holding back the laughter building in my throat.

"Stop being so stuffy, Stefan." Ruby sticks her head out the window. "You're ruining a perfectly good adventure."

After he has helped Leandra into the carriage, Stefan sighs and lowers his voice, "My sisters have both grown quite fond of you. Whatever you think of me, please, do not hurt them. Can we put aside our differences, just for today?"

I nod, and Stefan offers me his hand and we step into the carriage. When we are all settled inside, the driver urges the horses onward. The guards fan out and walk silently on either side of the carriage.

"How was your breakfast this morning?" Leandra asks me.

"It was eye-opening," I say, shooting Stefan a dark look and wishing I had also thought to mention our breakfast arrangements to Genevieve.

"I live to make you happy," he says, flashing a grin.

The carriage rattles over the cobblestone streets. The sky is overcast and smoke curls from several chimneys. When we pass a group of boys playing in the streets, they catch sight of us and one of them shouts. "Look, there she is! It's the Masked Princess!"

"So many new buildings," I murmur after we pass several construction sites.

"Yes," Stefan answers. "It is part of a building push. Each day more travelers enter Korynth, and many of them find the sea air agrees with them. We are working to accommodate."

I nod. "It's a remarkable city."

Stefan smiles, but quickly stiffens. "I suppose you prefer ancient cities with opal-flecked streets and gray stone buildings, with statues and plaques dedicated to the heroes who came before you?"

I should search my mind for something demure and Wilha-like to say. But in Stefan's liquid brown eyes, there's a spark of interest I haven't seen since our night in the kitchen. "Oh, I don't know," I say. "What if I prefer a newer city, where I might one day have a plaque dedicated to me?"

"Really?" A smile plays about Stefan's lips. "And what might that plaque say?"

"Look!" Ruby points to a crowd that has begun lining the streets. Several men and women call out their greetings. A few throw herbs and wildflowers and beg for a glimpse of the Masked Princess.

The carriage slows and comes to a stop. A guard's face appears at the window and says, "Your Highness?"

"Yes, Bogdon?" Stefan answers.

"We've been given a gift." He holds up a loaf of bread. "It came from a bakery nearby."

"It smells wonderful," Ruby says, reaching her hands out. "Can I have it?"

"You know what Grandmother says," Leandra admonishes. "You never eat anything that has not been tasted first."

"Shall we visit the bakery?" I ask Stefan.

"Why would we do that?" He frowns.

I roll my eyes. "So you can thank your subject for the nice gift. Or are you only capable of mustering up gratitude toward rich Kyrenican nobles?"

"That is not at all what I meant," Stefan replies, looking offended. "I only meant that it is difficult for the guards when—Oh, all right. Have it your way. Bogdon, please tell the guards we wish to visit the bakery."

The guards form a line that pushes the crowd backward, and several onlookers call out to us. I reach to open the carriage door, but Stefan grabs my hand.

"We do not exit the carriage until the guards signal that it is safe to do so. Surely it is the same in Galandria?" A strange expression crosses his face, and his hand tightens protectively on mine. "If something were to happen to you"—he says and then glances at Ruby and Leandra, who both stare at us with rapt expressions—"then . . . our kingdoms would most probably go to war," he finishes lamely.

"Of course." I snatch my hand away from his. "We can't

have that, can we?" I stare out the window, my heart thudding in my chest.

Bogdon signals to Stefan that it's safe for us to exit. Ruby scampers out of the carriage, followed by Leandra, and then Stefan, who turns and extends his hand.

"My Lady?" he says with exaggerated politeness.

"I don't need your help," I say, moving past him. "I doubt our kingdoms will go to war if you don't assist me."

From behind I hear him exhale loudly. "You are the strangest princess I have ever met."

Bogdon directs us to a small bakery. Inside are baskets filled with fresh-baked bread smelling of herbs. Behind a counter, an elderly man kneads a mound of dough over a flour-coated countertop.

"Be with you in a minute," he calls. A second later he looks up and his eyes widen.

"Your Highnesses." He comes out from around the counter and sinks to one knee. "I am honored you would come to my humble shop."

"We have come to thank you for your gift," Stefan answers. "My bride-to-be declares it the best bread she has ever tasted."

I glance warily over at Stefan, who shrugs and grins.

"Indeed," I add, "your loaf of bread is the first sincere gift I've received since arriving in Kyrenica." I make a point of running my hand over the bracelet Stefan gave me.

"Oh, Princess, please don't joke with an old man." The

baker's head is lowered, so he doesn't see Stefan flush.

"I've always wanted to learn how to bake bread," Ruby says to me and Stefan. "But Cook won't let me near the kitchen."

The baker hears, and with a delighted smile offers to give us a lesson. He stands and gestures to the back of the shop. Before I can join the others, Bogdon enters and addresses me. "Excuse me, Princess, but we have just received another gift. This one is specifically for you."

"Really, what is it?"

"An embroidered handkerchief and a book. The girl who gave it to me said it was for the Masked Princess." He holds up a thick brown leather volume, and my heart begins to pound. "It appears to be an old history book about Eleanor Andewyn," he says. "She said she was staying at the Sleeping Dragon, the inn next door, if you wished to speak to her."

CHAPTER 46

WILHA

The inn is mostly deserted except for James who walked back with me. Everyone, including Victor, has gone outside to gawk at the royal family.

"I don't understand why we had to drop everything just because some barbaric princess has finally decided to come down from her balcony and grace us with her presence," he says.

Upon seeing the hurt expression in his eyes, I ignore the slur and reach out a hand. "I was having a good time, James, I only—"

The door opens, and two guards stride in. Outside the window, several other guards have formed a line in front of the inn, preventing anyone from entering. Victor is shaking hands with one of the guards, and I remember that he used to be a soldier.

One guard ducks his head into the kitchen, then strides upstairs, while the second one addresses me, "Are you the young lady who gave the princess a book?"

I nod. "I am."

"The princess appreciated your gift and has decided she would like to meet with you. He turns a dispassionate gaze upon James. "In private."

James glares at the guard. Without a word, he stalks outside.

I wish I could go after him and explain, but Elara's visit to the city is not something I can ignore. I insisted we return to the inn, and hoped that an opportunity to contact her—to find out what is really going on inside the castle—would present itself.

And when I heard that their carriage pulled up at the bakery next to the Sleeping Dragon, it did.

The first guard returns and says, "The kitchen and upstairs are all clear, Bogdon." The two guards leave, and soon I hear Elara's voice speaking outside.

"I'm growing a bit tired and should like to rest in here while the crown prince and the princesses finish in the bakery. As this girl has shown herself to be a lover of history, I feel I may have found a kindred soul and should like to take tea with her. Could you wait outside with the other guards? I'd like to speak of things not proper for men to hear. . . ."

"Yes, Your Highness."

Elara enters the inn by herself. She wears the painted white mask with lavender opals and a lavender gown. Her hair is tied back in purple ribbons, and a thick jeweled bracelet I don't recognize is clasped at her wrist.

Standing so close to her, I think I now understand why it seemed so difficult for people to know me. With the painted mask and all the jewels, it is a little like staring at a ghostly doll come to life.

"You look well," I say, holding out her satchel. "You seem

to have adjusted rather quickly to being a princess."

"I haven't had a choice, have I?" she snaps, dropping her formal tone and snatching the satchel. She grabs my arm. "Come away from the window. Are you mad, declaring yourself like that? He's seen my face."

"I'm sorry. I only meant to—" I stop, as the rest of her words register. "*Who* has seen your face?"

"Stefan. And a couple of Kyrenican guards, though neither of them are here now."

"So then . . . the crown prince knows who you are?" I pause and swallow. I cannot bring myself to ask my other question. *Just how angry is he?*

Elara looks at me, blinking. "Has the ocean air addled your brain? He thinks I'm *you*, obviously."

"How can that be? Garwyn and the other guards in the city are searching for me." I pause. "I thought you sent them after me."

"No, they're searching for *me*," she says with a harsh look in her eyes. "Ezebo sent them after he heard how *your maid* escaped into the city. Lord Quinlan arrived a few days ago in Korynth and added a few of his men to the search." She laughs bitterly. "He said I'm a threat to the monarchy and can't be allowed to wander the streets."

"But that can't be right," I say. "Garwyn and—"

"Oh, what does it matter?" Elara glances outside. "We haven't much time. I can't do this much longer, Wilha. I can't be you. If you don't want to be you, that's your choice. But I can't go on pretending. Stefan is already suspicious. Sooner or later he is going to catch me in a lie."

"What is he like?" I can't help but ask. "Prince Stefan, I mean."

"He's fine," she snaps, sounding annoyed. "But don't change the subject. This can't go on, Wilha. You need to decide what you want. Are you ever planning to return to the castle?"

"Do you want me to come back?" I ask. "I've seen you, on the balcony, and I've wondered if, well . . ." I don't finish the thought, but I think Elara understands what I mean.

"Why in the world would I ever want to be *you*?" Scorn drips from her words. "I'll ask you one last time, are you coming back?"

I glance out the window, at the crowd straining behind the line of guards, just waiting to catch a glimpse of Elara. Of me. I shake my head. Neither of us, really. They just want to see a girl in a mask and a beautiful dress. My gaze fixes on Elara's mask.

"I don't want to be her," I whisper. "I don't want to be the Masked Princess."

Elara's voice softens, but only a little. "That's not who you are."

"That is all anyone has ever cared about," I say.

"But that's not your real name. Do you know what Lord

Murcendor told me before we left Allegria? He said the king and queen didn't bother to name me before they sent me away." The mask cannot cover the brief flash of pain I read in her eyes. "At least you have a name."

"I'm sorry." I swallow. "That is unforgiveable."

Elara says nothing. She is waiting for me to make a decision.

"What if I say no?"

Her gaze narrows. "Then I'm leaving the first chance I get. But you know what will happen if the Masked Princess disappears."

I close my eyes and I hear my father's voice. *Be a good girl, Wilha. Be a good princess. Kingdoms need someone to believe in. Let them believe in you.*

"I will," I say in a hushed voice.

"What did you say?" comes Elara's irritated voice.

I open my eyes and look straight at her. "I said yes. I will switch back."

"When?" she asks. "I need a definite time. When can we switch back? Tonight?"

I think of all the orders we still have to fill at Galina's and how I promised her I would stay up all night sewing, if she would just let me sneak away for a picnic with James.

"Not tonight," I answer. "Tomorrow night, at the masquerade. It will be easiest to make the switch then."

"I'm assuming you can get into the castle through the

passageway?" she asks coolly.

I nod. "There is an entrance near the sea. I will enter the castle through there. Then I will find you, and we will switch back."

"How do I know you'll keep your word? How do I know you won't run away again?" Elara asks.

"I said I will be there," I answer, tamping down a flood of frustration. "I swear it."

"Good," she says crisply, gathering up her dress. "It's too bad I didn't know we would be meeting today," she adds. "Otherwise I would have brought your letter." Her voice is carefully casual.

"What letter?"

"From Patric," she says, and my heart quickens at the sound of his name. "He was your trainer, wasn't he? He sent you a letter; I have it in the castle." Elara looks at me, and I read the calculation in her eyes. "I guess you'll have to wait to read it until you return." She turns to leave. "Until the masquerade."

I nod and curtsy for the benefit of the guards in case they are watching through the windows. Elara opens the door. A gust of ocean air fills the room, along with the shouts and cheers of people calling out to the Masked Princess.

When the door closes again, I am left with nothing but a chilling silence.

PART THREE

"In later years it would be her deepest held belief that, had she acted sooner, the tragedy could have been avoided."

ELEANOR OF ANDEWYN HOUSE:
GALANDRIA'S GREATEST QUEEN

CHAPTER 47

ELARA

*H*ow do you say good-bye to a life that was never your own? What do you take with you, and what do you leave behind?

I spread a few trinkets out on my bed, including a seashell Ruby gave me and a ribbon from a merchant in the city. On the bed too, are my dagger and the book from my mother.

I pick up the book and turn it over. Whenever I think of my mother it is still the vague image of a red-haired woman that I picture. Not Astrid the Regal. I can't bring myself to think of her as anything more than the dead queen who refused to name me.

I open the book and flip through a few pages. I can't help but wonder, if Eleanor Andewyn hadn't discovered Galandria's opals so many centuries ago, hadn't dropped the First Opal on her coronation day and it hadn't split in two, where would I be right now, at this very minute?

If Wilha and I had been born into any other family—one who viewed twins as a blessing, instead of a curse—how different would our lives have been?

As I continue examining the book, I notice something I haven't before. In the middle of the book, a few of the pages have been punctured with tiny pin pricks. How did I miss this before? It's almost as though someone deliberately—

"Your Highness?" interrupts Milly's voice from the sitting room. She knocks on my door. "I'm here to help you get ready for the masquerade. It's getting a bit late."

"I'll be right there," I call out to her.

Quickly, I shut the book and toss it onto the writing desk. Let Wilha—the favored twin—keep it. I tuck Ruby's seashell and my dagger into my satchel, along with the jewels I ripped from Wilha's dresses. I still plan to use them to start a new life. Whatever and wherever that will be.

When I'm finished, I open the wardrobe and pull out a blue velvet box. It's a new mask from Welkin, the betrothal present Lord Royce brought with him to Korynth. I open the box and examine the painted white mask encrusted with opals in shades of iridescent, powder blue and milky lavender, the colors of the Andewyn family. When I lift the mask, the opals catch the candlelight and seem to sparkle.

"Your Highness?" Milly knocks again. "May I come in?"

"Just a moment." I tie the mask on. Only a few more hours of pretending, and this will all be over.

∙◆∙

"*Y*ou look stunning, Your Highness," Milly says, holding up a small mirror.

A princess in an opal mask stares back at me. Wilha's silken birthday gown is a light, iridescent blue with a square neckline and draped sleeves. Stitched into the bodice and full skirt are lavender opals and bright, sparkling jewels.

A loud knock sounds at the door and Ruby bursts into the room, with Leandra following closely behind. Both of them are wearing silver masks and scarlet and black colored gowns, the colors of the Strassburg family.

Ruby twirls around, her skirt billowing like a bell. "How do I look, Wilha!"

"Girls," Genevieve says as she strides into the room behind them carrying a black box. "I'm trying to decide which of your great grandmother's rings we should wear tonight."

Ruby and Leandra turn back and bend their heads over the box. I stay where I am, until Genevieve says, "What are you waiting for? Come and pick some out."

I frown. "Oh, but I thought you only meant Leandra and Ruby. . . ."

"Nonsense. You are part of this family now, too." She grins conspiratorially. "Besides, it will quite annoy Eudora to see you wearing them."

I grin back at her. "Thank you." It's all I can say, because my throat is suddenly thick. I join Leandra and Ruby and we ooh and ahh over the rings. I settle on a gold one with a large sapphire.

"You're being too shy," Genevieve says. "You can wear more than one ring, Wilha. We can all sparkle together tonight."

And the moment bursts. Once she calls me "Wilha," I am

reminded that this is not my family, this is not my life.

"Now, girls," Genevieve says when we've all finished with the rings, "it is time you went down to the great hall. The doors are about to open and your father and I want you to greet the guests with us. Wilha will be announced later, after everyone arrives. Milly, will you escort them to the hall please?" Milly nods, and after they're gone Genevieve turns back to me. "You were given instructions, yes? King Ezebo wishes you to enter from the balcony that overlooks the great hall."

I nod. "He sent Sir Reinhold earlier to inform me."

"Good." Genevieve smiles. "You look beautiful, Wilha. Tonight, all eyes will be on you."

CHAPTER 48

WILHA

As I wrap the black cloak I borrowed from the dress shop around myself, I try to think of an explanation to give James and Victor for why I have to leave. Although I cannot tell them the truth, I can at least give them the comfort of knowing I am safe. Because once I make the switch with Elara, "Willie" will be gone forever, and come the next morning, I don't want them worrying about me. *My family has need of me, and I have to return immediately*, I compose the explanation in my mind.

It won't even be a lie.

I pick up the white and silver costume mask Kyra found for me to wear tonight and look around my room one last time, trying to capture the image in my mind. Perhaps one day, years from now, I will laugh at my adventure in the city, and it will not seem quite so painful, as it does now.

Downstairs, the inn is full and festive. Several customers wear costume masks and carry candles. According to town gossip, the Masked Princess is supposed to appear on the balcony at midnight while fireworks ignite over the castle. A gift from King Ezebo to those who were not invited to the masquerade.

It is with bitter irony that I realize the girl waving to the crowd tonight will be me.

"All set to go?" James asks when he sees me. Kyra told him we were meeting at the castle gates to pass the time until midnight.

"Yes," I say, and then surprise him by reaching out and hugging him tightly.

He hugs me in return and whispers, "I'll see if I can get Victor to let me off early, and I'll come meet you and Kyra."

I will myself to say the words, to tell him that I won't be joining Kyra at the gates after all. Yet as usual, my voice fails me and I keep hugging him, not wanting to let go.

"I'll be there as soon as I can," James says when we finally break apart.

I nod, ashamed of my own cowardice. With one last wave, I step outside the inn and close the door on one life. With a sigh, I tie on my costume mask, and once again, the world becomes a little smaller.

I step out into the night and head toward another life, the one I have been marked for since birth.

CHAPTER 49

ELARA

A guard pushes open the wooden doors and ushers me out to the balcony, which overlooks the party. The great hall shines; hundreds of lit candles hang from newly polished silver chandeliers. The wooden floors have been scrubbed and waxed until they glow like honey. A fire dances in the large hearth. Red and black banners of the Strassburg family crest alternate along the walls with Andewyn ones of powder blue and lavender.

Down below, the entire royal family is seated on the dais. Ladies dressed in vibrantly colored gowns twirl about the dance floor on the arms of elegantly styled men with all their faces hidden under masks. Some of the masks are decorated with jewels or sequins and bits of glass that glitter in the candlelight. Other masks are the faces of monsters and beasts bearing expressions of agony.

Near the staircase leading to the dance floor below, a man wearing a mask of silver, black, and crimson waves at me, and it takes me a moment to realize it's Stefan.

"I didn't recognize you at first." I laugh.

"No one could mistake who you are," he says, bowing deep. "You are beautiful." He steps closer. "Though you would be even more beautiful if you were not wearing your mask."

I struggle to keep my smile in place. I know he's probably only being polite for the benefit of the soldiers and servants behind us, but my heart constricts at his words anyway.

"May I present Their Royal Highnesses Princess Wilhamina Andewyn of Galandria and Crown Prince Stefan Strassburg," calls out a page.

The music halts, the dancing stops, and a hush falls over the crowd as everyone stares at us. King Ezebo rises from his seat on the dais and begins to clap. The rest of the royal family—except for Eudora, who remains stubbornly seated—follows suit and soon the ballroom is filled with thunderous applause. It's dizzying, listening to them all cheer for me.

Not for you, I remind myself. *For Wilhamina.*

Stefan bows to me again. "Ready to meet your public?"

I take the hand he offers. "I'm ready."

He gives my hand a small squeeze, and together we descend into the colorful crowd below.

CHAPTER 50

WILHA

Night has fallen at the ocean. An iridescent ribbon of moonlight spools across the Lonesome Sea and the tide has begun to rise. I step over jagged rocks, gasping when a wave rolls in and icy water seeps through my borrowed slippers. When I reach the moss-covered stone steps cut into the cliff, I hike up my skirt and begin climbing.

I haven't gotten very far when I hear voices coming from down the beach. I stop and duck down behind a boulder. The voices grow closer, and it sounds as though two men are fighting.

"We won't be caught—the entire city is focused on the masquerade. I've been given our orders. We are to wait here until the signal is given. When will your men arrive?"

With a start, I realize the voice sounds familiar. I chance a look over the boulder and see that it is Garwyn, along with Moran and the rest of the Galandrian guards. Garwyn is talking to Anton and Jaromil.

"In a moment," Anton answers tersely. "They'll be here soon."

"What is the signal?" asks Jaromil.

"At midnight, when the castle lets off fireworks, we are to begin. We are to start here, on the southernmost dock and spread out and work our way west. Tomorrow, Kyrenica will wake to a city burned."

"I still don't see how that will spark war," Anton says.

"It will when they see the Galandrian banners we'll leave in our wake. And if that isn't enough, he has something else planned."

Anton says something else, but his voice is low. I stand up cautiously to hear better.

". . . Don't know how, exactly," Garwyn is answering. "Someone in the castle could be working for him. Or maybe he plans to do it himself. But after tonight the crown prince will need to find himself a new bride."

After this there is silence, and I see the dim profiles of Anton and Jaromil turn to each other. "Does that mean . . . ?" Jaromil asks.

"Yes, slain on the very night of her own welcoming party. When Galandria gets word of it, they'll be chomping at the bit to go to war. And when Kyrenica realizes Galandria is responsible for the burning of their capital, they'll be all too eager to meet them."

"Never wanted a peace treaty in the first place," Jaromil says. "Your master, whoever he is, is a wretched bastard—a man after my own heart."

Horror washes over me and I duck down behind the boulder, putting a hand to my mouth to keep from crying out. It is possible that Anton and Jaromil are involved with illegal trading, and that Garwyn and his guards have been searching for me—but that is not what they have been recruiting men for.

They have been to help push Galandria and Kyrenica into war.

And I watched them do it. All the time they spent in the inn plotting, I watched them and did nothing. Not even when I was sure I read evil in their expressions. All I did was hide when I thought it was me they were coming for.

As a result, the entire city will burn, and Elara may be in danger this very moment. While I don't understand everything they have just said, I know that someone in the castle wants the Masked Princess dead.

All this time the mask was to protect Elara and me from people who would seek to use us to destroy our kingdom. The same type of people who will assassinate Elara tonight.

Unless I stop them.

Without hesitation, I rise and quietly begin climbing, hopeful that the men, draped in darkness and preoccupied with their evil schemes, won't notice me.

CHAPTER 51

ELARA

Wilha is everywhere, but nowhere.

When I glimpse a girl lurking near the fireplace wearing a mask shaped like a dragon's head, I'm certain it's her. Then I suspect she is the girl in the blue and green mask with peacock feathers who lingers by the platters of food, but never eats. After that, I'm positive she is the girl in the wolf mask standing quietly by the window.

But none of these girls turn out to be Wilha when I approach them.

Through it all, as I exchange pleasantries with noblemen and compliment noblewomen on their beautiful dresses, I expect a tap on the shoulder, a nudge in the ribs—some signal to let me know she has arrived and is ready to switch back. But as the night wears on, there's nothing. Where is she?

When Ezebo asks me to dance a waltz and everyone turns to stare, I wonder if she's here, biding her time. Hiding behind a mask and watching me, but saying nothing. Just as Lord Royce has done.

All evening, he's stood to the side of the room, near the orchestra, watching me. Of all the masks in the room, his is the most unusual. It is white and plain and completely un-adorned, almost as though he has no face at all.

But Lord Murcendor and Lord Quinlan have not been so content to stay in the background. Both of them have hovered just at the edges of the crowd surrounding me, both seemingly intent to catch my eye. It's been a complicated dance to avoid them all night, but a worthwhile one.

Wilha can speak to the Guardians after we switch back. I've had enough of them to last a lifetime.

After I finish dancing with Ezebo I stride over to the dais, hoping that with a better vantage point I'll be able to spot Wilha. Instead I find Ruby, standing alone, tears streaming down her face.

"Ruby, what's wrong?"

Ruby turns and presses herself to my side. "I went to give Grandmother a hug and I accidentally spilled her drink on her. She yelled at me and told me I will never make a good princess."

I look around the room, searching for Genevieve. Stefan, I notice with a flash of irritation, is surrounded by a group of giggly noblegirls. Again.

"Where is your mother?"

"She and Leandra accompanied Grandmother to her chambers so she could change into another gown," Ruby says through muffled sobs. "They were trying to calm her down."

I hug Ruby. As fond as I've grown of Genevieve and the rest of the Strassburgs, it's ridiculous the way they allow Eudora to push them all around.

Or maybe I'm the ridiculous one. Maybe it's the royal

way to let Eudora, as the eldest, spill her vitriol everywhere, regardless of who she hurts in the process.

But watching Ruby cry, I'm reminded of when I finally understood that even if I couldn't walk away from Mistress Ogden and the abuse she hurled my way, I didn't have to *hear* her, either. That was the day I shut my ears and started feeding her words to my imaginary kitten.

"And then Grandmother said—"

"—Your grandmother is an idiot," I interrupt, and Ruby's mouth drops open. "Ruby, listen to me." I crouch down so I am level with her. "When she speaks to you, I want you to nod, smile politely—and then dismiss every single thing she says. Your grandmother doesn't have an ounce of sense or kindness in her. Do you understand?" Ruby nods, and I continue. "Have you ever noticed how her neck wiggles when she speaks, kind of like a turkey?"

"I guess," Ruby says, hiccupping.

"Next time she yells at you, I want you to look at her neck and picture her as an oversized turkey. Gobble gobble. All right?"

Ruby's lips quirk with an impish grin. "Gobble gobble."

A waiter interrupts us and offers appetizers from a platter piled high with grapes and olives and figs. My eyes stray to the dance floor, and I see a girl wearing a dark cloak with her hood flipped up and a white and silver mask. She stands alone in the center of the dance floor watching us. Then she turns and strides from the room.

This is it. Time to go.

All of a sudden, it seems too fast. And the worst of it is I can't say good-bye to any of them, not even Stefan. They will never even know that "I" ever existed.

I hug Ruby tightly, and with one last smile, I step down from the dais and walk quickly through the crowd, passing Lord Royce, who's left his spot in the corner and is speaking intently with Sir Reinhold.

Outside in the foyer, the girl is standing in a dark corner under a portrait of Genevieve and Ezebo. But she's not Wilha, and she's clearly not alone. She is locked in a passionate embrace with one of the waiters, the one who just offered Ruby and me appetizers.

"Princess," she gasps when she sees me, and they immediately spring apart. "I'm so sorry. We didn't see you standing there."

The waiter utters an apology and hurriedly straightens his clothes.

"Please, Princess," the girl begs. "My father is determined to marry me into a good family. He would be so angry if he knew. . . ." Her eyes dart to the waiter, and she swallows nervously.

"Of course. Your secret is safe with me," I say, feeling like a dim-witted fool.

The girl smiles and curtsies. "Thank you, Princess. We were just about to get some fresh air." She pulls him away and they disappear into the shadows.

I linger in the foyer, gazing up at the portrait of Genevieve and Ezebo, and mentally catalog everything I'd like to tell Wilha, if I had the time. *Don't let Eudora push you around. Leandra is annoying, but means well. Genevieve is determined to like you and will make a good confidante. And Stefan is . . .*

A soft touch on my shoulder snaps me out of my reverie.

It's about time. I turn around, but again, it's not Wilha.

It's Lord Quinlan and Lord Murcendor, and I curse myself for my own stupidity. I should have realized the moment I detached myself from the crowd they would find me.

Lord Murcendor's expression is hidden behind his checkered black and gold mask as he bows deeply. "Truly Wilha, you light up the world tonight. Would you do me the great honor of dancing with me?"

I hesitate, wishing Wilha were here. I'm still not sure I can fool Lord Murcendor. And what would his reaction be when he realizes I'm only Elara, and that Wilha is currently unaccounted for?

"Actually, Princess," Lord Quinlan says, stepping forward. "I wonder if I might have a word with you in private somewhere?"

I edge closer to Lord Quinlan, thankful to have an excuse to get away from Lord Murcendor.

"Of course," I say.

CHAPTER 52

WILHA

I am halfway up the cliff side when my cloak catches. I give it a yank and the fabric tears. Several pebbles cascade to the rocks below.

"What was that?" comes Moran's voice.

"Your imagination," says Garwyn.

"No, I think I saw a shadow. There, up beyond them boulders there," Moran insists, and I press myself to the cliff wall as tightly as I can, pebbles digging into my hands. "I saw something; I know it."

"This beach is said to be haunted," comes Jaromil's voice. "They say the ghost of Queen Rowan roams these cliffs. See that large rock in the water there? It's been named after her."

"Shut up, all of you, and go look for some dry wood," snaps Garwyn. "Get a fire going. That'll scare away your ghost."

The men grow quiet as they begin hunting and I dare not move, certain that at least one of them is watching the cliff for shadows. When I hear Garwyn tell the others they have found enough wood, I resume climbing, trying to be as quiet as possible. My arms are shaking from gripping the steps for so long, and my cloak and dress are damp and heavy, pulling me downward. I remind myself that if I have lifted twenty-pound swords, then I can climb a staircase.

With one last burst of exertion, I scramble up the last of the steps and collapse in a heap once I reach the safety of the cave.

My palms are stinging and my legs are aching. The knowledge that a hundred feet below sits several men who wish me dead makes me feel faint. Yet I force myself to my feet, peel off the heavy cloak, and find the wall, where I'm quickly presented with another problem. Clouds have rolled in, covering the light of the moon, and I can't find the embedded opal. I feel around frantically, scraping my hands against the sharp edges of rock, until I have to concede that I just can't find it.

I slump onto the wet sand, exhausted. Perhaps I was a fool to believe I could save Elara. For what match am I really, against whomever it is that has his hand set against me?

I picture the imaginary shadowy villain I used to duel against all those nights in the Opal Palace. Who wishes me dead? Do Garwyn and his men take orders from a Galandrian? Or does someone from Kyrenica now command them?

From somewhere below in the darkness the melody of a flute begins to play. Perhaps one of the guards is entertaining the others while they wait. It is a lonely, sad sound. And I wonder at the other sounds we shall hear in a few hours' time. The hiss of burning wood, the roar of leaping flames— the sparks to ignite a war. The mourning of the Kyrenican royal family (will they mourn?) when the Masked Princess is discovered dead.

Though she may never know it, Elara has saved me these last few weeks. She gave me the time to find out I am not quite as useless as I always believed. Where now, is the person who will save her?

As if in answer, the clouds slide away, revealing the moon, a silver coin in a midnight sky. Moonlight spills and rolls over itself, illuminating the cave with silvery-white light. But only for a moment.

Another cloud rolls in, obscuring the moon, and the cave is plunged into darkness once more. But in that instant, I saw a faint glimmer, higher up the wall than I remembered. I feel around for several more minutes, and the next time the clouds shift, uncloaking the moon, I am ready. There, I see it! I press my thumb to the embedded opal, and the chamber opens. I swallow back my fear, and rush into the darkness waiting beyond.

CHAPTER 53

ELARA

"What do you need to speak to me about?" I ask Lord Quinlan, and suppress a shiver. I'm grateful for the chance to be away from Lord Murcendor, but the deserted corridor he's led me to feels drafty. And staring at me from behind his goblin mask, Lord Quinlan looks much like an overgrown gargoyle.

He clears his throat and shifts uneasily. "Princess I—"

He is interrupted by echoing footsteps. "Wilha? What are you doing?"

Stefan removes his mask, and his eyes flick from me to Lord Quinlan in obvious irritation. "Is there a reason why you have trapped the princess in a dark corner?"

"I didn't *trap* her," Lord Quinlan retorts. "I was merely going to ask—in private—how she is getting on here in Kyrenica. The Guardians and I have hardly had a minute with her since arriving in the city. You and your father seem to be purposely keeping her away from us."

"I am sure the princess is *getting on* just fine. I am also sure there is nothing you need to say to her that requires spiriting her away from everyone else."

Lord Quinlan begins to protest, but Stefan cuts him off. "I will remind you, Lord Quinlan, that you are here solely at the invitation of my family, an invitation that can be revoked at any time if we see fit." He regards Lord Quinlan coolly and continues, "At any rate, please excuse us. I need a word alone with the princess."

Lord Quinlan hesitates, looking as though he is bursting to say something, but finally leaves.

"What did he want?" Stefan demands.

"I don't know. He said—" I break off when I see Stefan's scowl, and a delicious thought occurs to me. "Are you jealous?"

"Not remotely," he snaps. "But I don't trust your father's advisors and would rather you stay away from them. And I hardly think it is proper for you to be conversing in dark corners with another man."

"Proper?" I scoff. "You're a fine one to talk. You've been surrounded all night by silly noblegirls."

"I wouldn't be if you would stay by my side for longer than two minutes. You have been flitting around the hall all night. What is wrong?"

Everything. Everything in the whole world. "Nothing. Nothing's wrong."

Stefan stares at me for a moment longer. "Come on." He turns away. "I want to show you something." I follow him down the hall, up a staircase, and over to a window. "It is beautiful, isn't it?" Outside, beyond the castle gates, a large crowd waits. Most people carry lanterns and candles, making the street an ocean of light. Stefan turns to me. "Tell me what is going on," he says. "And please do not say 'nothing,' because I know something is troubling you."

I want to tell him I'm not the princess he's being forced to marry. That, really, I'm the servant girl he met in the kitchen, the girl he could easily laugh with. Though I guess I'm neither. Not really a servant, not really royalty. I'm nobody.

I guess if I could tell him just one thing, it would be good-bye.

When I hesitate too long, he sighs and turns away. "So many people out there," he says. "And they have all come to see you."

"They didn't come to see me," I mumble. "They came to see the Masked Princess."

"Why do you do that?" he asks. "Why do you refer to yourself as that?"

"Because I'm not the Masked Princess." I close my eyes and lean against the window. I'm tired of pretending. Where is Wilha? Has she changed her mind?

Stefan sighs. "I know."

My eyes fly open. "What?"

He takes my arm and his expression turns serious. "Let me take you to your room. There is something I want to discuss with you."

CHAPTER 54

ELARA

What is the penalty for impersonating royalty?

When we reach my chambers, Stefan gestures to an armchair and asks me to sit. While he lights candles and makes a fire, my heart races. How did I give myself away? What small detail did I miss? Was it the note I wrote to Genevieve? On a table near the door is my satchel, packed and ready to go. I contemplate making a run for it, but decide I wouldn't be fast enough. Not with the weight from my mask and dress.

When the fire is roaring, Stefan lowers himself into the chair next to me. "I have been wanting to speak with you."

"Yes?" I scoot forward, prepared to fall to my knees. There's no role I can play here, no golden words I can speak that will make this better. I've impersonated royalty. A forgivable offense when we were on the road and security was a concern. Now, my actions will only be seen as treasonous and self-serving. The only card I have left is to beg and plead for mercy.

I can only hope that Stefan will have some to offer.

He takes a deep breath, and blurts, "I wanted to ask for your forgiveness."

"I—what?" I ask, stunned. "You want to ask for *my* forgiveness?"

"Yes." He stands, and begins to pace in front of the fire. "I have been thinking about what you said yesterday, how that loaf of bread from the baker was the first sincere gift you received in Korynth. Such pointed words, and they found their mark. I want you to know that—"

"Wait," I interrupt. "Just to be clear, you're not mad at me for . . . anything?"

"No, of course not. I told you, I am trying to apologize," he says, sounding slightly annoyed.

"Oh." I lean back in my chair, feeling shaky with relief. "Okay then. Continue."

"Where was I?" He starts pacing again. "I have not welcomed you to the city properly. I know that. It is just that I thought I was being forced to marry a monster."

"Excuse me?" Irritation flares in my chest.

He holds up a hand. "Please, allow me to finish. I considered it little better than a death sentence to marry you—"

"A death sentence?" I repeat. "Stefan, if this is your idea of an apology, then—"

"You know, this would go a whole lot faster if you didn't insist on interrupting every two seconds."

"All right," I say, leaning back in my chair again. "But let me know when you get to the actual apology part."

He shoots me an incensed look and continues. "Try to understand. I have grown up hearing horrible things about the Andewyns, about all Galandrians. That they are liars, barbarians wrapped in fine clothing. That they are gluttonous and swollen with their own vanity. Blind to the fact that their glorious kingdom has begun to decline." He pauses. "You heard similar terrible things about Kyrenicans, did you not?"

"Dogs," I say hesitantly. "Many Galandrians refer to Kyrenicans as dogs—but not every Galandrian feels that way," I add hastily when his gaze narrows. "Just as I'm sure not every Kyrenican holds such harsh feelings toward Galandria."

Stefan nods. "I am sure you are right. But can you blame me, if I thought that you, the Masked Princess, the most famous girl in your kingdom—indeed, in the whole world—might be the worst of the whole lot? Monstrous, not in your appearance, but in your heart. Many princesses are spoiled. They have been told since birth that the world is theirs for the taking. And I confess, the thought of spending my life with a girl like that was distasteful. But now I realize I was wrong. You are not the Masked Princess, you are far more than that. You are a puzzle to me, unlike any girl I have ever met. And so"—he drops to his knees, reaches for my hands, and heat floods my chest—"I am asking for a second chance. Forgive me, please, for all my unkindnesses? I have been rude, and I am sorry. And I want to ask you, really and truly this time, will you marry me?"

"Yes." The answer tears from my lips, though I know it's not me he's asking, although how can he be asking Wilha, when he has never met her?

My thoughts are tangled, and suddenly, his face is moving

toward mine—until his nose bumps against my mask. He laughs and tilts his head and finally, his lips land on my own.

The kiss is soft and gentle, and my arms wind around his shoulders. I let myself be taken away by it, and when he draws back he says, "Will you take off your mask for me? I would love to see your face." His fingers are fumbling to untie my mask.

"I . . . can't, Stefan. Not now." I grab his hands and hold them. I want nothing else. I want to stay here and let him take off the mask and let him look at me. But not when I'm leaving. Not when it will be another girl's face he sees tomorrow.

"Then, will you do something else for me? Will you allow me another kiss?"

I nod. Wilha will get a lifetime with him. But this moment is mine, this is my good-bye.

He tilts his head. And when our lips touch again, I could swear I smell the sea.

The sea.

Where did Wilha say the passageway opened out to? It was the Lonesome Sea, I'm sure of it. Which means . . . my head snaps away from him, leaving Stefan looking confused.

"Is something wrong?" he says. "Did you not like it?"

"No," I answer. "I mean, yes, I did. But we have been away from the ball for quite a while." I smile. "Didn't you just say everyone came here to see me tonight? We don't want to disappoint them, do we?"

Stefan grins. "One day you will make a wonderful queen." He stands and pulls me to my feet. Then he crosses the room, opens the door, and holds it expectantly. "Come. Your public awaits you."

I turn and with one last glance around the room, I whisper, "I'll come back, I promise."

But my voice is so low, I doubt Wilha hears.

CHAPTER 55

WILHA

*B*ile rises to my throat as I watch them kiss. The words I was about to speak, of the danger Elara is in, of the men plotting by Rowan's Rock, die on my lips. I quickly duck back into the bedroom, thankful that they are too engrossed in each other to notice me. But the image of them kissing is burned into my mind.

It is as though I have seen a vision of my future.

What is she thinking, to have let Stefan come into her chambers? Is this supposed to be a signal of some sort? A declaration that she is not switching back?

I'm taking what I can and then I'm leaving, I remember her once saying. At the time, I thought she just meant jewelry. I did not realize she was also prepared to take pieces of my own life with her.

"Will you take off your mask for me?" The words are softly spoken, yet I still hear them. Words I have longed to hear all my life, but they are not spoken to me. Elara has done her job well. Too well. Because when the crown prince wakes up tomorrow morning and it is me wearing the mask, and not Elara, will he find me dull in comparison? Will he smile at me, but secretly wonder where the radiant girl he has fallen in love with has gone to?

"Come. Your public awaits you."

When I am certain they are gone, I creep into the sitting room and kneel by the hearth. The fire is beginning to die out, so I grab the poker, stew the embers, and add some more wood. I remove my costume mask and hold up my palms, trying to warm myself and thaw the chill that is seeping through me.

I inhale, and work at putting aside the dull ache in my chest. Regardless of what I have just seen, Elara still needs to be warned. The Kyrenican troops need to be alerted, all without anyone learning of the existence of another Andewyn princess.

A slight draft caresses my neck.

"Wilha?" comes a voice from behind.

The sudden noise startles me. But when I turn around, relief floods my chest. "Lord Murcendor." I rise to greet him.

He removes his checkered gold and black mask, and I see that he is paler than usual.

"Wilha?" he says, sounding slightly confused. "But I spoke with—" He stops as realization dawns on his face. "Elara is here, isn't she? She is posing as the Masked Princess."

I nod. "We were going to switch back tonight."

His eyes take in my dirty dress, tangled hair, and damp bodice. My cheeks grow warm when I read his unusual gaze, for he is looking at me in a way he never has before.

I tug at my dress uncomfortably and glance at the bedroom behind him. "You know of the passageway?" I ask, though of course I realize he must. Yet why he used it or has come here at all, I don't know. But I don't have time to wonder. "Can you help me, Lord Murcendor? I need to speak to King Ezebo without him knowing who I am. It is urgent."

"King Ezebo is beneath you," Lord Murcendor says. "He is unworthy to even stand in your presence."

"Even so, I must speak with him. Elara could be in danger at this very—"

"All will be made as it should," he says. "Please, sit down." He gestures to the chair behind me.

"I can't. Not until someone alerts King Ezebo." I am frantic now, wishing I could make him understand. "We have to find him."

I move for the door, but he reaches out and grabs my arm. "Sit down," he says with more force.

The image of Lord Murcendor seems to change. It is as though I have been unknowingly staring at him through a kaleidoscope for a long time, and suddenly, the pieces have shifted, forming a new picture. A suspicion is nagging at me, but I refuse to acknowledge it.

Instead I sit down, hoping with all my heart, that I am wrong.

CHAPTER 56

ELARA

We take our time walking back to the great hall. Stefan stops to speak with several Kyrenican nobles. As the night has worn on, the guests seem to have fanned out around the castle. I should be in more of a hurry to get back to my chambers, and back to Wilha, but Stefan's hand is warm in mine, and I don't want to pull away. Not yet.

When we reach the great hall, Stefan turns to me and bows. "Dance with me," he says.

I hesitate. Wilha made me wait for days before she decided to return to the castle. Why shouldn't I make her wait, just a little longer?

"Princess, may I have a word with you?" Lord Royce appears, and bows to Stefan. "That is, if you do not mind, Your Highness."

Stefan blows out an irritated breath. "If you must," he says shortly. To me, he says, "But before this night is over, we will dance."

I nod, and after Stefan has left I say, "Yes, Lord Royce?" All around us, masked figures spin and whirl, and I wonder if he is also going to ask me to dance.

"Are you quite sure you have no idea of your sister's whereabouts?" he asks, surprising me. He uses a casual tone of voice. But staring at his expressionless white mask, it feels as though this is some kind of test. We are game players, each holding tightly to our own hand.

So I decide to play an unexpected card.

"In truth, Lord Royce, I know exactly where she is." *She's upstairs, hiding.*

His ice blue eyes search my own. "Where?"

"I told King Ezebo and Lord Quinlan she stole my jewels, but that was a lie."

"A lie? That does not sound like you, *Wilha*." Is that a dare I see in his eyes?

"It was Elara's idea, of course. But the truth is, I gave her the jewels. She intended to book passage on a ship and sail east over the Lonesome Sea. We both believed it was best for everyone if she simply disappeared." The moment I speak the words, I decide that after I leave the castle, I'll head further north, up the Kyrenican coastline.

"That is a pity," Lord Royce counters. "There were things I could have told her. Things your mother wanted her to know, a message she intended Elara to have."

Finally, he's showed his hand. This is a dare, plain and simple: *Confess who you really are.* He's not convinced I'm Wilha, so he has set a trap. And my mother is the bait.

This is his mistake. I am not so easily caught.

"If I ever see her again, Lord Royce, I will let you know." I curtsy and turn my back on him.

CHAPTER 57

WILHA

*L*ord Murcendor gazes at me with his dark eyes. "It kills me to see you here in this castle, in the heart of the enemy."

"The Kyrenicans are not my enemy," I say carefully, thinking of James, Kyra, and Victor. "Some of them are quite nice, actually."

"The whole country is diseased," he hisses. "They are a plague, one that needs to be wiped out."

"Wiped out?" Ice creeps through my veins. "What do you mean?"

"Kyrenica has no right to exist, no right to the wealth that Galandria has worked so hard to obtain. If they persist in stealing from us, we have no choice but to send them back to the dust in which they came from."

A wave of nausea passes over me and my suspicion blooms into confirmation: Lord Murcendor, the man who taught me how to read when others were too scared to come near me, the man who sat with me in the Queen's Garden, and the man who has been the closest thing I have ever had to an actual father, is also the man who wants me dead.

"You are the one who is sending Lord Quinlan's men to burn the city down? The one who has come to kill me?" I add quietly.

A man in his right mind might reasonably ask *how* I know about his plans to burn Korynth, and when he does not, I realize he isn't.

He doesn't *look* to be in his right mind, either, not with the twisted grin he flashes. "They are Lord Quinlan's men in name only," he says. "But in every way that counts, they are my men and they have come, as many in Galandria have come, to see my point of view."

He pauses to stare at me. His eyes are unfocused and his hand looks ready to unsheathe his sword. Truly, he means to kill me.

My stomach roils. All this time, he is the shadowy villain I feared would one day come for me.

But you have beaten him a thousand times before, in your own imagination. The thought comes from nowhere. The ice in my veins seems to melt and is replaced by something else.

Fire.

Does he think I will merely sit still while the tip of his sword pierces my flesh? Does he imagine I will be the good princess I have been trained to be, right up until the very end, too obedient to even raise a weapon in my own defense?

When you are facing an opponent, never pay attention to his words, I remember Patric once saying. *Use them to your own advantage if you can, but your attention should be focused only on his weapon.*

My eyes stray to the fire behind Lord Murcendor—and the fire poker lying right next to my white and silver costume mask.

"This point of view you speak of," I say suddenly, "the one you say Lord Quinlan's men have come to share. What is it?"

Lord Murcendor begins to pace about the room, his hand twitching at the hilt of his sword. "I have spent my life serving the Andewyns. Indeed, as a boy I could see no distinction between the two. By serving the descendants of Queen Eleanor herself, the greatest ruler this world has ever known, I thought I served my truest and only love, Galandria. Yet there comes a time when a boy's fanciful illusions must collide with the crushing weight of reality. Despite my devotion, it became clear to me that your blood—the Andewyn blood—had become watered down. Diluted by generations of weak men and women, who made even weaker monarchs. And I began to understand that something had to be done to restore the glorious kingdom that once was Galandria."

While he speaks, I lower myself to the floor and raise my palms, as though I am warming myself. The fire poker is only inches from me. I glance over at Lord Murcendor. His hands are no longer at his side; he is raking them through his hair.

"And then," he continues, "destiny gave me a most precious gift: your mask. Despite your father's incompetence as a ruler, his one stroke of genius was to place that mask upon your face, for through the rumors and intrigue of the Masked

Princess, a semblance of Galandria's glory and fame was restored. Peasants from around the world make pilgrimages to see you. Do you know what that alone has done for our treasury? You can imagine my shock and surprise when your father decided to throw it all away. To throw *you* away by betrothing you to the Kyrenicans, all to avoid a war he is too much of a coward to fight. A war we are sure to win. To lose you is to lose our kingdom's glory. And I was not going to stand for it. Kings have a way of being persuaded . . . or being assassinated." He gives a terrifying, twisted grin.

"You?" I gasp, forgetting about the fire poker. "You were behind the attack in Eleanor Square?"

"My men were ordered not to kill anyone in the royal family, merely to injure. And educate. I had thought with the king injured, with the evidence of Kyrenica's wickedness on display for all to see, the Guardians would come to reason and cancel the treaty. But I underestimated their stupidity. They would rather believe that Lord Finley's men were responsible, even though we had captured most of them by the time of the attack. And so, when it was determined that you were still to go to Kyrenica, I made a decision."

Pay no attention to his words, I remind myself and inch closer to the fire. "And what was your decision?"

"Surely you did not think I would allow the Kyrenicans— those diseased, filthy dogs—to have you? No, I would rather see you dead than married to a dog. Your sacrifice was almost too high a price, yet I considered it a testament to my faithfulness that I was willing to pay it. And so, I decided the Masked Princess would have to die—at the masquerade, murdered in the Strassburgs' own castle. My men were tasked with recruiting Kyrenicans. Worthless as they are, I knew if we paid them enough, we could hire them to burn their own capital down. It would have both Kyrenica and Galandria clamoring for war, and your father and King Ezebo would finally be forced to act."

His gaze strays from my face and travels down my dress. "Though perhaps, when the city burns, Kyrenica will finally rise up, and I will not have to part with you after all."

"What do you mean?" My hand closes around the poker. I raise it and stir the embers of the fire, my arm shaking.

"Seeing you now, ripening into a beautiful woman, I wonder if I have been too quick to deprive myself." He crouches down next to me, his long hair drapes over my shoulder, and his fingers graze my cheek. "Perhaps the Masked Princess does not have to die in the castle. Perhaps, instead her dear advisor saves her from being assassinated by a Kyrenican soldier." He leans close and whispers, "And the Masked Princess, moved by his devotion, insists upon marrying him." His hand travels up my arm and revulsion slides down my spine as he brings his lips to my cheek.

"No," I say, clutching the fire poker. I spin away from him and jump to my feet. I have made it around the armchairs, but he moves faster than I anticipated and blocks the door.

"What did you say?" His eyes narrow.

"I said no." I raise the fire poker. It is not nearly as sturdy as a sword, but it will have to do.

"Now Wilha, what do you think you are doing? Be reasonable. Be a good girl, and put that down."

"No." I move into position, just as Patric taught me.

He looks at the poker and seems to be amused. "This is supposed to be your makeshift sword? You're not even holding it correctly. You should have paid more attention during your lessons."

I ignore his words and instead watch his body. His feet have turned sideways. His hands are at his sides, but it does not look as though he means to draw his sword. Perhaps he doesn't consider me enough of a threat?

Just as he lunges to my right, I quickly slide to my left.

"Why so jumpy, Princess?" His grin has vanished, and he doesn't seem amused now. "Put that down. In less than an hour's time, Korynth is going to burn. You cannot stop that. But you can save your own life."

I shake my head. "I would never marry you."

He cocks his head. "You would marry a Kyrenican dog before you would marry me?" There's a dangerous edge to his question.

"I thought you were my friend," I answer. "You have always been my friend."

"Indeed, I have been the greatest friend the House of Andewyn has ever had, and I have served her truly. Now, it is time the Andewyns serve me."

He lunges right, but I had read his intention, and slip out of his grasp.

"Wilha, I cannot allow you to marry a Kyrenican." He extends his hand. "But I can offer you a good life with me. A life befitting who you are."

I shake my head and keep the poker pointed at him, trying not to be distracted by his words. "No."

"Then," he says, his voice quiet with resignation, "you will have to die."

He draws his sword and lunges. I block him once, and then twice, but far too late, I realize Patric was right. I never learned how to properly attack. The minute I advance toward Lord Murcendor, he knocks the fire poker from my hands. Then he grabs my arm and forces me to my knees.

"It doesn't have to be like this," he says, and presses the tip of his sword to my throat. "After all these years that I have cared for you, it is destiny that we should be together."

I don't have the strength or the skill to beat him. But I do have the power to say no. The power to die on my own terms, instead of living on his.

"No," I say.

He presses the blade deeper to my throat. I feel a sharp flash of pain, and a warm trickle slides down my neck.

There is a strange buzzing in my ears. Lord Murcendor stares at me, his eyes darkening with desire, his lips slightly parted, and I imagine he is looking at me—at the Glory of Galandria—one last time before he kills me.

In the end, my family's wealth was not enough to stand between me and the blade we all hoped would never come. So many times I have wondered if the queens of Galandria past, though long dead, could somehow see me. And if they have watched over me, have they been pleased with the life I have lived? And when I pass into their realm, will they welcome me as a fellow Andewyn traveler? Or will they deem me weak, and unworthy of them?

Lord Murcendor raises his sword above my chest. The room starts to spin, and the buzzing grows louder. Behind him, in a swirl of iridescent powder blue, I see a hazy shape grabbing the satchel off the table.

"History," Lord Murcendor says, breathing heavily, "will judge me as the man who restored glory back to Galandria."

Just as he begins to lower his blade, his features contort and his face whitens.

"History," comes Elara's voice, "will judge you as a madman." She raises a dagger coated with wet blood and stabs him—for the second time, I think—and Lord Murcendor falls away, striking his head on the table.

CHAPTER 58

ELARA

I just killed a man.

The words pound in my brain, insistent like a hammer. I just killed a man. I stabbed him with my dagger when his back was turned. The knowledge sends me to my knees, and I clamp my hands over my ears.

"Elara? Elara, are you all right?" Wilha is at my side, though she seems far away, and I stare at her through the black spots that dance before my eyes. She is damp and dirty and smells like the sea. *"Elara, take a few deep breaths and listen to me."*

I just killed a man. I'm floating away, being carried along by the wave of dancing black spots that beckon me into the darkness.

"Elara, I need you. I need you to stay with me." Her voice is soft and warm. I reach out and tether myself to it like a child clutching a kite.

I watch Wilha, seemingly quite calm. She steps over Lord Murcendor and pours a cup of tea from a silver pot, and thrusts it into my hands. *"Drink this, Elara. There is something I need to tell you. . . ."*

"I killed him." I can hear my voice, but it doesn't sound like my own.

Wilha is bending over Lord Murcendor. *"I don't think he is dead. . . . It is difficult to tell with his cloak. But his wound doesn't appear to be very deep. Perhaps he is unconscious from hitting his head?"*

I sip the tea and slowly feel the wave turn. It carries me away from the darkness and back toward Wilha. The black spots dissolve, and strength returns to my arms and legs.

She grabs my arm and gives me a shake, "Elara, I need you to listen. Lord Murcendor is not the worst of our problems."

"What?" I look at Wilha straight on, and realize that despite her calm voice, she looks panicked. "What do you mean?"

Wilha takes a deep breath. "He is planning to burn the city."

⌘

All of those old buildings. So flammable. So easily destroyed. That's all I can think of once Wilha finishes relaying the conversation she overhead.

"The city will burn fast," I say.

"What do we do?" She turns questioning eyes on me, and I realize this is my problem to solve. She has carried the message, but the decision to act must come from me.

"When did you say they were to start?"

"At midnight, when the fireworks begin."

I look at the clock above the fireplace. "That's less than an hour from now. Stefan must be told so he can send guards to the docks, but the streets are packed with people and carriages," I say, thinking fast. "You said the passageway leads directly to the beach by Rowan's Rock, and that the men are camped out near there?"

Wilha nods. A plan is beginning to form and I start calculating how little time we have if we are to prevent the city from burning.

I finish the last of the tea and stand up. "I'm going to alert Stefan. You'll be okay here alone?"

Wilha hesitates, glances at Lord Murcendor's body, and nods.

"Good. Have the passageway open and torches lit when I come back."

⚬✧⚬

The great hall has the air of a good party which has nearly reached its end. Candles burn low in the chandeliers and tired laughter mixes with the opening strains of a waltz. Many of the partygoers have removed their masks. Their once-crisp appearances are now rumpled and wilted.

"Finally you come!" Stefan says gaily, detaching himself from a group of men. His eyes stray to my mouth, and I can tell he's thinking of our last kiss. "Now we shall have our dance." He leads me to the dance floor, too merry to hear me protest. He pulls me close and whirls me around. "This is where you belong," he says, beaming.

I can feel everyone's eyes on us, so I smile brightly. Causing panic will not serve my purpose.

As we dance, I stand on my tiptoes and bring my lips to his ear, as though I want nothing more than to whisper sweet nothings. "Stefan, you must listen and listen well," I say, keeping my smile in place. "A handful of men are camped out near Rowan's Rock. They plan to set fire to the city at midnight. It is their intention that by destroying Korynth, they will force Kyrenica and Galandria into war."

Stefan goes rigid. He glances quickly about the room and continues dancing, his arms tightening around me. "And you came by this information, how?"

I hesitate. "It was Lord Murcendor who told me. The men are acting on his orders. His actions are in no way sanctioned by King Fennrick—by my father," I force myself to say. "Lord Murcendor is unwell, he tried to attack Wil—me—and—"

Stefan stops dancing. "He *attacked* you? Where is he? If he has harmed you in any way, then I swear I will—"

"That won't be necessary," I interrupt. "He's dead."

Stefan steps back and stares at me with an appraising look. "Dead? How, exactly?"

"By my own hand," I snap impatiently, not caring that this in no way sounds like the actions of Wilhamina Andewyn.

"If he's dead, then where is his—"

"We can deal with him later! You need to send guards to the docks *now*, before it's too late."

He looks at me a moment longer before nodding. "I will alert the guards. Until this is over, I would like for you to return to your chambers."

I smile, in what I hope looks like serene obedience. "Of course, my lord. That is exactly what I planned to do."

CHAPTER 59

WILHA

I press my thumb to the embedded opal and the wall slides back. I grab a candle from a table and venture yet again into the passageway, and light the first two torches I come upon.

When I return to the bedroom, I slump to the ground and lean against the bed, my heart hammering in my chest.

By now James should have left the Sleeping Dragon and will be making his way to the castle gates, safely away from the docks. But what of Victor and Kyra? What of Galina? What of the hundreds of other people who live near the docks? People who may not have enough time to escape if the men are not stopped and the fire starts.

A fire started by men from my own kingdom, for the express purpose of pushing Galandria and Kyrenica into war. All these years, I have heard Kyrenicans called dogs. But now, more than anything, I find I just want to see them saved.

From the sitting room comes the sound of anguished moaning.

I freeze and my fingers move to my cheek, where Lord Murcendor tried to kiss me. My breath starts to come in ragged gasps.

Soft thuds sound from the sitting room, followed by the

click of a door opening, and then closing.

It is a while before I can make myself stand up and creep over to the sitting room. Yet when I do, I discover that the place where Lord Murcendor had laid is now empty, his abandoned sword the only evidence that he was ever in the room.

CHAPTER 60

ELARA

When I fling open the door to my chambers I find Wilha staring at the empty spot where Lord Murcendor's body should have been.

"Where did—I thought he was dead?"

"I never said he was dead," she replies, white-faced. "I said—"

"It doesn't matter. We'll deal with it later. Grab his sword, we'll need it." I hurry into the bedroom. Wilha follows behind me, carrying the weapon. The passageway is open and a gaping black hole beckons me. I grab a cloak and pull it around me.

"What exactly do you plan to do?" she asks as we step into the tunnel.

"We're going to try to buy the Kyrenican guards some time." I lift a torch from its mount in the passageway.

"How will we do that? We can't stop them all with just one sword. We are outnumbered, and they have more weapons."

"But we have words. And we have legends and rumors. Put them together, and you have the most powerful weapon in the world."

When the tunnel wall slides away, I'm greeted with a blast of fresh, icy air. Wilha points to the edge of the cave.

"The men are just below there, at the base of the cliff. When I left there were about ten of them with more due to arrive."

I hand her my torch and creep to the edge. Rowan's Rock rises up in the distance, proudly battling the tide. To the north, the docks are eerily quiet. Deserted sailboats are tethered to port, and they float quietly on the water, like ghost ships. From far away I hear the sounds of laughter and carousing. It seems that anyone who's still awake at this hour has moved to the west side of the city toward the castle.

Down below on the beach several men, about twenty in all, stand around a campfire and listen to another man that I believe is Garwyn. He carries a torch and seems to be giving instructions.

From the west I hear a screeching, whistling sound, followed by a loud *pop!* Fireworks are exploding in the sky. Facing away from the castle, I can't see them, but the men below turn toward the cliff to watch, and I draw back further into the cave. I don't want to draw their attention. Not yet.

"That was the signal for them to start," Wilha whispers urgently.

"I know."

I'm standing at the edge of a moment. The instant the first act of war is committed. Or the instant I prevent it.

Don't I know how one choice, one moment, can echo across time? Eleanor Andewyn dropped the First Opal. Aislinn Andewyn chose to betray her twin. The ripples of both these women's actions continue on today in my own life. And here now is another moment. A hundred years from now, how will it be remembered?

I think of the book Queen Astrid gave me. I still can't reconcile myself to the fact that I'm an Andewyn, but I can understand this: Maybe the book was intended to be more than a feeble parting gift from a mother who gave me away. Maybe in its truest sense she intended the book to be a guide, something to help me set the course of my days. In this moment, maybe I can draw strength from Eleanor's story, the peasant girl who became a queen, and hope that her courage and determination will pass on to me.

"Light them!" Garwyn calls to his men, and they all step forward, each man producing a torch of his own. When the last torch has been lit, the men turn toward the docks.

As loud as I can, I yell, "Men of Galandria! Why have you come to wreak havoc upon my city?"

The men stop. They look up toward the cliff, and I draw back into the cave. I don't want to be seen, not yet. For now I prefer to be a voice in the darkness.

"Who said that?" comes Garwyn's voice.

I don't answer, and in the silence another man replies, "It came from there—from the cliffs. I *told* you I heard something earlier. Maybe it's the spirit of Queen Rowan herself."

"Don't be a superstitious fool," Garwyn retorts. He raises his voice. "I say again, who said that? Show yourself."

"Stay back," I whisper to Wilha. I flip the hood of my cloak up and step slightly forward. "Men of Galandria! Why have you come to wreak havoc upon my city?"

"There *is* someone up there—look. I see a shadow!"

"I know your plans," I call down to the men. "I know you mean to destroy this city and bring war to this land and to your own homeland. Yet what you cannot know, what you couldn't possibly know, is that the man who gave you this order is dead."

Silence meets my cry. And then, "She's lying. Moran, go up there and shut her up."

"I'm not going up there. What if it really is Queen Rowan's ghost?"

I step back and whisper to Wilha. "Give me his sword."

Wilha hands it to me. My arm immediately drops to my side and the sword clanks to the ground. "This is heavier than it looks," I say, cursing.

In the torchlight I see Wilha smile. "I know." She picks up the sword again—seemingly with ease—and as we stare at each other it occurs to me that maybe I've misjudged this quiet girl. The same girl who, now that I think about it, somehow managed to scale the cliff to reach this cave. The same girl who fled the castle and learned to survive in the city on her own, something I wasn't so sure *I* could do.

"I hid the letter from Patric in one of the velvet boxes," I say suddenly. "It's there waiting for you when . . . this is all over."

"Thank you," she says.

We continue staring at each other, but I look away first. "Throw the sword down to them," I tell her.

Wilha hands me the torch, and I fall back into the darkness of the cave. She steps forward, raises the sword above her head, and hurls it down to the rocks below. She returns and takes the torch from me.

I step forward. "Lord Murcendor, the man who gave you your orders, is dead," I call down to the men. "I offer you his sword as proof."

The men begin to argue. Two of them blow out their torches. And amid their bickering, the sound of horses clattering is carried along by the wind.

"I say again," Garwyn calls, "who are you?"

I remove my cloak and hold out my hand to Wilha. "Give me the torch."

I step to the edge. The ocean roars and a blast of wind hits my face. "I am Princess Wilhamina Andewyn, descendant of Queen Eleanor the Great, great-great granddaughter to Queen Rowan the Brave, whose presence still haunts these cliffs, daughter to King Fennrick the Handsome, future daughter-in-law to Ezebo, king of Kyrenica, I am, simply, the

Masked Princess, and if you do not lay down your torches I will curse you. You, and every last member of your family."

Illuminated by the campfire and torchlight, I can see the expressions of the men, their shocked, fearful faces as they take in my mask and dress.

"How is it that she's here?" cries a man with a Kyrenican accent, hysteria drenching his voice. "She's supposed to be in the castle."

None of the men seem to notice that the sound of galloping horses has drawn closer. "Are you surprised?" I call down to them. "Is it because you thought me dead? Easy prey, for a man such as Lord Murcendor? I tell you the truth, he is dead. Dead, by my own hand, for I killed him myself."

"That's not possible," Garwyn calls, though I can see doubt beginning to cross his face. "The Masked Princess is nothing more than a frightful and ugly girl, if the rumor can be believed."

"It can, though not the one you speak of." The sound of horses galloping comes to a halt. Behind the men, who stand transfixed while I speak, I see shadows creeping toward them. "It is true that I can curse, but I can also bless." I pause and hope that the men—especially the Kyrenican men—are still listening. "So I say to you now, lay down your swords and I will bless you. For just as my ancestor Eleanor Andewyn built a great dynasty, I intend to build an even greater Kyrenican dynasty with the Strassburgs. For a century our two kingdoms have been at odds. But starting tonight, can we not begin moving toward a lasting peace? I ask you again, will you lay down your swords? Will you join me, in protecting a kingdom that I have embraced as my own?"

In the dark silence that follows, a single sword is drawn, and a Kyrenican-accented voice says, "You know, Garwyn, if all your master cares about is starting a war, why didn't he have you and your men burn your own capital, instead of ours?"

Before Garwyn can respond, a red arrow strikes a guard's thigh, and he's brought to his knees. The shadows streak closer and morph into the form of Kyrenican soldiers, running toward Garwyn and the other men.

"She's deceived us!" screams Garwyn. "Arm yourselves!" Amid cries of outrage and confusion, torches are dropped and swords are drawn. Steel clashes with steel and a Kyrenican soldier falls under Garwyn's sword. Another Galandrian is brought down by a red arrow. He slips and falls into the campfire, screaming in agony before he rolls into the sand.

More Kyrenican soldiers storm the beach until they far outnumber the Galandrians, and soon Garwyn and his men all lie on the sand either dead or surrendered.

A shadowed figure approaches the campfire. One by one, each Kyrenican soldier drops to his knees before him. When he steps into the glow of the campfire, I see that it's Stefan.

"How in the world did you manage to get yourself up there?" he calls.

"Magic, my lord," I call down to him. "And when you return to the castle, you shall find me in my chambers as though I never left at all."

Stefan laughs. "I am sure I will. And when I do—with your permission, of course—I wish to kiss the girl who has saved our city this night."

"The permission will be granted," I say. What else can I say, when all the soldiers are watching? I look back, wondering how Wilha will react. But the cave behind me is empty, and the passageway is open.

Wilha is gone.

CHAPTER 61

WILHA

"*Men of Galandria! Why have you come to wreak havoc upon my city?*"

Elara's words twist and turn. She summons truth and falsehood with equal ease, weaving them together into an enchantment that strips the Galandrians of their will to act.

Standing behind her, I watch her as she speaks. Her chin is lifted and her shoulders are thrown back. She seems to be a living copy of my mother's statue in the Queen's Garden.

I had come back to the castle intent on saving Elara, believing her to be in danger. I remember the fierce, animal-like look on her face as she stabbed Lord Murcendor. She did not need to be saved, after all.

I did.

And the thought that has fluttered at the edges of my mind now bursts forth like an uncontrollable gale:

What if, sixteen years ago, a mistake was made? What if the true Andewyn daughter, the one to be named Wilhamina, was not the twin who slid first into this world, but the one who was never supposed to exist in the first place?

Wilhamina Andewyn, the Masked Princess. The name has always seemed like an intangible, ethereal cloud, floating above and around me, covering me completely. And yet never truly becoming a part of me.

As I watch Elara speak, watch the Galandrians fall under the greater numbers of the Kyrenican soldiers—but defeated, really, by the power of Elara's words—I find that cloud rising up from around me and nudging me back into the cave. It dissipates into nothingness as I sweep into the darkness, filled with a new resolve that moves my arms and legs until I am back in the Masked Princess's chambers.

I find Patric's letter in the velvet box, just as Elara said.

Princess Wilhamina,

I regret the hastiness of our last training session, and that I did not have a chance to properly say good-bye. You are competent with a sword, far more so than you give yourself credit for. Remember this when you face your new life in Kyrenica. I also wish to beg your forgiveness, in that I did not grant the request you made of me. As my sovereign, your request should have been my command. As a devoted servant of Galandria, and of the Andewyn family, I can wish for no greater happiness than this: that you should find joy in your life in Kyrenica.

His words reach somewhere deep inside of me. I *am* more competent than I once believed. I remove a cloak from the wardrobe and tuck the letter away. I go to the sitting room, pick up my white and silver costume mask, and tie it on.

Once upon a time, I stood in this room and chose to run away from my future.

But tonight, I choose to run *to* my future.

CHAPTER 62

ELARA

After I return to the castle, Ezebo summons me to his study and I explain to him how Lord Murcendor attacked "me" and told me of his plans. I promise him that Lord Murcendor was working alone and that Galandria has every intention of honoring the peace treaty. Ezebo orders the guards to search the city for Lord Murcendor, and then finally, I am dismissed and return to my chambers.

Dawn's early rays peek through the castle windows by the time I enter my bedroom. When I open the blue velvet box to take off the mask, I find a letter tucked inside. Not Patric's letter, but another, also addressed to the Masked Princess. I quickly open it, all thoughts of removing my mask forgotten.

Dear Elara,

Tonight you saved the city from an unimaginable fate. Indeed, your actions may well have saved both Kyrenica and Galandria from an unnecessary war. I know you do not consider yourself an Andewyn, and for this, I cannot blame you. Yet in you I see so much of our ancestors. Indeed, far more than I have ever glimpsed in myself.

You say you have no name, so I beg of you, take mine. For in these last several days you have worn it with more grace and vigor than I ever have. Take my name and build for yourself the life that should have been yours sixteen years ago. Become the Masked Princess. I have seen you and Stefan together, and it is clear he has claimed your heart and you his. Someday we will meet again, and on that day I hope you will forgive me for choosing a life outside of the castle.

Somewhere in your heart you must see that this is the logical end to this matter.

Wilha finishes the letter without a signature. Fitting for someone who has just walked away from her identity. I stride to the sitting room, start a fire, and sink into the armchair, considering her words.

For all Wilha's persuasion, she forgot to mention there is still a peace treaty, still a war that would very likely be fought if I choose to leave. But despite all this, Wilha has made her decision.

Now I must make mine.

I read the letter one more time and then I rise. I toss it into the fire, where it curls and blackens, turning in on itself. Until there is nothing left but ashes and embers.

A knock sounds at the door, and I hurry to open it before Milly awakens. Stefan enters the room. His eyes droop with exhaustion.

"The guards can find no trace of Lord Murcendor in the castle, or in the city. They will continue to look, of course, but I fear we may not find him. Lord Quinlan has sent several pigeons bound for Galandria. He seemed eager that your father should know of Lord Murcendor's actions. Indeed, that was what he wanted to speak to you about in private earlier. One of his men saw Lord Murcendor in the city yesterday speaking with Garwyn, and he was troubled when Lord Murcendor did not report it to my father."

"Where is Lord Quinlan now?" I ask.

"Packing. Both he and Lord Royce mean to leave Korynth at once. As it was some of his own men who joined with Lord Murcendor, Lord Quinlan in particular is anxious to return to Galandria and explain these events to your father in person. Both he and Lord Royce have asked to speak to you before they leave, but I told them I myself would convey their well wishes." He pauses. "After what happened with Lord Murcendor, I am not eager for any of your father's advisors to meet with you." He sighs. "Unless of course you wish to?"

I hesitate, remembering Lord Royce's words: *There were things I could've told her. Things your mother wanted her to know. A message she intended Elara to have.*

I don't think Lord Royce knows anything. If my mother gave me up so easily, I doubt she had anything to say to me, other than giving me the book. And even if she did, I'm not sure I care. Not after she decided I was worth so much less than Wilhamina.

Nevertheless, the temptation to speak to him is strong. Just, I think, as Lord Royce intends. I imagine him not very far away, waiting for me to come to him. Waiting for me to play into his hands.

He'll have to keep waiting. The farther I stay away from the Guardians, and Galandria all together, the safer I'll be.

"No," I say. "I have no wish to speak to them."

Stefan nods and reaches for my hand. "You are the most wondrous woman I have ever met. Do you want to tell me exactly how you managed to appear on that cliff at just the right moment tonight?"

"A woman can't give away all her secrets. Surely you must know that," I say with a bat of my eyes.

He pulls me close, cups my chin in his hands, and whispers, "I look forward to a lifetime of learning your secrets." His lips meet mine and a thrill passes over me, split into equal parts of joy and fear. Joy that he wants me.

And fear that he will find out my biggest secret.

But I push those thoughts away and give myself over to the kiss. It's *me* he wants, and *me* he will marry, the only twin he has ever known. And if I have to trade one name for another, does it really matter? Because standing on that ledge and addressing those men as the Masked Princess didn't feel like deception. It felt like the righting of so many wrongs.

"I meant what I said earlier. I intend to make a new start," Stefan says when we pull apart. "I intend to put aside our families' differences and love you." He traces a finger down my mask. "Loving you, I suspect, will not be a difficult thing to do." His face is hopeful and expectant, and I know he wants me to return his sentiments.

Instead, I bring my lips to his for another kiss. Of all the words in this world, *love* is the most powerful of them all. It's a word I can't say. Not yet, anyway.

Not until I know it comes from the deepest, most sincere place in my heart.

CHAPTER 63

WILHA

*T*he masquerade lasts until dawn. When a servant ushers the remaining guests from the great hall, I rise up from the corner I have been hiding in to join the crowd that is now streaming out the castle.

The streets of Korynth are damp and dirty from a night of reveling. Several men are passed out near the castle gates. Empty bottles of ale and half-burned candles litter the cobblestone streets.

I pass a couple slumped together on a wooden bench. The girl wears a simple, powder blue dress and a lavender costume mask. Instinctively, I change direction and turn north, set on a new destination.

When I reach the Broken Statue I kneel down, my eyes almost level with Queen Rowan's stone gaze. I remove my white and silver mask and tilt my head to the wind, enjoying the feel of fresh, salty air on my face.

Queen Rowan's broken, beheaded statue stares at me silently. For once, I don't think she is judging me to be unworthy of the Andewyn name. I think she is watching, curious to see which path I shall take.

"No matter where I go," I whisper to her, "I will always be an Andewyn. Always."

I leave the mask at the foot of the statue. Then I rise and turn eastward, and head for home.

I don't know what will happen today, or the next day, or the day after that. I only know, for the first time ever, I have the chance to *choose* the life I want to live.

And for right now, that is everything.

ACKNOWLEDGMENTS

For years this book was my "Secret Project," the story I played around with when I needed a break from my formal work-in-progress. It would still be my secret project today had my agent, Kerry Sparks, not suggested that I "start writing my YA book" during a phone call when I was whining about having writer's block. Thank you for all your encouragement and direction, Kerry!

Marlo Scrimizzi, my editor at Running Press, believed in this project even in its earliest stages. Marlo, every author should be so lucky to have an editor like you!

The entire team at Running Press has been a joy to work with. Thank you to Teresa Bonaddio, the genius behind the cover and map. To Suzanne Wallace, Susan Hom, Emily Epstein, and Stacy Schuck: Thank you all for helping turn my manuscript into an actual book and seeing that it gets into the hands of readers.

To my early readers: Douglas Coleman, Lisa Allen, Ruth Gallo, Nancy Winkler, Pam Carroll, Stefanie Wass, and Deanna Romito, thank you so much for your encouragement and feedback. It means so much!

In order to reach the deadlines on this book I often had to call in reinforcements. Thank you to Pam and Tom Carroll, Nancy and Gerry Winkler, and Lisa and Bryan Allen for watching my boys when I had to sneak away to write.

To all of my friends and family who have supported me on my writing journey, thank you, I am so incredibly lucky to have you in my life.

To my Grandpa Jim, who is in his nineties and is convinced I'm famous: Thank you for always trying to sell my books at your senior center!

To my husband Ryan who is always willing to help me carve out more writing time: Thank you for always being my biggest fan, and especially, for not being picky when it comes to housekeeping! I still feel so lucky to be your wife.

And finally, highest thanks to God, the First Storyteller, and the author of my own journey. May I live a life that increasingly reflects your love and commitment to this world.

WATCH OUT FOR THE SEQUEL TO

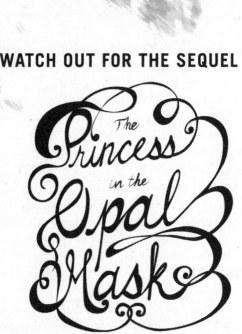

AVAILABLE FALL 2014